Friends Always

Corinne Arrowood

First Edition, 2022

Published by Corinne Arrowood
United States of America
www.corinnearrowood.com

ISBN: 979-8-9851087-2-9 (paperback)
ISBN: 979-8-9851087-1-2 (ebook)
ISBN: 979-8-9851087-3-6 (Hardcover)

Cover and Interior Design by Cyrusfiction Productions.

*This book is dedicated to those who fought to be themselves
in a world that fought against them.*

Chapter 1

I knew I had a secret – even though I had ignored a lot of red flags. The music I liked didn't jive with most kids my age, I wasn't girl crazy like my friends, and my ever-present thought wasn't on getting my hands inside some girl's shirt. My mom told me I was a late bloomer, but deep down inside, I knew something was off. I was in denial. I just didn't want to know; however, the summer of 1972 opened my eyes.

Every summer, my family—Mom, Dad, my sister Sarah, and me—visited Mom's family on the East Coast. One word described the annual trek—boring. Moan. Moan. Sharing the back seat of the Mercury Grand Marquis with Sarah was cramped and most trying on my nerves. Leaning against the window, I stretched my legs into her well since she was curled in a ball reading some teen magazine.

"Bradley, do you have to take up my seat as well as yours?" she asked, putting her feet on mine, but I acted like I didn't care. "Mom, can you tell him to move his legs? He's taking up the whole back seat."

Dad pulled the car into the next rest stop, Mom got out, and Dad and I took a moment to stretch our legs. "Bradley, you sit in my seat, honey; you'll have more room. Sarah and I can have the back seat." Mom was sympathetic to me when it came to dealing with Sarah's bitchy, whiny tendencies.

Dad and I were almost the same height. I knew he had hoped I'd be a basketball star and get a free ride to college. Truth be told, I was pretty good, and if I had put any energy into it, I would've been really good, but I had no desire to play basketball or any sport for that matter. I loved horses, and I owned the ring on my steed.

For the first leg of the trip, we had stopped in Virginia at Mom and Dad's college friend who lived close to the ocean. Like the previous years, my parents and their friends hinted at some made-up romance between their daughter and me. Dad winked at me, nodded his head, and said something like, "Why don't you two go see what new yachts are in the harbor?" Lisa and I had as much in common as I did with the seagulls. The overnight stay was torture. Inevitably, Sarah would excuse herself and go to the restroom.

The next day was another long drive. We were finally about an hour away from my cousins' house outside New York City in Scarsdale. Nearly everyone in their subdivision commuted by train into the city for work.

My cousins didn't like us, or so it seemed. They all lived mere miles from one another and had grown up together. Julie was Sarah's age, Louise a year younger, and Debbie a year younger than I. Leslie, the oldest, had graduated from college and had gotten engaged around Christmas. She was cool, loved both of us, and was sensitive to my sister feeling left out, even though Sarah couldn't give two shits. On the other hand, Sarah and I were from New Orleans, *the South*, as though there was still a stigma attached to the name, and just the sound of it tasted foul.

To make matters worse, my cousins all looked alike and were beautiful with manes of thick black hair, a dramatic contrast to my sister in all her natural blondeness and slow Southern drawl. Whatever she said sounded sweet, even if it was moody as hell. The adults loved her, which pissed off the rest of us even more, so our stay was no picnic for her. And then there was me: Can you say square peg in a round hole? One boy in a sea of girls that hated me, or so I thought, why, I don't know. I gotta give it to my sister; she was either too unaware in her own Sarahland or was just that confident, and it didn't matter.

We arrived to great fanfare, with everyone coming out to greet us. I felt my heart swell and had fought tears when Mom, her sisters, and Gran, her mom, cuddled, hugged, and squealed. New York was Mom's home, and these were her people. Dad and Uncle D. were close as brothers and gave each other manly bear hugs. I don't think there was a moment of silence the whole trip unless everyone was sleeping.

Uncle D. shot over to me, "Kiddo, you're getting as tall as your old man. I hear you've been blazing a trail with Trumpet." He hugged me, and I felt my body stiffen like a board because I wasn't a touchy-feely kind of person. Mom was the only one who hugged me regularly. Dad was more arm-around-the-shoulder kind of guy, probably where I got my standoffishness.

I backed off a little. "Trumpet is amazing, Uncle D., and we've been collecting a lot of blue ribbons." I was all smiles. I could talk for hours about my horse but refrained.

I made my way to Gran, my grandmother, short in stature but larger than life. I loved her more than I could ever express. I always looked forward to the nuggets of wisdom or tidbits she shared with me. "Bradley, Bradley, Bradley, you're growing up too fast. Look at you. I think you're going to pass up your dad soon."

She was full of kisses and cheek pinches. I was pretty sure I had dark red lip prints all over my cheeks. It was obvious the cousins came out to greet us by instruction. I nodded; what else would I do? Sarah hammed it up and exaggerated her drawl and prissiness. I'm sure to hear Uncle D. say something about his beautiful Southern belle. My sister didn't earn any brownie points for sure, at least not from my cousins or me. You could almost hear everyone groan. Oh, so, Sarah!

I was looking for Leslie, but my aunt told me that she and Del, her fiancée, would be back a little later. After Dad, Uncle D., and I removed our luggage from the car and sported it to the assigned rooms, we joined the women for a welcome snack. Even though carrying luggage wasn't a fun activity, it made my cramped muscles begin to feel normal again. The big news since our last visit was the new family down the street; in particular, my aunt and uncle laughed with raised eyebrows, the new teenage boy. The grown-ups were interested in the fact that the dad was from Amsterdam and the mom from Paris, but all my cousins talked about was the boy. Evidently, he was a heartthrob.

Because there was nothing to do but play Scrabble with my grandmother, my dad took pity and let me take off on one of my cousin's bikes, just to get away from the hens. I pedaled down the street and noticed a guy with shoulder-length golden hair washing his red Cutlass. Could that be the guy my aunt was talking about, I wondered. I didn't want to keep looking at him, and his bare chest ripped with muscle, but I couldn't stop. He was the coolest kid I'd ever seen, and it took all I had to stay on the bike. He smiled and nodded as if to say hello. I nodded back but kept going. *Did he really just nod at me? Man*, thinking to myself, *you're a weirdo, Bradley.* I rode a short distance and then turned around and went back. He was still washing the car, so I stopped.

Chapter 2

He looked up from wiping the back bumper and smiled again. He had one of those smiles. He could have been a model for a toothpaste commercial. "You new around here?" he asked. For some reason, I had trouble speaking. All I wanted to do was look at him. *What the hell is wrong with me*, I thought. I felt nervous as all hell. I'd never been overly social, but I did know how to say hello to someone I didn't know. Something about this guy was different, and it gave me butterflies.

I had to swallow the frog out of my throat. "No, just visiting my mom's family." I gave a look of disgust because it was how I felt. I would've much rathered stayed in New Orleans and ridden my horse. "Is there anything to do around here?" Was that the best I could do? I should have been cool and said something like, how goes it, or what's up? I sounded like the weirdo I was.

"No, not really. You can hang out with me. I bet you're from the family with all those girls." He grinned.

"You guessed it. By the way, I'm Bradley." I realized I was still straddling the bike and felt even more awkward.

"Cool. I'm Berit. Berit Jensen."

He and I talked for a while, and he seemed as lonely and bored as I was. He told me he was going into twelfth grade at the local public high school. He was originally from Amsterdam and wasn't a big fan of the

U.S. As he talked, I noticed a slight accent. I listened and tried hard to stop looking at him now that I was off the bike and standing right next to him. His bare chest was tanned, his hair was a mixture of blond and brown, and his eyes were a light shade of bluey-grey. At six-three, I made him look kinda short, but he was muscular and around six feet, so not short at all. The picture of a California surfer popped into my mind. I envisioned him riding a wave or even sitting in a lifeguard stand like I was watching a teen beach movie.

I told him I was from New Orleans, was only sixteen, but I did have a driver's license because, in New Orleans, fifteen was the driving age. He thought it was cool. I told him I went to an all-boys military school and how much I hated it, but I figured I could make it another few years, and then I'd be out of there.

For not knowing each other, we jived, talking about a lot of stuff. Plain old ordinary conversation. He was easy to talk to, and the more he spoke, the more I dug his accent.

I sat on the driveway chasing an ant with a twig and watched him as he continued cleaning his car. "I have three friends in the entire world, and they're from the neighborhood. The two boys are named Ricky, and then there's a girl, Cindy. We ride horses together. All our parents are friends, which made us automatically friends. You don't have any choice in the matter."

Berit looked up through his hair. "Do you have a girlfriend?"

"No, but I have gone to two dances with one of Cindy's friends," I said a bit defensively.

He shrugged. "Okay, I was just wondering. I don't have a girlfriend, and you have two more dates under your belt than I do." To me, it didn't compute. Here was this good-looking guy who had no girlfriends. That just seemed odd.

"Hey, I need to finish washing the car. You mind helping?" Berit flashed his smile.

"Sure," I said, grabbing a wet cloth from the suds-filled bucket.

Just as we were about finished, Berit sprayed me with the hose. It took me aback, but I had to laugh. The thought crossed my mind that even though I'd known him for only a couple of hours, we had gotten along better than I had with the two Rickys.

We walked into his house, and he handed me a towel. "Had to do it. You looked too perfect. Here I am, half wet and sweaty, had to unpretty you some." He had a light-hearted, friendly laugh. "How long will you be staying?"

Still trying to shake the pretty comment out of my head, I managed to answer him. "Ten days."

"Bradley, we're going to find things to do with your ten days. There aren't many guys around here, and the few I've met from school talk about boring. They're into hanging out, trying to look cool, and getting a piece of ass. I'm not into those games." We had a fun time, and it was great making a friend.

After returning to my aunt's, I walked into the kitchen and dining room, where everyone was visiting. No one seemed to have missed me—except Mom. I told her I met the new neighbor kid, and he was great.

"That's nice, honey," she said and patted my arm.

The next morning, the girls had planned a shopping trip, the dads were going to play golf, and there I was. *Who am I to tag along with and be completely miserable?* I pondered. Before I decided, the doorbell rang.

"Bradley, Berit's here for you," my uncle called up to me. My eyes popped open, and my heart pounded. Cool! I actually had a friend to hang with and wouldn't have to go to the mall or around the golf course.

I could see my cousin Debbie look at Louise. Their eyes shifted back and forth from Berit to me to each other as I walked downstairs. Yes, all the girls were green with envy, including my sister. Here dorky Bradley was going to hang with Mr. Heartthrob. They giggled hellos to Berit and tried to act like they'd known him. He was polite but focused on me. Berit smiled as he saw me approaching. "Hoi, vriend."

I got it. "Hoi!" I smiled back.

"Want to hang out?" I kept thinking over and over, *my savior, no mall, no golf, just guy time, and I have a friend.*

"Sure." I introduced Berit to my parents, but I wanted to get out of there and fast.

Once outside, I knew I had to remain composed because he was a senior and I was a lowly sophomore. I couldn't seem too overboard and freak him out.

I tried to sound calm and mature. "Berit, I owe you, man. My choices were shopping with the girls or golf with the dads." Inside I wanted to jump along, asking, "Where are we going, huh, huh?" but I knew I had to remain collected.

"I thought you might like to go to the lake. Nobody goes there, or hardly anyone. You'll dig it." We walked down to his house, hopped in his car, and took off, windows down, radio turned up loud. I wasn't the strange kid that didn't play basketball or football. I was a guy riding in a car with my seventeen-year-old cool friend listening to music.

He pulled up to an old house-turned store.

"C'mon in," he said, getting out of the car. "There's cool stuff inside." I followed inside to a room full of objects I'd never seen or imagined; the small signs told me what they were. The store had an assortment of water pipes and shotguns, which were glass tubes with a small hole on the top and open ends. Great posters were plastered on the walls– Queen, Cher, Leon Russell, and Jimi Hendrix. The place had a strong musky smell of incense, like nothing I had ever smelled before, but I sensed it was living on the edge, and it was exciting, like being on a steep roller coaster slowly chugging up to the top waiting for the plummet at breakneck speed.

"I have to pick up some rolling papers," Berit said.

After he paid the clerk, we returned to the car and were soon flying down winding roads until he pulled over and stopped. We walked through the woods. Even though it was summer, a blanket of leaves crunched under our feet as we plodded to the lake. He was right; it was incredible. We were totally alone.

Huge boulders overlooked the water, and we climbed up. "You smoke?" Berit asked.

Me, being all cool, "Sometimes, when I feel like it."

"This is good shit," as he proceeded to roll a joint. I had never smoked pot in my entire life.

I watched as he lit it, and I copied him, but after one puff, I started choking.

He grinned at me. "What'd I tell you? Some good shit! Two tokes, all you need."

Trying to gauge what my reaction would be to the pot, I forced conversation.

"You come here much?" There was a slight tremble in my voice.

"Some. It breaks up the boredom. It's cool though, you like?" He smiled.

He ended up telling me about Amsterdam and how a person could do pretty much anything he wanted, like smoking pot. He said he missed it and would have to take me with him sometime if we stayed friends.

My mind raced, wondering what it would feel like when the pot hit me. *Am I going to fall out?* I wondered. Nothing seemed to happen.

He stood up and stripped off his clothes. "The water is fucking freezing, but you'll get used to it." He jumped in.

Oh shit, I thought. I stripped down and quickly jumped in, hoping Berit hadn't noticed my boner. The cold water promptly got rid of the problem. "This *is* freezing."

He laughed. "You think this is cold? You should feel the water back home." When he referred to his home, I could see his mind linger to some memory.

I splashed him. "Maybe one day I *will* go to Amsterdam with you."

He told me I was the first friend he had made in the States. He talked about a close friend in Amsterdam named Han and how leaving him was hard. His voice changed, and I could tell that they had been close.

I don't know what came over me, but I ducked down under the water and swam through his legs, came up behind him, and shoved him under the water. He bounced back up with a deep belly laugh and splashed me. After a splash and dunk frenzy, I swam to the edge of the big rock, climbed up, and laid down, waiting for the sun to warm me. I was hoping he would stay in the water, but he also got out. I managed to keep my dick under control this time.

Berit's body looked strong like a state wrestling champ, whereas I looked like a lanky weakling. He reached over to his jeans and pulled out the joint. After lighting it, he took a few more drags. When he offered it to me, I found the balls to say I was good, but thanks.

After a few minutes, we dressed and drove to a local pizza place.

"I'm bored sick since moving here, but I've managed to build a car engine. Other than that, I've smoked dope and jerked off."

My jaw almost hit the table.

I was too embarrassed to tell him how the two Rickys would get one of their dad's *Playboy* magazines, open it to the centerfold, and the three of us would jerk off. I'm sure the two Rickys assumed I did it for the same reason they did, but it wasn't. Even when I was doing it, I knew I was somehow different. Who wouldn't want to jerk off to the Playmates? I didn't. Sure, I could see they were beautiful, but jacking off on them did nothing for me. What was wrong with me, I often wondered.

I looked blankly at him.

"You okay?" he asked.

"Yeah, when I smoke pot, I sometimes get quiet."

"Oh."

Before he could ask why, the waitress brought our pizza, and we scarfed it down. Meanwhile, I was on a tightrope: Do I tell him? He was so casual about his personal stuff. Could I trust him? I figured who the hell would he tell? My aunt? My parents? Hardly.

"Berit, you and I are different. You say whatever and don't give a shit. I don't want to sound even weirder than I am. It's hard to explain, but I'm not you. I'm the last guy picked for anything. I'm that guy, ya know?"

He sat there looking at me and then started to laugh.

"Brad, you make me laugh. Why care what high school kids think about you? You're only going to be there for another couple of years. Don't you get it? You'll be a man a hell of a lot longer than you'll be a high schooler. What difference does it make what people think? That's what my friend Han told me, and it made sense."

After finishing the pizza, we went back to his house to listen to records. He first put on Cher. That's something I'd listen to, I thought. I liked the Beatles too, but in total privacy, I'd listen to Liza Minelli and Diana Ross. The things I did were embarrassing to myself, like standing in front of the mirror watching myself mouth the words to Streisand.

He flopped on the sofa next to me. "I think we're more alike than you think, and I think I know why you feel like a weirdo, as you put it. I used to until Han told me what my problem was. It blew me away, but then I got it slowly, not at first, and was pretty pissed he'd said what he said to me. He was only trying to be a friend. He was older; he knew things."

"What'd he tell you?" I had to know what the magic answer was to the question of me.

He seemed to be looking through me. "Brad, you're not a weirdo. We're different from many, but I don't think weird. Just different. You're great. Look at you. You're a big guy and handsome. I don't want you to get pissed at me. Just forget it."

I couldn't leave it at that. I had to know what the secret was. I desperately wanted anyone to tell me why I hated myself so much. Why did I have to be different from everyone else? Everyone liked my sister. She was popular and, tried as she did, she couldn't make me one of the in-crowd. She had tried, but if this guy had the answers, I wanted them. Maybe kids were smarter in Amsterdam.

"No, tell me. I won't get pissed. What's the secret?"

I could see the gears grinding in his head, looking for the best way to say it. He looked up at me, sized me up, it seemed, got up to put on another record, and turned toward me. "You like dick." He was blunt. At first, I couldn't comprehend what he said, but it started to sink in. He was right. I was pissed. He was calling me a queer. He said it out loud.

I know my face showed anger, embarrassment, humiliation. How dare he say I was a queer! My silence probably gave away that I was furious.

"See, I told you. You're pissed at me. There's nothing wrong with it. I'm gay, and once I got over the shock of admitting it, my life changed, and the picture became clearer. Being gay is more accepted in Amsterdam. As I said, anything goes. It's harder here, and you can't tell people. Couldn't you tell I was gay? That I was attracted to you? How could I not be? You're cute and funny and so innocent."

I didn't know what to say. What do you say to someone who's just called you a queer, I thought. I liked this guy. After all, he had been major cool. I didn't care, as he put it, that he liked dick. He was easygoing and fun to hang out with.

"You're right. I'm pissed. I'm not trying to be insulting, but—"

"Wait. Stand up, turn around, and please promise not to deck me." He first put his hands on my shoulders, then my back, and returned to my shoulders. "Do you feel creeped out? Like ants running all over you or like you're gonna throw up?"

The truth was, no, I didn't want to throw up, and no, it didn't feel bad. More noticeably, I could feel my rock-hard cock in my pants. He touched my back again, this time reaching under my shirt. Waves of heat passed through my body like the first few seconds after getting in a steamy shower; it was the perfect heat to the innermost part of my being. I started to break a sweat, my heart raced with exhilaration, and I could feel my face turning bright red. Fuck, I was a fag. He was right. A fucking fag.

"It's a lot to take in, and maybe I'm completely wrong, in which case, I'm sorry."

I felt defeated, lower than low. I wished I could disappear, and then, shit, I started crying. Yeah, no doubt I was a fag. I should have punched him in his pretty-boy face and gotten out of there, but no, I cried instead. I still hadn't said another word to him.

He turned me around and looked me in the eyes. "Bradley, it's not the end of the world. If anything, it should make you feel better because I bet it answers some questions or explains some of the things you did when you were a kid." My tears were slowing down, and I was listening. "When I was a little kid, I used to put my mother's fur coats on and run my hands up and down the fur. I sometimes even put her high heels on and pranced around in the fur coat and heels," he said, starting to laugh.

My laughter broke through the tears. "Yeah, I was in a Mardi Gras ball once and had some gold and purple costume with a turban. I loved that costume. Any chance I had, I locked myself in the bedroom and put it on. One time I didn't lock the door, and Mom came in. She was a bit startled but said, 'Don't you look cute! You don't have to lock yourself in the room to wear your costume.' Berit, I don't know if I like guys or not, but I know I don't like girls, at least not like, you know."

"Do you mind if I touch you again? I'll stop right now if you don't feel comfortable." He resumed touching my back again. "Did you like it when I did it? It's okay if you didn't."

I paused. "Seeing you naked jumping in the water gave me a hard-on."

"I saw, but I didn't want to say anything."

For the first time in my life, I felt like another person finally saw me for who I was. Someone accepted me, and he didn't expect anything but friendship in return. He was the first person ever to touch me so gently, and he had been right. Deep down, I knew I was gay. I wanted him to touch me more.

"We can take things slow," he said. "I don't want to overwhelm you." His hand on my thigh was like sparks going off in my body, raising my body's temperature. What I had thought felt like a hot shower before was nothing compared to this. He undid my jeans and pulled the zipper down, all the while looking into my eyes. I dropped my jeans. The bulge in my underwear made things uncomfortable, so I slid them down. His whispered touch on my stomach caused me to nearly gasp as though getting ready to hold my breath, but it was all involuntary. I wanted his touch. I could feel my pulse throb in my dick that had never been so hard. He must've read my mind because he moved his hand straight to where I needed it.

"Oh God," I moaned. I had never felt anything like that before. He had the perfect grip on me: He knew when to slow down and when to speed up. All the while, he never lost eye contact until the magic moment, and I came hard with such force my eyes rolled back in pure euphoria. It felt like electricity was running through my body. "Oh God," I said again. I couldn't think of anything else to say. Should I say thank you? That would've sounded lame, nor did it express how outta sight my body felt.

I could tell that he had enjoyed giving me pleasure. I better return the favor, I thought, but I wasn't quite sure how to do it. My curiosity took over, and I moved my hand to touch him. My hand was shaking at first, but he put his hand over mine, and something about it felt right. I began to jerk him with his hand guiding mine, which hardly described the feeling of doing it to someone else or having someone do it to me. My hand no longer shook as I touched him. I knew the pace and grip that he made perfect for me. I wanted it perfect for him. I must've been doing something right because he dropped his hand off of mine. Soon his hips flexed upward, and he clenched the sofa with both fists. I felt the pulsing as he unleashed his load.

"Un-fucking-believable, you're brilliant," he said, breathing heavily and collapsing beside me. "You were fantastic." After a few minutes of silence, he stood and kissed the top of my head. I wasn't sure I wanted any kissing, but the top of my head was okay, but I definitely wasn't ready for lips, no way. I still wasn't convinced I was gay. I just thought I was attracted to Berit, not because he was a guy, but because of who he was as a person.

The record had long stopped playing, and the last one had dropped.

"Wanna go for a ride?" he asked. "There's a cool cave not far from here."

"Sure." I'd go anywhere with him.

Fifteen minutes later, Berit pulled off the road to a densely wooded area. We walked deep into the woods until we came to a cave at the bottom of a hill. We had to hunch over to enter, and after we were inside, we could stand up easily. It was a real cave like one a bear might hibernate in during the winter. I wondered if, in fact, this was a bear's cave, and it'd come back and make us his dinner. The cave was damp, cold, and dark and smelled like a dirty horse's stall. I could barely see Berit, who was only a few feet in front of me, until he lit a couple of lanterns.

"Welcome to *my* cave," he said. I could see he had put his mark on it. The cave walls were covered in his drawings, including a peace sign, a four-foot flag with a red, white, and blue stripe, some odd zigzags, and HAN, written in big letters.

"Have a seat here," he pointed at a rock that was the perfect height and large enough to lounge on. "I call these rocks 'squats.'"

Being there felt primal like an early caveman. He lit up, passed me the joint, and I toked it twice. I didn't know people usually got high the second time they smoked pot, but I quickly found out. I was a living testimony of the second-time high. Once I got used to it, I accepted death wasn't imminent.

"I have to confess," I said. "Today is full of firsts for me, including smoking pot."

"It's all good. I kinda figured," he said and smiled.

We sat in silence for a few moments, enjoying the high and company, until he asked what I liked to do. I could talk an easy mile when it came to my horse, Trumpet. I told him about the shows, and he couldn't believe how much Trumpet cost. I told him all about the pomp and circumstance and the trophies.

"Can you believe that the trophies, for the most part, are silver tea service, platters, bowls, and the like?" I asked. "Of course, you get a blue ribbon, too. They attach it to the bridle." I rambled on for a while about how I felt with Trumpet. "What do you enjoy doing?"

"I liked playing football back in Amsterdam, but it isn't a thing here in the States," he said.

"What do you mean? Football is very popular here."

"No, the real football—what you guys call soccer."

He was right. I didn't know of any teams, and it certainly wasn't popular.

"So I've taken up nature and hiking, which explains how I discovered my cave," Berit said with a grin.

I sat cross-legged on one of the squats. "How often do you come here?"

"Not much. When I first found it, I came a lot. That's when I wrote on the walls. The first thing I wrote was Han. I missed him, and in my mind, I created a picture of bringing him here, but it didn't work out that way. Not at all. Later on, it bummed me out to come here, but I thought you might like it."

He was pulling out all the stops to entertain me. He talked a lot about Han.

"Do you stay in touch with him?"

"We did at first, but over time it became less and less until we only wrote every few months. My parents said they wouldn't pay for any more long-distance calls. Even though they didn't know who I had been calling, they said it had to stop. I got furious at the time because I missed him and wanted to talk to him. I didn't know anyone here, at least no one I wanted to know."

We talked about our dads: his dad was an ad executive dealing with foreign cars and made good money. Mine worked in a land development business and did okay. That ended the dad talk.

We laughed hysterically at the flickers of the lanterns on the walls. "Shit, that one looks like a caveman did it. Watch this." I made animal shadows with my hands like we did during a slide show at school. He laughed even though I acted childish as hell. I felt I had lived more since I met Berit than I had my whole life.

After we started to come down from our high, we ventured back toward the car. Judging from the sun, I realized it was getting late. The evening sky had started to darken, and I worried my parents might be worried. I didn't want anything to spoil my day of liberation.

Two pristine foreign cars were parked in the driveway when we got to his house. We pulled in. His dad came out the front door and seemed surprised to see me.

"Dad, this is Bradley. Bradley, this is my dad," Berit said.

"Nice to meet you, Bradley," his dad said in a strong accent.

"Thank you. You as well," I said.

The front door opened, and Berit's mom walked toward us. She didn't look like anybody's mom I'd ever seen. She looked like one of the women I had jerked off on in *Playboy*. Berit introduced me to his mother, and his parents asked about me. I shared about being from New Orleans and staying at my aunt's.

I noticed my dad and uncle walking down the street toward Berit's house. They saw me and walked over to us. Soon all the grown-ups were talking, and my uncle invited them back to the house for cocktails.

How typical, I thought. Adults lived for cocktail time like kids lived for Saturday mornings. Berit's parents accepted the invite, but Berit and I chose to stay at his house rather than enter the realm of girls.

Once in his room, he dug in the back of his closet and pulled out a photo album. He flipped through, showing pictures of Amsterdam and the outer area where they had lived. Everything looked like it was from a movie. He showed me his voetbal pictures and then some photos of a woman.

"This is my real mom," he said. "My mom died when I was young, and my dad married Gabrielle, who's Parisian. I call Gabrielle Mom." Gabrielle was probably most men's dream of a woman: beautiful, French accent, with a lot of cleavage and wiggle to her walk, not at all like a real mom. His real mom looked kind, and I could see where he got his killer smile. She had blonde hair and light eyes.

"Do you remember her at all?"

"My memories are more from pictures, I think, and I know it sounds crazy, but somewhere in my heart, I can hear her laugh."

Berit then flipped to the pictures of a guy.

"This is Han," he said. I inspected the photos. Han wasn't at all as I expected. The pictures showed Berit maybe fourteen or fifteen, and Han looked almost like a grown-up like he was twenty or something. Han was tall, or appeared to be, had dark hair and a friendly smile. In every picture, he had his arm around Berit's shoulder or was holding his hand.

The last pictures were from Berit's bon voyage with Han. I was surprised because Berit still looked to be maybe sixteen at most. For some reason, I thought Berit had just moved to the States. I felt sad for him because he'd been starving for a friend for more than a year. I, at least, had the two Rickys and Cindy, even if it wasn't ideal. He had no one.

"Berit, how long have you lived here?"

"A year here, six months in Manhattan, and before that six months in Chicago." What I thought was a cool guy was a lonely boy just like me—the only difference was he looked like a movie star or teen idol. He continued to stare at the last picture before slapping the book closed.

"What'd you think?"

"Amsterdam looks happenin'. I can tell you miss Han."

"Yeah, but ya gotta keep on truckin', man."

His short answer indicated he didn't want to talk about it even though he wanted to show me the pictures. He laid back on his bed. "Brad, you had a good day? There's a place around here for horseback riding if you want to go tomorrow. I've never been, so you'll have to teach me. Cool with you?"

"Man, that sounds so cool. I'd love to." I loved riding and couldn't think of anything I'd like better—well, maybe getting naked and swimming in the icy lake. I wanted to see his body and touch him. I felt my woody coming on again.

Quickly I changed mental images. "Where'd you meet Han?"

"I had a school project and was researching at the nearby college library. Han was in college working on his master's, and I met him at the library. He offered to help me, and the next thing I knew, we were at his place. He was a smooth talker and put the moves on me. Han was all over me, removed my pants, took off his own, and introduced me to the world of gay sex. Later I was confused but look at me now."

Berit seemed amused by it now, but I found it a bit disturbing.

"At first, I was overwhelmed," he said. "I didn't enjoy some of it until maybe the third or fourth time. Han really dug me." I couldn't stop my mind from thinking, yeah, I bet he did like you!

"He knew me. He knew my story, and he accepted me right from the start. He loved me when I needed love. I understand now. He moved on after I moved to the States and got a new lover after a while. He never made me feel like a piece of ass, maybe because he was my one and only. I went to visit my grootmoeder back home over the school break. Being home and breathing the air felt good. I wanted to surprise Han at the college, but I'm the one who was surprised. He was doin' some chick in his office. He didn't skip a step and wanted to know if I wanted to join in. I couldn't get out of there fast enough. He was shaggin' a girl. A girl! I felt wronged. Had it been some guy, it would have been different. I think he's one of those people. He can do males or females. Truly, anything was cool in Amsterdam. You wouldn't believe some of the things people did. Blows my mind to think of it."

I felt sorry for him, but I didn't want to. He was too cool to have anyone pity him. I decided not to talk about Han anymore. Just thinking of him infuriated me.

We stepped out on the patio, toked again, and headed back inside. While watching TV, we scarfed down five hot dogs each and a whole tube of Pringles. We both must have passed out because the next thing I felt was my dad's hand shaking my shoulder. Berit's dad also shook him, telling him to go to bed.

On the way back to my aunt's, my dad said he liked Bram and Gabrielle and that they seemed like good people.

"What do you think of their son?" he asked.

"Berit's cool. I like him a lot." If he only knew.

Dad told me Berit's parents said they'd been worried about him. He hadn't had a friend in two years. He barely talked, they said. I told him I knew, and we, Berit and I, shared a lot in common, and it had been fun so far. My dad skipped over my comment, or so I thought.

"Berit's dad said Berit already has enough credits to graduate from high school, but he and Gabrielle are too worried about him to send him away to college. He mentioned Berit wanted to go back to Amsterdam, but he changed his mind since his last visit, so I want you to keep an eye on Berit and see if you notice anything noteworthy. Maybe his parents are overcautious and worrying for nothing."

What did Dad expect of me, I thought. I don't want to betray Berit, and I don't want to argue right now. Berit was a new friend, and it didn't feel right for his parents to talk to my parents like that after having just met. What did Mom and Dad say about me, I wondered. I'm sure the cocktails were flowing, and they babbled. I flashed back to the cave, and I giggled inside, thinking about Berit and me stoned and laughing at all the shadows. I could never imagine my parents stoned; seeing them stoned would be hysterical or maybe the most fucked-up thing imaginable. "Sure, okay, Dad," I said.

Chapter 3

When we walked into my aunt's house, Sarah was playing Scrabble with my aunt, my mom, and my grandmother. We connected eyes, and she rolled hers.

"Sarah, when you get a second, can you help me?" I asked her. I had a great plan, but I'd have to see if Berit would go for it. For once, I felt sorry for my sister. She was cute, funny, and smart like the All-American girl next door. She had a bubbly smile that was contagious, and she was every parent's dream girl, or so they thought. Grownups found her sweet, cute, funny, and polite. She was a grown-up magnet. Although Mom and I knew the bossy, condescending, bitchy Sarah, she hid it beautifully from Dad and the rest of the world. Even though I loved her, I usually resented the hell out of her.

She jumped at the chance to have a legitimate reason for quitting the game. When she got to our room, she thanked me.

"So what's the dirt on Berit? Tell me everything. Does he have a girlfriend? How old is he? Where'd you guys go? It's so cool."

I ignored her questions. "Good night," I said and rolled over in the twin bed. I was exhausted after a full day. As I lay there, thoughts swam through my head, and I took a mental inventory of the day: I had hung out with someone from Amsterdam, learned some Dutch words, had a male to talk to who wasn't a dad, got high on pot, swam naked in a freaking freezing lake, found out I was gay, gave a hand job and got a hand job. Yeah, it had been a heck of a day. I looked forward to horseback riding, but mainly I couldn't wait to see Berit again. I could picture him, all of him, and it made my whole body tingle. Gay or not, he was it on a stick, and he was my friend. I just knew it.

I woke up groggy, and I heard the girls making plans to go antiquing with the moms and lunch. I threw on a shirt over my shorts and went downstairs. They were already dressed and almost ready to leave.

"Good morning, Pumpkin," Mom said, "The ladies are going out for the day—"

"I'm going horseback riding with Berit and won't be back until late."

"Okay," she looked puzzled. "Be careful." She dug in her purse and handed me some money.

I could hear them leaving and my aunt telling my mom about the riding stables, their voices muffled as they went.

I ran back upstairs and put on a pair of jeans, even though it was hot. We were going to be on horses, and from my experience, I knew bare skin against a saddle could leave a mean chafe. I checked myself in the mirror from every angle. I hadn't changed since the day before; there were no signs saying fag or homo on my forehead.

I left the house and started walking toward Berit's house, and he was coming my way. We both smiled and did the guy nod in acknowledgment.

"Hoi," he smiled.

"Hoi back at cha." I was a New Orleans boy, and it reared its ugly head when I let my guard down. Most people not from New Orleans found our slang strange, but then again, I was with a guy who said hoi, dank je, and a bunch of other odd words.

"Ready to learn how to ride a horse?" We walked next to each other with long strides.

"I think I'm gonna hold off on the toking until I get the hang of the horse." He flashed his Pepsodent smile.

"That's a wise move."

The drive to the stables lasted about thirty minutes, so we had plenty of time to talk. I told about my sister dying from boredom playing

Scrabble. "My cousins haven't included her really; I mean, they have their lives and all, plus she's miserable. I thought she could maybe hang with us one of the days or part of a day. That's if you're okay with it."

"Why not? I can do one better. I can pretend to be interested in her – that'll drive the others nuts. When I first moved in," he laughed. "They would walk or ride their bikes past my house five or six times a day trying to get my attention. Not that I didn't find it a boost to the ego, I—"

"Are you into girls too?"

"No, no way, man. I can appreciate beauty, but I won't get a rise in my Levi's over a pair of tits," he said, grabbing my hand and looking at me. "Now about your sister, you think she'd want to groove with it, or would she freak? I'm gonna have to tell her the truth." I was horrified, and he saw it. "You think I'd do that to you? Your secret is safe with me. I'm stoked I helped you find the yellow brick road, Dorothy. I feel honored."

We pulled into the stables and discovered we could opt for a trail guide or go on our own. I knew what I preferred, but I let Berit choose because he was the novice and had been easy on me regarding other things. He was all-in for the private experience, which gave us time alone on the horses. The staff gave us a map with different trails and pointed out which ones the guided riders took.

While they saddled the horses, I quizzed him with questions like was he scared and whether he had ever ridden at all. He answered no and no, so I went through a brief do and don't list. He was a fast understudy and had no trouble mounting and gaining control. Soon we were riding at a steady pace.

He was on a chestnut mare that was mid-age, if I had to guess. His horse was lively with an energized prance but well-disciplined. They put me on a brown and white paint gelding. The horse was way too small for me but had spirit and was stubborn, unlike most trail horses that plod along the usual path. No, this little paint, Tonto, hadn't been broken in long, I could tell, and maybe it was why they put me on him after I'd told them I was experienced with the reins. Perhaps it was for their amusement, but I'd broken enough horses over the years I could've handled him in my sleep.

I watched Berit, and he was a natural like he'd been riding most of his life. As we rode, we planned out the whole Sarah thing. I hoped she would go along, and I didn't think she'd rat him out to Mom and Dad. I knew she had tried pot before and seen her in some heavy making-out sessions with a boy I knew. If she got weird, I could always pull out the I'll tell-on-you card, but I didn't think it would come to that.

According to the map, an open field was nearby.

"Do you want to try going full tilt?" I asked him.

He didn't answer. All he did was signal his horse, and off he went.

I kept right up with him. "You sure you've never done this before?" I yelled.

"No, but I *will* do it again! This is great. Hey, will *you* do it again?"

He made me laugh, "You know it." I wasn't quite sure what we were referencing. Of course, I'd ride again, but maybe that's not what he meant.

After some time, a rider from the stables rode up to us. We both burst out laughing because we hadn't realized anyone might be joining us. It could have made for an embarrassing situation.

"Time's up, guys," the guide said. "You need to come back in."

We raced back across the open meadow and slowed down as we neared the stables. The guide was a good guy; he had given us an extra half hour for free.

"Do you want to go to the lake?" Berit asked me in the car on the way back to his house.

"Hell yeah." We were sweaty, and I wanted to see him naked again. I wondered if we'd touch each other again, but it wouldn't be my suggestion; it would have to be his. As my mind wandered through different scenarios, a picture of him kissing me popped into my head, and it disturbed me. I had never seen two guys kiss like a guy and a girl. I wondered why I could understand the other things, but not a kiss? Something I needed to think about.

I could feel him give me an occasional look. "We were flying on those beasts."

"Yeah, I'm my best on my horse. I feel in control. It's been my escape, man."

"I dug it," he said as he pulled off the road. The walk to the lake seemed shorter than before. Berit was like a little kid pulling his clothes off as he walked to the rock ledge. I peeled mine off at the same rate, and we both took a running jump into the water. The shock of the cold water almost took my breath away. He came up with a shout and flicked his hair like a dog shaking off water.

"How'd you find this place? It's not like you can see it from the road." I wanted him to talk to me like he had before, like two regular guys.

"The guy from the head shop told me," he said. "He and his girlfriend are old hippies. One day I asked them about places to go, and they told me about this lake, which was cool because they also became my source for pot and hash.

"I've gotten high with them a couple of times, but it's weird. They were at Woodstock," he said. "And I've caught them out here swimming. Not a pretty picture, trust me."

Soon we were talking like we had been before.

"What's New Orleans like?" he asked. "I've heard it's a kickin' place, especially for gays. Now you'll have more things to check out since your revelation. Maybe I could visit sometime." His parents were okay with him traveling alone; evidently, it happened a lot in Europe. He'd been to all kinds of places like Spain, Italy, Greece, Belgium, and France. He wanted to go to Australia and New Zealand.

We lounged on the rock, drying off in the summer sun. We talked about anything and everything while we toked on a joint. I could see the definition of his muscles; his chest was pumped, his abs formed indentions, and his arms were cut. He wasn't muscle-bound like one of those monster bodybuilders or anything. He was my live, in-the-flesh statue of David. I noticed him checking me out and thought he probably saw how white and skinny I was. We went over the plan again for Sarah. I'd bring her with me the next morning. I was happy about doing it, but I also regretted mentioning it. I didn't want to share him.

Riding back to his house, he grabbed my hand and held it for a minute. I was kinda uncomfortable with hand-holding, but I'd let him hold other things, so it was strange that I was a tad uneasy. He turned on his record player back at his house and showed me his eight-track tape player but said he preferred records. Besides, he only had a few tapes.

He turned up the volume and led me into his bedroom again. He dug in his closet, and I hoped I didn't have to hear about the ultra-cool Han. Instead, he brought out a couple of magazines like *Playboy*, only with naked men. I had never seen anything like them before. I couldn't help but look, and it was an eye-opener. I flipped through one and noticed toward the back pictures of men performing different acts on each other. The more I looked, the more aroused I became, but he remained calm like it was no big thing.

He tipped up my chin, moving my eyes from the page. "See anything of interest?"

What was the right answer? I was like a deer in the headlights. What should I say? He cupped my crotch and smiled. Of course, it was hard. What did he think would happen after showing me those pictures?

"Have I made you feel—"

"I don't know where we go from here. I feel awkward, like yesterday things happened like unplanned, ya know?"

"Bradley, there *is* no plan. Do what makes you feel good. It's not complicated. I liked everything about yesterday. Today doesn't have to be anything else or anything at all. Or if you want to do that, we can," he pointed to a picture of one man on his hands and knees and the other kneeling behind him. "It's cool either way." He tossed the magazine back in his closet.

He could still sense my awkwardness, so he whispered that everything was okay and smiled at me with kind, patient eyes. He told me to tell him no if I wanted him to stop touching me. Of course, I wanted him to touch me. After a few minutes, he leaned me back on the bed and unzipped my fly, then stopped and took off his pants. He squirted some kind of gel in the palm of his hand, grabbed my dick, and stroked up and down as he covered my entire erection. He climbed onto all fours like the man in the picture and talked me through the experience. I pushed my dick into him, and no words could describe the sensation that I was home. He didn't have to tell me what to do. All on its own, my body began sliding in and out, building intensity with each thrust. I couldn't control the sensation pouring through my body until I cried out and shot my load. My knees became weak, and I collapsed beside him. Nothing could have prepared me for that feeling.

He was patient and kind, even though I was the only one gratified. All he was left with were my remnants and the sticky gel everywhere. I felt guilty. I was sure he wanted to do me, but there was no way I could fathom him putting his dick up my ass. He hadn't acted like it hurt, but it had to, I mean, things that hard and big can't seem to fit there. He rolled over and smiled.

Day two of my gaydom had been outstanding.

"What'd you think? Ever felt so good before? I dug it," he said as we lay on his bed, catching our breath. How could he say he liked what I did, I wondered. It was beyond understanding to me. I tried to picture what it must've been like, but I couldn't wrap my head around it. I wanted to say not to expect the same cuz no way was I going to do it. As long as I was getting the big thrills, I liked being gay, but I drew the line at sucking someone's dick or letting someone ride me. I couldn't even be good at being gay.

"Berit, didn't it hurt? Maybe I'm not cut out for this. The thought of you doing that to me, no offense, just hurts to consider it. And how you said you dug it, shit, no way."

"Don't worry. With time you'll feel differently. Han fucked me before I had my first go with him, and yes, it was painful at first, but I knew he enjoyed it. He wasn't very gentle, though; it was more of wham-bam." He shrugged his shoulders like it was no big deal, but I was pissed.

What a bastard! I thought. *Han, the pervert, had made Berit his whipping boy.* Just the thought pissed me off.

I liked us being regular guys, doing guy things like friends, with no one ever knowing our little secret. I felt accepted when I was around Berit. For some reason, deep down, there was a connection like no other. It was like milk and cookies; nothing else would suffice. The thought of doing those kinds of things with anyone but Berit was a big fat zero. He could visit New Orleans, and my family would always come to my aunt's at least once a year. Because he was seventeen and close to being an adult, maybe my parents would let me go somewhere with him. I'd save my allowance for a trip to Amsterdam, or maybe we'd go to Australia where he wanted to go.

As he sat on his desk and opened the window, he started to light the joint again, but I stopped him because I thought I had heard a car coming up the driveway. Sure enough, two minutes later, his mom entered the house and called him.

"Berit?" she asked, knocking on his door. He looked like he was going to crack up laughing, which made me start to laugh. That's when we both saw the mess we had left on the bed at the same time, and I instinctively jumped on it as she opened the door. Berit stayed sitting on the desk.

"You boys have the music blaring. I'm surprised you can even hear yourselves think."

By then, I couldn't hold back my laughter.

"What's funny, Bradley? Your mom complains about your wild music, too?"

"Yes, ma'am. She does." Berit looked at me. *Good cover.*

Before leaving the room, she turned down the volume.

Berit started to laugh. "Way to act quick and hide the evidence," he whispered. He pulled me up, checked the back of my pants, and then laughed some more when he started trying to wipe off the sticky mess. "I knew I'd get a piece of your ass."

As I was getting ready to leave, we firmed the Sarah plan again, like it was an act of espionage. I'd ask her when I got back to the house, and I was sure she'd say yes.

As I walked back to my aunt's house for dinner, Dad met me and asked if I wanted to invite Berit to go out for dinner. Hell yes, I thought, but I didn't want to put Berit on the spot or make him feel funny around my parents or cousins. I told Dad that I'd run back and ask Berit, and I'd either meet him back at the house with or without Berit, depending on his answer.

Berit's mom greeted me at the door before I could knock. "Forget something?"

"No, ma'am, I wanted to ask Berit something, that's all." She called for him.

When he got to the door, he was wearing a towel wrapped around his waist. His hair was wet, and he'd obviously been showering, even though I had only been gone a couple of minutes.

"We're going out to eat. Ya wanna come? If you don't, it's cool, and if you do, that's cool, too." I could see him debating the pros and cons.

"Why not? I'm just warning you I'm not great in crowds. Be back in a minute." He was back in a flash.

As we walked to my aunt's, we resumed talking. He was easy to talk to. We again laughed about his mom and the timing of everything. Had I not heard his mom, Berit would've been toking away. "Thanks, man. You saved my ass, Brad."

I laughed. "If that's what you call it."

I don't think I had ever been as happy before, and it kept getting better the closer we got.

For not being at ease in big groups, he seemed just fine. My cousins giggled at everything he said and went on about his accent. Sarah sat quietly until the hype had settled. In her sweet southern drawl, she asked, "Berit, what do y'all do all day?"

"We hang, *y'all*," he laughed. "Say, why don't you hang with us tomorrow?"

Fuckin-A, I thought. It couldn't have gone any better.

"Y'all sure?" I could see the twinkle in her eye.

"Well, I wouldn't have asked." He flashed his pearly whites at her. If I wasn't seeing things, he may have even winked at her. His winking at her and his laid-back demeanor made my stomach tickle. I was attracted to him. Why hadn't I seen who I was long ago? My life would have been far less confusing.

Dinner went well. Berit was the kind of person to get along with everyone. All his traveling around Europe made him conversational with the adults. He knew a lot about things like world history and politics, which was way off my radar. He spoke with my cousins about living in

Amsterdam and how some fashion trends began in Europe and then came to the States, without saying Americans were a bit behind the times; anyone with half a brain could pick up on it.

Even though he was my friend, I was a little jealous. He was the whole package—cool, smart, athletic, funny, and personality plus. Coming from my stupor into reality, I saw him looking at me. He looked like he was trying to read me. I knew I had never been one to hide frustration or anger well—my parents had told me that time and time again. I felt like my feelings were out in the open for everyone to see. Could he see my jealousy? My insecurity? Was I that transparent? My thoughts of being a walking billboard brought me to wondering if people could tell I wasn't into girls. Certainly, my dad hadn't figured it out after the episode with his friend's daughter in Virginia Beach.

After dinner, my parents dropped Berit at his house. As he got out of the car, he reminded Sarah and me not to forget about the following day.

Sarah and I went up to our room upon returning to my aunt's house.

"What's up with Berit's invitation?" she asked.

"He and I talked about how this trip is never a great one for us." I then hesitated. I had to tell her about Berit, but I didn't want to blow her away completely. Besides, it was part of the plan. "There's something I gotta tell you, but you have to swear you won't tell anyone, and I mean anyone."

She rolled her eyes, "I promise."

"You can't tell *anyone*."

She was getting annoyed. "Okay, Bradley, cross my heart and hope to die. Good enough?"

"It's important…what I'm gonna say, oh shit, Sarah, Berit's gay, and we figured it would be fun if he acted like he was interested in you."

"Wow, what a waste….Don't worry. His secret's good with me, but that's such a waste. He's gorgeous and his body—"

"He thought you needed to know, so there were no mixed messages." I had to cut her off because I didn't want to hear what she had to say. I didn't know how far she'd gone, and I sure as shit didn't want to know or hear her thoughts on his body.

For a quick second, I wanted to add, "You're not kidding! His body's outta sight."

The next morning, Sarah and I headed toward Berit's house where there'd be less scrutiny. Fresh out of the shower, his hair was still wet, but he'd managed a pair of cut-offs. His parents were gone, the stereo was blasting, and it was more than evident he was high as a kite. My mind started wondering. Would he smoke in front of Sarah? Would I smoke in front of her? I had to chill out. I was such a freakin' weenie.

We listened to the rest of the album, and then Sarah started with the questions. "Do you have any brothers or sisters? What sign are you?" She then flat-out said what I had told her. "What a waste! I would've liked to get you in the sack." She laughed. "Have you ever been with a girl?" She cocked her head as she twirled her hair, trying to give sexy eyes.

"I'm an only child, and I'm a Libra," he said. "I guess, thanks for the compliment, and if I floated your way, I'm sure I would've taken you up on the offer in a New York second. Last night you asked what we did all day, I didn't want to say it at the table, but we swim at a hidden lake. It's kind of private, but I didn't want to give up the secret if anyone knew the area. Hope you're not worried about getting your hair wet." He shoved his hands deep into his pockets and fished out the car keys.

We got in the car, he opened the passenger side for her in case there were any prying eyes, and I climbed in the back begrudgingly. I kept my thoughts and feelings to myself. The radio blared as we sped along the road. She was far more inquisitive than I had ever imagined, and I didn't know if I felt okay with it all.

"Do you mind if I smoke?" she asked.

"What are you planning on smoking?" He laughed.

News flash. I didn't know she smoked cigarettes, and even though I knew she'd smoked pot, I didn't think she was a regular pot smoker. Apparently, I didn't know much about my sister and didn't want to know.

"I've got some killer weed." He offered as he pulled his stash out of the glove box.

"I'm game. " Sarah was all in on the adventure.

She loved the trek through the woods to the lake. "Y'all, this is super cool! How'd you find this place? I mean, it's like we're in some freakin' movie. Ya know, like three kids in the middle of nowhere. This is so exciting. We don't have anywhere even close to this at home. It's the best!"

We reached the lake, and he started to strip. I wasn't sure how far he'd go. Oh, but he took it all off. Sarah started taking off her clothes and called him a tease. Shit, I hadn't seen my sister naked since she was seven and I was five, nor did I want to. She was all woman, that was for sure. I never realized her tits were so big. She could've been in one of those magazines if she'd been that kind of girl. Hell, maybe she was that kind of girl, I thought. After all, she did tell Berit she'd want him in the sack. Fuck, perhaps this wasn't a good idea at all.

"Come on," he called out to me from the water. "What are you waiting for? Get your ass in here."

I turned the other way, quickly stripped, and jumped in. She probably said, "What a waste," at least three more times. The last time she said it, he said, his boyfriend certainly didn't think it was. She giggled and told him touché. She'd never thought of it that way and said she had a couple of guy friends who were gay and had told one of them the same thing, but he ignored her comment.

When we got out to sun, Berit lit up again. By this time, the odd situation didn't seem quite as strange. At least everyone put on their underwear, thank God. The way Sarah was acting, I could tell she thought he was cool, and maybe I had gained some cool by association. I almost felt like hippies at Woodstock, letting it all hang out when we were swimming.

Passing the joint, she grabbed his arm. "What's that about, Berit?"

On the inside of his wrist was a scar. Why hadn't I noticed it before? He became quiet as if she had crossed a line.

"Sarah, mind your own business," I scolded. "Sorry, Berit." I saw the same sadness in his eyes, like when he spoke of Han. I took his other hand and held it right in front of my sister. I didn't care. I wanted to let him know I was more than just his friend, and I cared. I had wondered if it had been me he referred to as boyfriend, which didn't sit easy with me. It felt, well…queer. I hadn't gone far enough down, as he put it, the yellow brick road, to claim to have a boyfriend, but I wanted to make his sadness go away. *Thanks, Sarah*, I thought, *for bumming him out.*

Before she could say anything, he stood up, stripped, and dove into the water. I looked at her and told her to stay put. I then stripped and jumped in. I wanted to do something to let him know I cared and wasn't going to betray him. I imagined the scar had a matching one on the other wrist, and they had something to do with the Han crap. He had hurt Berit. I swam right up to him, face-to-face. I closed my eyes and did it without even thinking. I kissed him. It was not like a full-on make-out, but I could feel his pain and wanted to make it go away. I tried to bring out the free, fun-spirited Berit back again. He kissed me back quickly. "I'm sorry Sarah pried, Berit."

He looked me in the eyes, and I could see his sparkle had drained, and his ever-present smile had vanished. All that I saw was a somber, sad boy. "After seeing Han with the girl, I felt cheap and used. I thought we were special, not like I was a piece of ass. God, it hurt to the point that it made me vomit. He had taken something from me, which at the time I was willing to give because I thought—" He paused. "Forget it. It doesn't matter what I thought. The truth was, he used me, and what I had expected of our closeness was shit.

"After I left him, I went to the Red Light District where you can buy any kind of sex; it's an abundant commodity. Basically, I paid for sex. Afterward, I felt gross. I went to my grootmoeder's and cried. Who I'd become sickened me, and I decided to end it all. I went into the bathroom and filled the bath. She heard me and probably thought it was odd that I was taking a bath at that hour. When she didn't hear any noise, she forced the door open. I had just opened my wrists. She bandaged me and didn't make me feel bad. She nursed me back to health and listened." Treading water was making his speech choppy, but he continued.

"She told me I was the way I was, and she loved me no matter what. She advised that I learn to love myself first and be selective with who I shared my body and soul with, and there was nothing in this world insurmountable. Hearts could stand more than one break. She made me promise never to attempt it again; it wasn't my life to take. Man, her advice was solid. I decided to embrace who I was and be thankful to have my life. I take things as they come, enjoy each day, and don't worry about anything. I roll with it. I have been, for the most part, selective with whom I have shared my body. First and foremost is friendship, and Bradley, you're a real friend, I can tell."

"I'm glad your gran saved you," I said. "You truly are the coolest person I've ever met, and I hope we can be friends forever." I knew how I sounded, but I didn't care. I was the opposite of cool, and it showed in what I said. He could've said the same thing, and it would've been cool.

"Thanks, Bradley, for everything. It means a lot to me."

The Sarah day ended up being fun. Although we had only the closed-eye kiss, I felt like Berit and I got closer. Whether she saw me kiss him or not, I don't know. She never asked me if I was gay. Just as well, I wasn't ready to fess up.

The days passed quickly. From Berit and my friendship, my aunt and uncle befriended his parents. Berit continued to be reserved around my cousins, except Leslie. She and her fiancé, Del, freely gave their friendship. I had been right: Leslie came to love my Berit, like a big sister.

On our last night, we returned to the cave and talked about our friendship and the possibilities of seeing one another in the future. We talked about the necessity to be careful and not take chances. I wrote on the cave wall, "Friends Always," and signed it. We fooled around a little, but not as much as we had on some of the other days. While the sex was outstanding and opened a whole new experience for me, the most important thing was the bond we had, the friendship we ignited. What we had wasn't a summer fling. It was far deeper. I knew for sure it was real.

When it was time to leave the cave, I didn't want to go. The ache hurt intensely in the pit of my stomach. My family was leaving before sunrise, so we wouldn't have any more time together. God, it was painful, like someone ripping out my heart and stomping on it. I didn't want to say goodbye. Berit said it was more like, see you next time. I was afraid all the big plans we had made to keep in touch might fade away with time, and Berit would forget about me even though he promised and swore he wouldn't.

He was my first love.

Chapter 4

Once home again, life was back to the same humdrum. Nothing new had happened in the neighborhood while we were on vacation. Riding Trumpet was my reprieve from missing Berit. I doted on Trumpet while telling him all about my new friend and our secret. He was a magnificent chestnut beast, statuesque at almost eighteen hands. Together my pleasure gaited gelding, and I made a tight appearance. Judges loved him; he had personality, and they could see it. We made a good team. My parents hired a trainer, which I never understood because Trumpet and I took first more times than not.

Pelim, the trainer from Turkey, had a thick accent that was easy to make fun of, but he had mesmerizing eyes. He and the horses were one in spirit. Even though he played it up with all the women at the barn, I could see him watch me. On occasion, he came to dinner with my family. More than once, he'd had too much to drink and made a disguised pass at me. I ignored his overtures. I think he was probably like a Han. He didn't care if the flavor of the night was male or female. I couldn't dig that; besides, my feelings for Berit were heavy on my heart.

I wrote Berit and sent three photos: one of Trumpet alone, one of me posed on him, and an old action shot my dad had gotten from one of my earlier shows. The letter flowed as if I were there talking with him. I reminisced about the first time at the lake, but as I had heard my mom tell Sarah, "Don't put anything in writing; you're not prepared for the whole world to read," I didn't mention anything incriminating regarding the pot or the sex. When it came time to end the letter, I had a hard time.

Sincerely was too formal, and love was too gay, so I just signed my name, stamped the envelope, and mailed it.

A week went by, and I hadn't gotten a letter from him. Surely, he had received mine. I felt heartbreak and dread. Had it only been a summer fling? For me, it hadn't, and I found myself crying in my room.

After a few more days, I had all but given up hope when my mom told me that I had a letter. I could hardly breathe. He must've sent it right after we left because it looked like a herd of elephants had trodden over it. Who knows, it could have been lost forever, but it wasn't. I tore open the envelope and devoured his every word. As I had, he also had written in code. He, too, referenced the lake but also wrote about the cave and how much fun he'd had with Sarah and me. He had the perfect close—friends always, just like I had written on the cave wall.

I worked up the nerve to ask my mom if I could call him and that I'd pay for the call out of my allowance. She smiled and said okay but not to make it a habit. My heart was bounding out of my chest as I dialed. I figured his parents were at work, and he'd be alone, so we wouldn't have to censor anything. He picked up on the fourth ring.

"Berit, it's Bradley. I got your letter." I made the phone call from my parents' room and had locked the door.

"Hey, it's good to hear your voice," he said. "I got your letter and the pictures. Trumpet is huge, I mean, like giant. You look so professional on him in your suit. Quite dapper, my friend."

"That's why my parents bought him. I looked ridiculous on the average size horse. We make a statement when we enter the ring, not to brag, but we do." Hearing his voice was a dream come true. It hadn't been a summer fling and what we had was real.

"Have you investigated any of the gay hangouts in the French Quarter?"

"No, because I don't have anyone to go with me. Wanna hear something weird? My parents hired a trainer for me. His name is Pelim, and he makes these disguised passes at me, especially when he's drunk." It felt good to be able to tell someone who would understand.

"You're smart to stay away from him."

I glanced at the clock on my dad's bedside table and knew that I had been on the phone long enough and that Mom would be telling me to get off the phone, so I blurted out, "When are you coming to New Orleans? Before school starts?" I sounded like a boy-crazy girl.

"Let me talk to my parents, and I'll let you know in my next letter. You should be receiving two more letters within days."

"Ha. I thought you might have forgotten to write. I just got your first letter today. The envelope was crumpled like it had been caught in a machine." Before I could finish telling him how I'd started to feel sad, he stopped me.

"You must have felt as though I had Han'd you." That was the term we had come up with for people who used people.

"Thanks," I said, feeling relieved.

"So, how has the jerking off with the two Rickys going?" He laughed.

I had to laugh right back. " Surely you're joking, Berit. I haven't even seen the two Rickys, and let's just say that chapter in life is over and done. Now that I got the real thing, shit, it's all about us being together, at least to me."

" Same here," he said.

"Okay, I gotta go," I said. "Friends always?"

"Yes, friends always."

As he said, two more letters arrived within days apart. My mom noticed and sat me down.

"Do you worry about Berit? Have you noticed that he seems sad?" I knew what she was getting at. "Gabrielle told us what he did when he was at his grandmother's house the last trip he took to Amsterdam. I was shocked she would mention it, but, at the same time, I know how levelheaded you are, and maybe it's good he has someone like you as a friend. If you hear anything, Brad, you need to tell me, promise?"

I couldn't believe Gabrielle would have been so casual with people she had only met. "Yes, Mom, I promise I'll tell you, but Berit told me all about the whole thing. He was in a bad headspace at the time and promised his gran he'd never do it again. He promised me, too. Mom, he's the most unbothered person I've ever met. Y'all have nothing to worry about." I hugged her; she truly cared. "Since we're talking about Berit, any chance he could come down toward the end of summer to visit?"

"That's a *marvelous* idea," she said. "Sarah will be excited too."

I nodded as my stomach did flip-flops in excitement.

The two Rickys came to the house and wondered why I hadn't been hanging out since I had come home from vacation. They filled me in on the neighborhood happenings: a dog had bitten a neighborhood kid, and our favorite drug store was closing. Dang! What a bummer! I loved to ride my bike there for a nectar soda plus a dollar's worth of penny candy; they were one of the only real soda shops left.

Other than our magazine activity, which wouldn't happen again, we loved water balloon fights. The two Rickys and I had a system: We were the youngest of the neighborhood kids, and our system made us victors almost every time and had for years. The only problem was the bigger kids were no longer into playing, so we usually had a bucketful of water balloons and no one to battle.

Fat Ricky had the brilliant idea to hide behind bushes and throw them at passing cars. "It wouldn't hurt anything," he said. "They'll hit the window and splash! Whoop-tee-doo!"

So after loading a bucket of water balloons, we headed two blocks over to a busier street where Fat Ricky hummed a full balloon at a passing car. We realized the old man driving, Mr. Ellis, had his window down as it was about to hit. Shit! He was a dick. A mistake this grand was gonna be punishville if he got us. Fat Ricky might even get the belt. We hauled ass to my house. We ducked in, ran up to my bedroom, and laughed our asses off.

Five minutes later, while we were still busting a gut, my mom called upstairs, "Bradley, come down this minute." Thank God I hadn't gotten wet. I kicked off my shoes and grabbed one of the letters. I had been laughing so hard I was crying; maybe I could play the miss-my-friend crying card.

I walked into the kitchen, wiping my eyes, "Yes, Mom?" Fuck, Mr. Ellis was standing in our kitchen. Mom had given him a towel, but his shirt was soaking wet. I managed to hold it together.

"Bradley, are you okay? What's wrong?" She drew to my side with a hand on my shoulder.

"Nothing, Mom. I'm fine." Her attention on Mr. Ellis had switched to me, her precious boy, the kid who never did anything wrong. Most of the boys in the neighborhood were mischievous, but not her Bradley.

Mr. Ellis cleared his throat, "Son, do you know anything about kids throwing water balloons at passing vehicles?"

"No, sir." I lied.

I could tell from his scowl that he didn't buy it for one second, but Mom did, and nobody wanted to mess with my mom, especially concerning me. "I coulda sworn I saw you," he said.

I looked at Mom, and she turned to Mr. Ellis. "James, if Bradley said he didn't do it, he didn't do it. I'm sorry somebody hit your car with a water balloon. Can I get you some ice tea or lemonade while you dry off?"

He kept eyeballing me. "No, thank you. Boy, if you hear of anything, you make sure to let them know I'll be on the lookout, then they'll be messing with the law." The door closed behind him.

I turned to go back upstairs, "Bradley Davis, you left wet footprints on my carpet. I suggest you and the two Rickys take some towels and dry my stairs off."

She knew *she knew*! Shit, I was gonna be in deep crap when Dad got home. "Yes, ma'am," I said and slithered upstairs. When I returned to my room, the two Rickys were still dying, holding their sides. "Y'all old man Ellis was downstairs. He hunted us down. He knows it was us, but my mom covered for us. Shit, I hope she doesn't tell my dad. Oh, and she said we have to dry the carpet."

After we dried the carpet, Mom sent the two Rickys home and me to my room, which was okay because I could read and re-read the letters. I started to write another letter to Berit and knew he'd get a kick out of our shenanigans. I wrote about the drug store, the nectar sodas, and the history of our water balloon wars, including that day's debacle. To think about it, I was probably too old for water balloon wars. The two Rickys were a year younger than me, but they were immature for fifteen, which meant I was an even bigger loser—the kind that enjoyed water balloon fights at sixteen.

A few days later, another letter arrived. Berit's parents agreed to buy him an airplane ticket to visit around the first or second week of August. How long did I want him to stay? I read the line over and over. I wanted to say, "Just freakin move here," but I settled for, "If you can come for two weeks, that'd be dynamite!" He told me he had been going horseback riding because it reminded him of me and our fun day together.

I realized our letters had begun to lose some of the code and sounded emotionally charged. I'm sure anyone with half a brain would have read them and said, "Get a load of these queers." It wasn't fair. Most people would have looked at a young boy and girl the same age as us with a sentiment of isn't young love sweet. Two guys were a whole different kettle of fish. Nothing was sweet; we were twisted and disgusting. We'd be an embarrassment to our families.

The dates Berit sent me were perfect, and both sets of parents agreed to the two weeks. Mom gave me permission to call. It was the weekend, so it was a crapshoot about who would answer the phone.

His mom picked up.

"Hi Mrs. Jensen, this is Bradley Stedman. Is Berit around?"

"No, I'm sorry. He's out right now, but while I have you on the phone, I just wanted to let you know how thankful Berit's dad and I are for your friendship. Are you sure about him staying for two weeks? Berit can be sulky and extremely moody at times. Two weeks might be pushing it. I better talk to your parents. If they need to send him home early, we'd understand."

I was pissed! I wanted to yell into the phone that moms aren't supposed to knock their own kids. Instead, I stayed calm. "Berit and I are a lot alike, Mrs. Jensen. We know how to deal with each other's moods. We both had our moments when I was visiting New York." I had kinda lied, but I bet part of his moodiness was like mine at home, sheer boredom and frustration.

"If you say so," she said. "It's a nice thing for you to invite him to New Orleans. He's never been." She paused for a moment. "Wait, he's walking in the door right now. Here he is," she passed the phone. "Honey, it's Bradley from New Orleans."

I could hear him thank her. "Hey, how's it going?" he asked. "I'm stoked about the trip to New Orleans. Can't wait." I could hear him walking with the phone and a door closing. "I was just at the cave and started thinking. Do you need me to bring some pot, or can you score?"

"I don't think I can, but I bet Sarah could. I'll check. By the way, I think we need to keep the language in our letters a little more coded. I don't think my parents would go through my things, but just in case."

"Do you think they know deep down?" The question made me wince.

"I don't think so," I said. What a horrid thought! I sure as hell hoped they hadn't a clue. That'd be embarrassing!

"Oh, okay. I don't think my parents know, but they kinda suspected something was up when I didn't go to the spring dance with anyone. A lot of girls had called the house asking me to go." He paused for a moment. "I'm going to tell them after the trip to New Orleans. I'm surprised Gran didn't tell them back then. I've often wondered what she told them about my wrists. I've never brought it up, nor have they brought it up. You'd think they woulda been curious or want to know."

We stayed on the phone for a few more minutes, although I knew I'd be getting the *scream* to get off the phone soon. My job was to find out about the gay bars, which were good and not so good. We hung up, both excited about his upcoming visit to The Big Easy.

I had no idea how many people he had been with, and I didn't want to ask, but I was curious inside. He had been my one and only. All those horrible fears ghosted their way to my mind: Was I as well equipped? What kind of friend had I been? I had only been on the benefitting side of the equation. I knew our relationship eventually would be equal in the sex department, but right now, the thought of either of the other activities turned my stomach.

I didn't think I could do them. Berit had given me several blowjobs, and I'd had ridden him a few times, but the only things I'd done for him was a hand job. It's like he wanted to suck my dick, and he wanted me to have sex with him. I didn't ever suggest either because I knew I didn't want to reciprocate. Crap! What did Berit see in me anyway? I knew I loved him and yet was hesitant with showing it. Was I gay, or wasn't I? As a gay guy, wouldn't I want to do all those things for my lover? The answer should've been yes, but it was, hell no. Berit said I would change in time, but I didn't see any chance of it.

Mom's voice interrupted me. I'd have to schedule my self-deprecation for another time.

When I walked into the kitchen, Mom was ready for a serious talk. Shit!

"Do you have any concerns about Berit's visit?" she asked.

I told her no.

"So what are you planning to do when he's here? Where are you going to take him?"

Deer in the headlights, deer in the headlights…emergency…think fast! "Um, I planned to take him to the stables and see if Cindy would let him ride Prancer. If not, we may go on a trail ride through the park. I want to take him on the Sunfish, go fishing by the lakefront, or head over to Bayou St. John, and definitely go to Pontchartrain Beach." I kept listing things I thought might seem the right answer. I very well couldn't say we were going to cruise the gay scene in the French Quarter and probably engage in some sexual activities while getting stoned.

"Bradley," she looked with serious intent, "honey, you know Berit is well-traveled. He's been all over Europe. I'm sure he'll want to tour the French Quarter with all its historical value and also go to Cafe du Monde for beignets. Your dad and I will pay the bill for a couple of dinners at nice restaurants. As I'm sure you've gathered, his family is well to do. His dad has many European car clients and heads up the U.S. division of the agency. Berit's not your run-of-the-mill kid."

"You don't have to tell me, Mom. I got to know him pretty well on vacation." She wouldn't believe how well we got to know each other, I thought. In fact, I could safely assume she'd be in shock, maybe horrified, if she found out how well we knew each other. "We're a lot alike, both kinda different. Loners. We get each other."

She went about her business listening to me, but I knew how she could go through the motions and not actually listen. Many times, her "skill" was a saving grace. If I got caught doing something questionable, I'd play the I-asked-you-and-you-said-uh-huh card. She knew she did it, so she would buy it almost every time. Both Sarah and I used it to our advantage when we needed it.

A couple of days later, I was out at the barn, and Cindy worked on Prancer. I asked her if she minded Berit riding Prancer. She hesitated but eventually agreed to one time.

As I was walking back to Trumpet, I noticed Pelim and Mark, a guy who helped clean the stalls, feed, and groom the horses, go into the tackle room. They both had quickly looked around before sneaking in unnoticed, or so they thought. I waited about seven or eight minutes and barged in. As I suspected, Pelim and Mark had their pants down with hands on each other's cocks in a rather passionate kiss. I calmly said, "Excuse me," and quickly darted out. They freaked when I startled them. I had set the trap to ask them questions like how'd you know and where do y'all go out? I could play the naïve kid and get the info I wanted for Berit's visit.

About ten minutes later, Pelim came out straightening his hair and trying to compose himself. He made eye contact with me and signaled he wanted to talk to me

"Bradley, what you see, you tell no one," he whispered in his heavy Turkish accent. I realized if I had waited one more minute, they would've maybe been in the act, and I could've milked it better.

"Pelim, I didn't see anything. I don't know what you mean," I said and coyly smiled like a Cheshire cat. He knew I knew, but I was willing to watch him squirm.

He exhaled and said, "I take care of you. You say nothing?"

I played dumb like a champ, "Huh?"

He was frustrated. "I give you hand job, blowjob, what? I tell no one, and you tell no one."

I had him in the crosshairs, "No, why would I want you to do that?"

He was coming unglued. He started hammering me with questions about my sexual experience and told me a man could make another man feel much better than a woman. I asked why he would even think to do such things because I knew he had been with some of the women from the barn. I actually said the word, *queer.* I asked where queers like him went to meet other queers. Certainly, there weren't a lot of queer places. He told me something like there were many more than I would have guessed, and then he began to rattle off the names of bars and clubs in the Quarter.

"The clubs are *far* more *be*-autiful than the clubs for men and women. The dance music far superior, the drinks the best in the city. Let me show you how a man can make you feel," he said.

"Thanks, but no thanks, Pelim." There was no way he was touching any part of my body.

"Let me know you change your mind. Bradley, shhh to no one."

"Right, shhh." I rolled my eyes and went back to the tackle room to get a bridle. The cheering was almost deafening in my head. I did it! I did it! The Bourbon Pub Parade.

I realized I needed some hipper clothes to wear clubbing and ones that made me look eighteen. I knew I was tall enough to pass. Berit could pretend to speak broken English or not understand anything at all. I'd remain silent as a mute. They'd assume I was with him and think I didn't understand English at all. I convinced my parents to give me the credit card and went to Jeff's Haberdashery.

Jeff's was the place to go. I had heard of it but never been. It smelled like expensive cologne, and a good-looking salesman with Harris on his nametag approached me. I wanted something like his outfit because he looked completely put together. While I didn't have tuned-in gaydar, as Berit called it, I was pretty sure he was gay.

"How can I help you today?" His smile made me feel at ease.

"I have a friend coming in town who is originally from Amsterdam and a little older. I want to look like we're the same age.

"Sounds good. In what kind of setting, casual or more sophisticated?"

"We'll be eating out at some of the nicer restaurants downtown and then maybe going to some clubs."

"I'm Harris, and you are?"

"Bradley Stedman." I smiled.

"Want to go out and show him the Quarter?" I nodded. "You'll want to look smart but stylish. I have a few options over here." He picked out several outfits and then set me up in the dressing room. "Would you care for a glass of wine?"

"Um, no, thank you." I put on the first outfit, a pair of black flared pants and a printed tight-fitting shirt with wide lapels. Being used to military uniforms and riding clothes, I was a duck out of water. I stepped out, and he saw my confusion.

"Given your height, Bradley, you can wear almost anything and look fantastic. We don't want to put big bells on you, but just enough to be stylish yet subtle, not too trendy." He sold me the outfit like his and another a bit simpler but sharp—white linen pants with a white linen jacket and a bright red dress shirt. "You can't go wrong with the look."

"We're going out, and I'm not eighteen yet, but I want to look like I am."

"Don't worry," he said. "No one will question your age." I figured he was a bit older than Berit, but not much, so he knew. "Just to make sure, wear a pair of tinted glasses." He inspected my face in the light. "Because of your dark hair, you could probably grow a stache. How much time do you have?"

I figured I had about a month, and my hair had already grown a bit during the summer. It hardly was regulation for school, but I only needed the look for his visit. If the mustache, or stache as the guy said, looked shaggy, I'd get rid of it. All I wanted was to look sophisticated, older, and mysterious. The inner voice reared its ugly head: *Who the fuck are you kidding? You're a weirdo, skinny, and the exact opposite of cool.* I gave Harris Dad's credit card, thanked him, and left to shut up the voice harassing me in my head.

To prepare for Berit, I decided to start exercising with a set of my dad's dumbbells and laying out in the sun. What miraculous changes I expected were unrealistic, but I could improve and was determined to do so. We didn't have any places like the hidden lake or abandoned cave to be alone. Although it wasn't nearly as cool as Berit's with its rebuilt engine, I did have a car. On the other hand, mine had A/C. I had already programmed the hip radio stations.

Like all the other Fourth of Julys, the neighborhood families gathered at my house to set off fireworks. The parents would all drink too much, which left the opportunity for Sarah and me to sneak a drink or two, and this year was no different. A couple of gin and tonics later, and my tongue loosened up.

"I'm really excited for you to have Berit coming here," she said. "What do you have planned?" I went through the same list as Mom's but added I would take him to a few bars.

"Please don't tell Mom," I said. "By the way, can you help us score some pot?"

"Um, I don't know. Why can't Berit bring some with him?" She paused for a moment. "I'll see what I can do. If I can find some, I get to hang out with you guys at least once. You know I really want to kiss him just once when he's here. He's so hunky." Her free talking was making me uncomfortable. She wanted to kiss him…hmm…I *had* kissed him. All I could think was she was so into being Sarah that she didn't have a clue Berit and I were more than friends. The kissing thing still wasn't in my comfort zone. Would it ever be?

Day after day, I lay in the sun for a half-hour on each side, and I slowly was getting color. I may have imagined it, but the muscles in my arms seemed to be getting more developed, too, although my chest was still hopelessly undeveloped. My hair growth was substantial, and I actually was doing okay on the mustache front, or so I thought. I heard my parents quietly mention the new facial hair on a few occasions.

About two days before Berit arrived, Dad took me to the side.

"Your mom and I have noticed the longer hair and the beginning of a mustache. We understand, but as soon as Berit leaves, the hair and mustache are going too. Remember this: You have to be comfortable with yourself and not let other people lead you. You need to be a leader and your own man."

I wanted to tell him I had never been a leader and probably would never be and that I had always been a weirdo. I kinda knew why now, but the day for *that* conversation hadn't yet arrived. I didn't know when or if ever we'd have the conversation. He'd hate me for sure.

Dad was a man's man through and through. I got my height from him and figured that the weight would come on as I got older. He had been a jock. From what I understood, he played a mean game of football and was near pro level in basketball. I knew he had high hopes for me. I was better than okay at basketball, but I hated it. I loved horses, especially Trumpet. I'd had two others, but neither of them compared to Trumpet. Together we were winners. When Berit was here, I would let him ride Trumpet at least once to feel what power and grace felt like under the saddle. I knew he'd had a good time with the trail horses, but nothing was like my majestic champion.

On the other hand, Mom would accept me being gay possibly hurt. She incessantly talked about one day being a grandmother. I was her baby, and she overlooked a lot when it came to me. If anyone were to understand, it would be her. We shared a close connection. She'd make Dad come around; I knew he loved me no matter what.

What Sarah knew was beyond me. Had she seen me kiss Berit? Did she suspect anything knowing how he buttered his bread? The truth was, did she give two hearty shits? She was still trying to figure out who she was and what she wanted in life. I knew she desperately wanted to go to college and join a sorority, but she wanted to feel accepted more than anything. Why she didn't realize she was well-liked was anyone's guess. There had been a few guys in her life, but none serious. I knew she eventually wanted to get married and have a family, but she wanted to marry well and wouldn't settle. She had never been a just-settle kind of girl. Sarah was a driven person. I learned more about her during the day spent with Berit, and I liked my sister, bitchy and nosey as she was. I always knew she had my back, period.

Chapter 5

The big day finally arrived, and after three sets of directions to the airport, which I knew already anyway, I left the house. My stomach was in knots of anxiety, butterflies of excitement, and scared all at once. What if I wasn't the guy he remembered, I thought. I never realized that he could be thinking the same thing.

Parking was easy, and I arrived at the gate fifteen minutes early. I watched as the plane landed and taxied in, and then the stream of people deplaned. What a funny word, I couldn't help but think. I envisioned people flicking little planes off their arms and shoulders. I was grabbed from behind, interrupting my thoughts.

"Jesus, I didn't see you get off the plane. You scared the shit out of me."

"Obviously," he gave me a big friendly hug. "Shit, look at you. Could you look any better?" He squeezed my arms. "Somebody's been working out. Your hair looks great, but I have to ask, what is this?" he asked as he patted the hair on my face.

"Don't like?" I asked as we walked to baggage claim. "You haven't changed. Still too cool for your own good."

"I don't know if I like it or not. It takes away some of your boyish charm," he said and laughed.

"It can go, but I thought it might help to get into the Parade."

We got his bag and headed to the car. No more than two seconds in the car, he grabbed my face and kissed me, once again, not like a make-out kiss, but nonetheless, a kiss. His hand briefly glided over my crotch.

"Oh!" he smiled, "You still feel the same way, Bradley, and am I glad. I've been wondering if you would remember me and still feel—obviously, you do." His smile was purely Pepsodent. The A/C kicked on. "Nice. I wish I had A/C in my car. As you know, mine is a work in progress, maybe one day."

The interstate was clear, and before long, we pulled up to my house. He gave my mom and Sarah a big hug when we went inside. My dad was working in the yard, but Berit went out to shake his hand.

Mom asked if he wanted some ice tea or lemonade, her fridge's usual suspects. I brought his bags up to my room, taking a last glance to make sure it looked up to snuff. I could hear him and Sarah laughing in the kitchen, and I got jealous. When would this ridiculous insecurity leave me? He came to visit *me*. I needed to get a handle on my crazy.

I went out on the landing. "Up this way, Berit." I put on a record, one I bought with thought, Judy Garland's "Somewhere Over the Rainbow."

He walked into the room with a huge smile and said, "Too fuckin' much, Brad, too fuckin' much. That's hilarious. You're a thoughtful young man."

I shut the door, locked it, and then hugged him. "I've missed you, and I know I sound way gay, but it's true. Thank you for coming here."

He continued to hold me and whispered in my ear, "Are you kidding me? The picture of you and Trumpet has given me many pleasurable moments, and now I have you in the flesh. We're gonna have a blast." He started to unzip my pants, "May I?"

"Uh-yeah, sure." He pushed me on the bed and pulled off my underwear. It didn't last long. After he finished, I looked up at him. "We have to talk, Berit. I've been thinking about our time together. It's always been me getting the better side of the deal, and it's not right. I want this to be a two-way thing. I want to give as much as I get."

"All in good time, Bradley. I'm not going to force this too fast. I don't care if anything happens or not. Your friendship means more to me than anything else. Anytime you want to touch me or whatever, it's all up to you. I don't want you doing anything you're not completely comfortable with." He lay next to me on the bed, propping himself on his side.

I undid his pants. He helped to lift his body so I could pull them down. I grasped his dick. I wanted to feel the warmth of his skin in my hand, his firmness, and the throbbing of his desire. I worked him methodically. I remembered he liked a firm grip. I obliged, and when it was time, I knew he was about to come; I wanted to feel his explosion. I cupped the head of his dick as it pulsed into my hand. Of all things, I then put one of my fingers in my mouth. Step one: I passed the taste test without losing my lunch, yes! He looked at me and smiled. It was apparent he found amusement in my finishing touch.

I imagined at some point I would accept other things, but even with our day-to-day time together in New York, I had done what I had done and nothing more. Berit seemed to think I'd be ready for more one day, but I wasn't too sure of it. Everything Berit did to me and let me do to him was great, but the thought of putting his dick in my mouth or assuming the position was frightening. What if I gagged when he released down my throat or screamed like a girl when he penetrated me? I was a wimp, plain and simple, and he was my adventurous hero. I couldn't imagine my feelings changing, but then again, look how far I'd come. I had felt extremely uncomfortable with a kiss, and now, while I wasn't into a big make-out, I did enjoy the closeness.

We spent the rest of the day sightseeing. We rode around the neighborhood, and I took him to the lakefront. He was impressed by the size of Lake Ponchartrain. We then headed to the barn, and I introduced him to Trumpet.

"Wow, he's amazing," he said as he stood next to Trumpet. "He's huge! You were right. He is majestic."

We were hungry by then, so I introduced him to sno-balls and po-boys. Even though it was hot, a nice breeze at the lakefront cooled us off. After we ate, we took a few tokes as we walked along.

"Where do you see this going from here?" I asked. I was confused about the future and how it all worked.

"Bradley, you stress over the details. I enjoy our time together. We're friends. Can't that be enough?" He looked over at me with a smile. He was sincere in his every word.

"When you told Sarah your boyfriend didn't think it was a waste you were gay, who were you talking about? Me?" I slowed my pace; my strides were faster the more nervous I became.

"Have you been hung up on that all this time? Shit, you're a boy, and you're my friend, right? That's all you need to think about, understand?" He wasn't condescending, but I could tell he hardly took it seriously.

I stopped. "Berit, I want to talk seriously because this is all new to me," I said. "I don't know any other gay people to ask. Besides, you're the only one I trust." He walked away from me and sat on the sea wall, and I joined him.

"We're close—close as I can get to someone. Now that you know you're gay, you'll catch the subtle glances, and I'm sure when we go to the Parade, you'll be a hot item. There'll be lots of guys wanting your time. Monogamy is rare in our circles, and in-the-moment sex frequently occurs. The advice to be selective with who you share your body with is the name of the game. Be elusive, and don't be easy. Otherwise, people will talk, and your heart will get broken, your self-esteem will go down the toilet, and you'll get depressed. Friends are more important than anything, and if someone won't hang with you without sex, then that person isn't your friend. Just walk away. Have fun and relax. Now no more serious talk for the rest of my time here, okay? Just fun together…like you say, two plain old guys." He smiled and laughed.

We sat looking at the lake. I don't know if it was because we were stoned or what, but the lake seemed brighter, more inviting. The reflection of the blue sky made the lake even bluer, and the sunrays sparkled like diamonds. Just like a picture from a travel brochure, I realized. Several boats were sailing, and there was the occasional breaking white cap. Even though I'd seen it all my life, being with Berit, I felt like I was seeing old Lake Ponchartrain for the first time.

I pointed to one of the big clouds. "Doesn't it look like a big dick and balls?"

"You horndog. I know what you have on your mind, and friend, it's right here." He grabbed his crotch. "All yours for the next two weeks." We started with the nonsensical laughter induced, no doubt by the pot. I wanted to ask him if he had been with anyone since seeing me, but I better leave it alone, I thought. Do I want to know? No. Besides, I had to remind myself: He didn't have anyone else to hang out with; then, I felt guilty for my thoughts.

The following night I planned to take him to the club. I probably was more excited than he was like a kid on Christmas Eve, but he also seemed to be looking forward to it.

I dressed in the bathroom to unveil my new outfit and put on the glasses as I entered my bedroom.

"Ta-da! So, whaddaya think? Glasses or no glasses?"

He smiled as he inspected me. He looked sharp in a blazer, T-shirt, and jeans. He wreaked of posh, no matter what he wore or did. Here I was dressed for the night and still felt like the ugly duckling.

"*Everybody* in the place is gonna want a piece of you and to think; you're with me. Child, I'm not letting you get more than three feet from me." He looked me up and down.

"Mom made reservations at Galetoire's and gave me her credit card. I don't know how much drinks are at the club, but I do know there is a cover charge."

"I have the cover and drinks," he said. "No one buys us drinks, and don't ever put yours down, *ever.*"

We went downstairs and headed for the kitchen.

"You both look great," my parents said as we entered. Dad cleared his throat and said in a raspy whisper, "make sure if any girls try to pick you up that they don't have an Adam's apple."

Berit laughed at the joke. "Not much I haven't seen. Amsterdam is a smorgasbord of diversity." I wasn't as quick, but I finally figured it out.

"I bet you've seen your fair share," Dad said.

Before we headed out, they gave us the warning speech: Don't go on any side streets, stay aware of surroundings, and park at the Royal Sonesta Hotel.

After fifteen minutes or so, we pulled on Royal Street.

"The nuance of this place is incredible," he said. "We *have* to take a tour during the day. This place is enchanting and romantic. The buildings are quaint, like old-world. I've seen tons of pictures, but they don't do it justice. The whole place is like from another century. You don't come down here just to romp? If I lived in New Orleans, I'd be here quite a bit." He pointed in amusement, "Look at the kid over there tap-dancing on the sidewalk. You gotta love the street performers everywhere. There's so much soul. Doesn't the Quarter make you feel alive? It has energy down here."

Who talked like that and sounded cool, I thought. Not me, for sure. I'd sound gay to the highest power, whereas Berit came across as sophisticated and worldly.

We ate at Galatoire's, which he compared to some restaurant in Paris. It was good, but I was never into sauces or vegetables. The wine he ordered for dinner tingled on my tongue. I wasn't sure how it would go with a drink at the bar, though. He grew up drinking wine with dinner, so it came naturally to him. I would've preferred a Coke, but I needed to act older, so I drank the wine.

After dinner, we walked to the club, both of us having long strides. I watched the heads turn as he walked by. He could've had any one of a couple dozen women. He was freakin' unbelievable. I had to admit; a few people even sized me up. I could barely contain the excitement. I'd never been to a bar, let alone a club, and a gay club at that.

Nothing could've prepared me for The Parade. The guy at the door didn't even ask to see my driver's license. I had never seen so many gay people at one time in all my life. I had looked in some of the open doors along Bourbon Street before, and they seemed nasty and dirty, but The Parade was anything but. It was sophisticated and modern, with a few platforms hung from the ceiling trimmed with neon rope lights. The cages were for one or two dancers with impressive physiques, hardly wearing anything. Every attractive person must be here. I thought as I took it all in. A mass of half-naked bodies gyrated to Elton John as lights flashed in sync with the beat. So, this is it, the ultimate in clubs? I sensed a definite stir from the patrons when Berit and I walked in. He grabbed my hand and led me to the bar.

Berit ordered some drink on the rocks for us and sounded like my dad. After the bartender had served the drinks, Berit raised his glass. "To you and tonight," he said. Then out of nowhere, he put his arm around me and pulled me in for a *real* kiss. I didn't throw up in my mouth, but I *did* take a big swallow of my drink to wash it down.

"With all the eyes on you, I marked my territory," he whispered in my ear. "Tonight, you're not up for grabs. Virgins might as well have a neon sign on their forehead."

I looked around the packed bar. More men were kissing men than I could shake a stick at. The dance floor was shoulder-to-shoulder people, including some women.

"Many of those girls are fag hags, girls who liked to hang with gay guys," he said. "I've never understood that concept. Who knows? Maybe they're trying to conquer the unconquerable."

I finished my drink, and he got me another. "Slow down there, Tiger. Nurse your drink. There's no rush." We sat close, his hand on my thigh. The alcohol started taking effect, and my inhibitions were waning. My body wanted to be touched more than ever.

"Let's dance," he said, pulling me out to the dance floor. Dancing was cramped, though, because it was packed. I had a much easier time dancing at the formals I had gone to with Cindy's friend. Berit's body rubbed against me, and the feel of his package through his pants turned me on. His body was taut; I could feel his muscles through his jacket. Every time he would lean in to talk to me, his breath tickled my neck, and my dick got harder and harder. I must have appeared self-conscious.

"It's okay," he assured me. "No one knows but us. You can try to relax." Just after he said it, some guy grabbed my butt, which startled me. He looked over my shoulder with menacing eyes. Then, another guy, obviously drunk, started rubbing himself on me.

"Fuck off, asshole," Berit said, moving me aside and looking down at the much smaller drunk guy.

I watched as the same guy moved on to another group of guys and did the same thing. Well, I guess it wasn't personal, I thought. After a few dances, we took a break, and two men, both maybe upper twenties and clean-cut, approached.

"Hey y'all, I'm Stuart, and this is my partner, Leighton." Stuart was shorter with a round face and great dimples when he smiled; whereas, Leighton looked more like a distance runner or cyclist and seemed a few years younger than Stuart. Both were as friendly as could be. "Are you guys from out of town? We've never seen you before."

"I'm from New York," Berit said.

"Cool. Your accent doesn't sound like from these parts." How they detected his accent, I don't know, I wondered.

"Yeah, I'm originally from Amsterdam."

The three of them continued talking, and I felt left out. Berit must have sensed it and put his arm around me.

"How long have you two been together?" Stuart asked. "We're celebrating our one-year anniversary today." They kissed. I wasn't sure I liked all the kissing, touching, and groping in the club. Maybe I wasn't gay after all and just liked someone else jerking me off. Maybe I only wanted Berit and no one else. He watched me as the thoughts raced across my face.

"Lighten up, Brad. You've got to roll with it. Wanna dance again?"

I followed him to the dance floor. Dancing helped me lighten up and not feel quite so stiff and odd. Before long, I immersed myself into the music and occasionally Berit's eyes. He was all smiles and pulled me close. "You move me." My heart raced, and I felt tears welling in my eyes. I could feel his affection for me in each word and touch. Wait, more like love, I realized. He loved me, and I loved him. Wow, what's going on? I'm so emotional…maybe because of the drinking. I've won the best blue ribbon ever, I thought.

We must have danced for at least an hour and were both sweaty messes, so he ordered two club sodas with lime to cool down while watching the go-go dancers. The scantily clad young guys seemed to turn on many bar patrons, but they didn't do much for us. The dancers amused us more than anything because many appeared slightly older than me. Meanwhile, I could overhear many comments made by other people, and they made me uncomfortable. Was this the world I was entering? Did I want this kind of world with these types of people? I thought not. It wasn't me. I liked the horse world.

I felt a tap on my shoulder. "Hello, Bradley. Who is your friend?"

Shit, Pelim! I turned and introduced Pelim to Berit. Running into Pelim would only open the door for more gross passes from him. I watched him undress Berit with his eyes and wanted to deck him. He was definitely a Han, a user.

"Bradley, why did you act peculiar when—"

"Because I'm *not* like that," I said.

Berit touched my back to calm me. I was sure he knew who Pelim was from my description. He had warned me that Pelim was the kind to screw anyone and avoid being alone with him. Berit had made it abundantly clear to be selective with whom I had sex. In my world, my brain and my heart were the same. For me, I had one interest, and it was Berit.

"Can I buy you guys a drink?" Pelim asked, but we declined. I wondered if he would share seeing Berit and me with Mark and whoever else he was diddling at the barn. That wasn't how I wanted my family to find out. The question remained: Was I gay or infatuated with Berit and our friendship?

We left soon, and a million questions were flying around my head during the walk to the car. Maybe because I was still buzzed, I blurted out, "Is there anyone else besides me right now in your life? Are you doing it with other guys because I don't know if I'm gay or if it's just how I feel about you? I didn't want to be touched by anyone in there, and some of them grossed me out."

He started laughing and then stopped. "I'm sorry to laugh, but you're funny."

"I'm not trying to be funny. Berit, I want to know." I stepped in front of him on the sidewalk to block him.

"Brad, get a grip and calm down."

I entered an open door, and he followed me. I ordered a drink and then realized all I had was my parents' credit card. As I started to hand it to the bartender, Berit grabbed the card, changed my order to a Coke, and ordered a soda and lime for himself. "I hardly think your parents would appreciate an alcohol charge." Hardly anyone was in the bar, so he grabbed our glasses and headed back to one of the open booths.

"Sit." He sounded pissed. "I get it. Tonight was overload for you. Maybe it was too soon, but I'm glad I was with you. Maybe it's not your scene. Who knows? I like to go clubbing now and then because I like to dance, not to pick up people, and because I was in New Orleans, I wanted to see what the city had to offer. By the way, it was one of the better clubs I've seen.

"Bradley, I'm not seeing, doing, or whatever anyone right now. *You* are my friend. I have more fun with you, and as I told you, we don't have to do anything. Do I think it's just me? No, Brad, I don't. You're gay, my friend, and it's okay. Love yourself for who you are. Many of the men in there creeped me out too. They're prowling. You can feel it. And as far as Pelim, he's disgusting. I wouldn't even want to shake hands with him. I don't want to make you feel insecure, but it's your problem, not mine, so stop trying to make it mine. I don't know any other way than to say it: You are my friend. I don't have any other friends. Can you move on from this, please?" He took my hand and kissed the top of it.

He was right; it was my problem. I felt childish and foolish. I thought, why do I need to keep having these feelings. Why does he want to be friends with someone like me? "I'm sorry, and you're right. It's my problem, not yours. I'm gonna try to move on. Would you buy me a damn drink?"

He didn't and wouldn't because I was driving, but he hit the joint in the parking lot as we got to the car.

The next morning, Mom called to wake us up. I thought having the two Rickys come over to hang out would be amusing.

"I can't wait to meet the two Rickys," he said. "I hope they didn't bring a Playboy with them. That ain't happening." He laughed.

"Damn, my head hurts," I groaned. "The thought of food makes me want to puke. I had a blast last night, and I'm sorry I–"

"Shh, he said, walking up to me and putting his hand on my lips. "I remember the beginning of my journey, and it wasn't *that* long ago, so I get it." He reached in his shave kit and handed me two aspirins. "Just think how bad you would have felt if I'd have let you get the last drink. You'd probably be worshipping the porcelain god."

We headed downstairs and entered the kitchen where the Rickys were waiting impatiently. I was glad Mom hadn't told them to come on up like she had so many other times, maybe because of Berit. One couldn't help but be taken back by Berit, and the Rickys were no exception. They immediately started asking questions about Amsterdam and him.

Soon we headed out into the backyard.

"So, is it true that all the girls in Amsterdam are beautiful and into sex?" Fat Ricky asked.

Berit burst out laughing. "Um, do all Southern girls walk barefoot and fry chicken?" The two Rickys burst out laughing.

"Seriously, American girls are equally as beautiful as the girls from the Netherlands. I particularly like Southern girls and the way they talk. They always sound so sweet, even if they aren't." He then looked at me. "Bradley tells me you guys, I mean *y'all*, are killer in water balloon fights. I've never been in one. Can we play with four people?"

Right then, Sarah, who had spent the night at a friend's house, walked through the gate with her friend Sue Sue.

"Whacha doin', y'all?" Sarah asked. Even though she knew about Berit, I could tell that she still loved flirting with him. He teased back, knowing she knew the score.

"Do y'all want to join us in the water balloon fight?" Berit asked. Sue-Sue was all about joining.

The two Rickys and I didn't waste another minute, and Berit saw firsthand our stellar system in action as we started preparing the balloons for the fight. Before long, we had two huge laundry baskets filled to the brim with ammo. The two Rickys were captains and picked their teams, with Berit being the first one chosen. I was then picked, followed by Sarah and Sue Sue. The battle commenced, and within minutes we were all soaked, a perfect way to cool off on a hot summer's day.

"I am so wet you can see everything," Sue Sue said, drawing attention to her white T-shirt.

The feigned embarrassment got the two Rickys' attention for a couple of seconds, but to avoid being pummeled, their attention quickly returned to the battle.

Berit climbed up a tree and told Fat Ricky to toss some up to him. He bombed me with a torrent of balloons, but I returned the fire. Even though the tree gave him an initial position, he couldn't move away from the barrage of balloons I threw at him.

Some of the older kids must have heard the commotion, seen the battle in session, and joined in. The girls were put on the duty of loading more ammo. If a balloon didn't explode, it was a mad dash to get it, usually ending in tackling the man with the balloon. Before I knew it, each side had five boys and one girl, and it was the best water balloon fight I could remember. Everything was better with Berit.

When we finished, some of the older kids announced they were going out on their Sunfish because they were already wet.

"Are you game?" I asked Berit.

"Sure. I've never sailed on a Sunfish."

The girls went inside to change, but Sarah made sure to give Berit a quick wet hug. I could see the jealousy ooze out of Sue Sue. Sarah couldn't help but giggle to herself. I was sure she thought if she only knew.

Eric, a neighbor who lived two doors down and Sarah's old crush, took half the guys in his VW van, and the other kids split in another car with Berit and me following alone in mine. Berit talked a little about his dad during the drive after seeing the VW van. His dad happened to be the ad manager for the U.S. division of Volkswagen, and some of his other clients were BMW, Volvo, and Saab.

"Why don't you drive an import?" Not that I didn't think his car was outstanding.

"I'm all about the fast car," he said. "European cars are boring; it's all about the American muscle car. I wanted a Corvette, but my dad wouldn't buy me what he calls 'a death trap,' so I bought my Cutlass Supreme, rebuilt the engine, and got to know it inside and out. My determination impressed my dad so much that he agreed to pay my insurance."

When we pulled up, the lake looked still with a slight breeze. The club wasn't fancy like the Metairie Country Club or the New Orleans Country Club, but the waiting list to get in was miles long. Located on the point overlooking the lake, the Club was perfect for people to hang out on the seawall and sneak a beer or two.

The Sunfish was a one-person sailboat, lightweight, and easy to get in the water. I handled it while Berit looked around at the harbor; the number of expensive boats seemed to fascinate him. I explained New Orleans, being surrounded by water, was a fishing and boating community. I figured we'd lag since everyone else was on their own boat, and we were two big guys on mine, but surprisingly we caught the wind and tacked out the harbor pretty fast.

I tightened the sail to the max, and soon we were heeling close to going over and moving at a good clip.

"What happens if it flips?" Berit asked.

"It's made to flip. See?" I pulled the line tighter, and over we went.

"Shit!" He yelled.

"Berit, we're okay." I showed him how to put it upright. "Sorry if I scared you. We're perfectly safe. I'd never risk hurting you or myself, for that matter." I thought for a quick second about what I had said and wished I could've taken it back.

He must've seen my face. "You're cool. I was stupid and won't flip out again. Get it? *Flip* out again." He started laughing.

"Haha! You're a real comedian," I said and laughed. "Seriously, if you're worried about sharks or anything like that, don't worry. The lake only has sand sharks, and they stay at the bottom. In truth I've never seen one except once when some old guy caught one while he was fishing at night."

"Do you mind if I try navigating?" he asked. I gave him the basics, and he took over. We went over two times until he got the knack of how far he could heel. He was doing well until suddenly he flipped her over. When we came up for air, he was right beside me in the water, his body next to mine.

"I'm dying to touch you," he said. I knew not much could happen in the water because it was awkward as all hell, but he slid his hand down my shorts, and I reciprocated. We went under the water, and I kissed him. He came up laughing. "Underwater, really? Hey, I'll take your kiss anytime I can get it."

We righted the boat and were back on track.

"Berit, what do you want to do tonight? I don't want to go back to the Quarter. I still feel a little hungover. I guess I'm not much of a party boy."

He ran his foot along my leg, "We can hang with your parents for a while, maybe go see your old fisher guy."

"Maybe we'll be lucky, and he'll catch a sand shark. They're only this big, or at least the one I saw." I held up my hand maybe eighteen inches. "Or," I raised my eyebrows at him, "We could watch the submarine races." He had no idea what I was talking about. "Submarines are underwater, Berit, so you can't see them. It's like lover's lane, only New Orleans style." I grinned at him. "Let's head back. I'm starving."

"Think fast." I knew he liked Pringles, so I tossed him a can. After pigging out, we went upstairs to shower, he in the hall bathroom and me in my parents' bathroom, and then toweled off in my bedroom. I thought about his comment earlier and pulled his towel off.

Berit leaned back on the bed in all his nakedness. I hadn't even touched him, and he already had a boner. I closed my eyes and began to touch him as I had the first time. I couldn't believe what I was about to do, but I dropped to my knees. I was afraid I wouldn't do it right or that I was gonna lose it because my gag reflex had already been triggered a couple of times. He moaned as he got closer, and I didn't stop. I didn't puke, but I couldn't swallow.

I grabbed the nearby towel and wiped my face.

"Kiss me?" he asked.

I wondered if he realized I still had his jizz on my mouth.

"Kiss me?" he asked again.

Okay then, I thought. I was sure he realized the situation, so with my eyes closed, I kissed him. He stuck his tongue deep into my mouth. I wasn't sure how I felt about it, but when he grabbed my dick, the kiss made the jack-off more intense. I then started to understand. Making out while doing anything else was like plugging in a string of lights: it took an ordinary tree and made it magical.

"Bradley, you're priceless. Whoever ends up with you will be one lucky man," he said and smiled. I could feel his authenticity. He meant every word he said.

"I was hoping it would be you," I said. Berit smiled again.

"You're sweet and innocent, but long-distant relationships never work. We'll always be friends, but someone will come along and turn your head, and that's okay. I'll always be happy for you if you're happy," he said matter-of-factly. However, the thought of him being with someone else tore out my heart. I didn't want to hear or think about it. The tears started forming in my eyes. Why did he have to say that right after being so close and sexual? It was unfamiliar territory for me, and it meant a lot, not just some, as he said wham-bam.

"No, no, no," he looked genuinely upset. "Don't cry. Why are you crying? We just had a wonderful time. Did I say something to hurt you? Oh God, I hope not."

"Don't ever talk about me being with anyone else but you. I'll make this long-distance relationship work. I won't do these things with anyone else. I can promise you."

He put his fingers over my lips. "Shhh. No, you can't promise me that. I know you want to, but there'll come a time when I'm yesterday's news."

"Shut up. Obviously, you don't know me. You will *never* be yesterday's news. You're Berit, my one and only love. I know you loved Han, and it didn't work out, but I'm not you, and you're not Han. Don't say it again." I turned my back to him.

He sat up. "Let's get dressed and go watch the old man catch a shark." He acted calm, cool, and collected, and I was anything but.

I got dressed, but I was angry and hurt. How dare he jump to those ridiculous false conclusions, I thought. I guessed our relationship was more important to me.

We drove to the lake and sat on the seawall to watch the old man fish. Berit knew I was angry. I had said maybe five words to him since our not-so-nice conversation. To think I had just done what I said I'd never do, and that was his reaction.

"Brad, talk to me." He turned toward me.

"About what? How you don't want to make this relationship last? Are you already looking for someone else? Are you bored with me? Am I not experienced enough for you?" I could feel my body tremble. No, I wasn't gonna cry again. No.

"Not at all. What did I tell you the most important thing was?" He inched closer.

I had to think because he had said so many things. He was an endless stream of words of wisdom.

"C'mon, Bradley. I've said it a hundred times. It's the most important, above all else." He looked at me as though trying to will the words from my mouth.

Then it hit me. "Friendship." I got it. He would always be my friend. He would always love me. No matter the situation, he was my friend. How could I be so blind?

"Brad, I would lay my life down for my friend. There is nothing better or closer than the love between friends. It's what we all want. A friend to the end, get it? Neither of us knows what the future holds, do we? But we can agree to be friends. Nothing will come between that, right? Don't get me wrong; I have no intention of looking for anyone else, but lovers may come and go for either one of us, but friends are forever. If you're not friends, you're nothing."

"I get it. I do, but can we not talk about or hypothesize about either of us being with anyone else? Can we, Berit?" I turned my head from staring at the water.

"Yes, what I said I meant as a compliment because the performance was incredible. For your first time, I wanted to let you know that you were dynamite." His eyes told me without saying anything else that he meant every word.

"So, for my first blowjob, I did okay?" I timidly asked.

"Okay? No, it was perfect. You're a lot more sexual than you think."

We sat and watched the old man until he quit for the night. By then, my eyes were getting heavy, so we headed home.

We spent the next several days riding and sailing. Another day we hung out with Sarah for a bit. She got him into one of her what-if conversations. I knew them all too well. She could go on for hours.

I sat there mortified, wanting to throttle her, but I knew Berit wouldn't hesitate to put her in her place.

"Berit, you never answered my question from before: Have you done it with a girl? If not, how do you know you wouldn't like it?"

"Sarah," he shook his head. "I've had more experience than I care to share. I've learned what I like and what I don't like."

"But, just sayin'—"

"For Christ's sake, Sarah, shut up!" I had heard enough of her.

"Mind your own business, Bradley. You—"

"Not to be rude, but your naked body wouldn't make me hard enough to give you a go."

She threw her hands up, "Well, you don't know what you're missing."

"Believe me. I'll live without a roll in the sack with you. I care for you like a sister. Please tell me you wouldn't want to fuck Bradley." I could see his smirk.

"Berit, I can't believe you even said that. That's so gross!"

We sat in silence for a few minutes until she started again. She never once asked if Berit and I were lovers. I thought for sure she would. I guess it never occurred to her that her younger brother might have a sex life.

On the second-to-last night, we decided to go to the club, even though I felt bummed at the thought of him leaving.

"Let's go dancing and live on the edge," he teased. I hoped we didn't run into Pelim again. We went to Antoine's, another famous New Orleans restaurant courtesy of Mom and Dad. I could tell Berit appreciated fine food; a burger and fries from Bud's would've served me fine, but he was the guest. I was munchie ravenous, and the food tasted better than anticipated.

After dinner, we headed to The Parade, and again no one carded me at the door. The crowd wasn't as large as it had been the first time, maybe because it was Thursday and not Saturday. While ordering a drink, we ran into Stuart and Leighton, and the four of us hit the dance floor.

We all exchanged phone numbers. They were surprised to find out my age and imparted some words of wisdom about clubbing.

"Keep our number handy in case you ever need anything," Leighton said. "Being gay and being young as you, life may throw you some curveballs. And one other piece of advice: Don't go to the club alone. If you want to go, let us know. We live right down the street and can meet you here."

"So, what are some of the gay events in the city?" Berit asked.

"Halloween is huge," Stuart said. "It's a zoo. And then, of course, there's Mardi Gras. If you haven't been, you must come for a visit."

"Stuart," Leighton added, "Don't forget Night of Decadence at the Country Club." I guess he saw my confusion. "Not your parents' country club, Bradley." He started to laugh. There's a huge, fabulous house just outside the Quarter owned by a wealthy man. Around Labor Day, he has a huge party, and boy is it a night of decadence! Great music and food, but those are the main gay events. We have a large gay community in New Orleans and not just in the French Quarter."

"Halloween sounds like a gas, and I've always wanted to see Mardi Gras. I'll have to come back." I was happy to hear Berit was thinking of other visits to see me. I had to depend on Mom and Dad to travel anywhere.

I couldn't have imagined a night any greater.

As we left, I spotted none other than my school vice-principal. I diverted eye contact and headed out the door. I felt his business was his, and mine was mine. I never gave it another thought.

I woke up the next day sad because it was Berit's last day, but at least I had Halloween to look forward to and then Mardi Gras. My family would go to New York sometimes for Christmas, depending on the weather. With any luck, New York would have a mild winter, and I could see him then.

The day flew by way too fast, and soon he needed to start packing. He was standing right in front of me, and yet I missed him already.

When we were ready to go to bed, I made sure the door was locked and cuddled next to him in the twin bed he'd been sleeping in. It was a tight fit to sleep. It had been adequate for other activities, but sleep was a different story. Around 3:30, I gave up and moved into the other bed.

"Brad," he quietly whispered.

"Yeah?" I whispered back.

"Can you come back over here?" he asked. I got up and nuzzled next to him. His accent was distinct for some reason in the dark, and he sounded more like a little boy.

"I don't want to go."

"I don't want you to go." It was my turn to be brave. "October's not too far away." He held me tight.

"Friends always?" he asked.

"Friends always, Berit. That's a promise."

Chapter 6

More than a week passed, and I hadn't heard from him. Although I was busy getting all my uniforms and school supplies because school was to start in a week, my feelings were hurt that I hadn't heard from Berit. As sad as he had been when he left, I figured he'd be writing a letter on the flight home. Each day that went by, the harder it was to hold back my fears. I felt totally sickened. My parents had received a letter from Berit's parents thanking them for their hospitality and hoping they'd see them on their next trip to New York.

I couldn't take the waiting any longer. "Mom, can I please call Berit?"

"Yes, but don't talk too long."

Berit's mom answered the phone. "Hi Mrs. Jensen, this is Bradley Stedman. May I speak to Berit?"

"I'm sorry, Bradley, but Berit is in Amsterdam."

"Oh…um…when will he be back?" He hadn't told me anything about Amsterdam. I found that strange.

"He won't, dear." My heart sunk.

"How can I get in touch with him?" I needed to know.

"You can't. I'm afraid." She had no inflection in her voice. What does she mean I can't get in touch with him, I wondered, beginning to worry. Indeed, she knew how to reach him.

"I'm sorry, Mrs. Jensen. I don't understand how you don't know how to get in touch with him."

"I do, Bradley, but I'm afraid I can't give you that information. I'm quite busy, so I'll need to get off the phone, dear. Good-bye." I wanted to scream into the phone, Fuck you, bitch! I hung up and went to my room and sobbed in my pillow until I finally figured it out. He had told them he was gay, and they had kicked him out. He was at his grandmother's, but how the shit was I going to get in touch with him there, I thought. She didn't live in Amsterdam. She lived outside in the country; everyone just called it Amsterdam.

I went into my dad's study, pulled out the world atlas, and looked for Amsterdam and started madly writing the names of the surrounding cities and anything with a name, but some small villages weren't on the map, and I thought I remembered him saying she lived in one of them. Shit! I was frantic.

Sarah came in and noticed I was upset. "What are you doing in here? They'll kill you if they find you in here."

"I don't give a shit," I growled.

"What's wrong?" She seemed sincerely worried.

"I think Berit's family kicked him out after he told his parents he's gay, and they sent him to Amsterdam to his grandmother's house. I bet they kicked him out, those fuckers." I didn't use that word, especially in front of a girl, but to hell with manners and being polite.

"Bradley, calm down," she said. She looked at the map and called out the towns where I left off, helping me strategize. "I'll help you find him. Don't worry, you'll find him."

I called multiple travel agencies asking for tours of the countryside originating in Amsterdam. One agent inquired as to why I wanted the information. I lied, saying I knew what one of the big projects in school was, and I wanted to get a head start while I had time. She said she thought I was a bright young man. Right.

My closest friend was, poof, gone. What I didn't understand was why he hadn't written. He had my address. I knew his by heart. Surely he knew mine, but nothing. I wasn't excited about starting school or the big horseshow coming up in Tennessee. I couldn't relish anything until I spoke to or heard from Berit. I felt as though my life had come to an end. Before I met Berit, I was a big zero, and I was back to being a big zero. My cool had vanished with him.

A week later, on the first day of school, I didn't feel like talking to anyone or doing anything, so I just went from class to class. Before I realized it, the final bell rang. I was supposed to go to the barn to train with Trumpet for the upcoming show, but nothing mattered. I still hadn't heard from Berit. I felt like I'd never see him or hear from him again, all because of his fucking parents.

I went straight home, skipping the barn. I didn't even want to train with Trumpet, and he had always been my go-to for everything. Resting on the pass-through from the kitchen to the den was a letter for me. I saw the postmark, ran upstairs, locked the door, and opened it.

Hello my friend,

Let me start this by saying the trip to New Orleans was sensational, and I will hold it close to my heart forever. I'm sure you're wondering by now why I haven't called you. Remember I told you I was going to come out to my parents? Let's say…it didn't fair well. They were ashamed and told me I had to move out of their house. The sight of me repulsed them. I couldn't help but think one minute I was the apple of their eye, and the next I was detestable. Love is supposed to be forever, especially parent love.

My grootmoeder welcomed me. She couldn't believe her son, my dad, had acted so selfishly and without thought. She said she loved me no matter what. I told her all about you and us, probably more than she wanted to know. She held me while I cried. I miss you. I don't know when we'll be able to see each other again. You can call, but I won't be able to phone you because she can't afford it. 0031205264777. Remember the time difference. I'm seven hours ahead of you.

I'm sure you'll be starting school soon. I wish I could be there with you. I can't believe my fucking parents. They boxed everything of mine and went ballistic when they found my stash of pot, photos, and magazines. They returned my photo album minus the pictures of Han and me. I'm sorry our plans for Halloween will be in the crapper, but you go and have fun.

Stuart and Leighton seemed on the up and up. You should call them. I'm sure they wouldn't mind. Don't go to the club alone, though. Remember, you're easy pickings right now, especially if you're half as upset as I am. Don't give in to anger sex or get-even sex because you'll only hurt yourself in the long run. Believe me, I have to remind myself, and it's so easy here.

I'm sorry I didn't tell you enough. I wish I had. I love you, Bradley. I was attracted to you the first time I saw you ride by on the bike and got a rise in my Levi's. I bet you're smiling right now. You've got a great smile, beautiful, caring eyes, and great other parts, in case you were wondering.

We'll see each other again. I know it. Be careful and safe. Don't take chances, and please write. Don't give up on me. I'm going to get a job to help out here, but I'll save what I can to visit you.

Friends always,

Berit

I read the letter over and over. My emotions ranged from tears of sadness to tears of anger to, yes, Berit, a smile for the Levi's. Although Sarah aggravated me often with her constant intrusions to take Polaroid pictures at inopportune times, at least I had the photos of the two of us together. I put my favorite photo of Berit and me in an envelope and wrote him. I was pissed at his parents, and I didn't hold back. My emotions were all over the place, like one of those rides at the beach where I'd be thrown continuously around forward, to backward, then sideways. It was out of control and unpredictable, but this was fucking life, very real, and I couldn't get off. I had written three pages before I even realized it, the longest anything I'd ever written besides a term paper, and those were filled with a lot of quotes from my encyclopedia.

He was the best friend I ever had, and I was determined not to let our friendship fall away with time. I hadn't ever felt as much anger toward anyone as I did his parents. Their reaction made me think about what my parents might do when, and if, I ever told them. I couldn't imagine them kicking me out. Would they? Sex wasn't a topic in our house. Obviously, they had sex at some point because Sarah and I were born, but they were never affectionate except for an occasional kiss on the cheek. On the other hand, I felt like I couldn't keep my hands off Berit. If I wasn't touching him, all I could think about was touching him.

I had a ton of beginning-of-school paperwork to fill out. Even though doing it took every bit of concentration I had, I finished. That evening I told Sarah about Berit's parents. She said it was horrible, but she wasn't shocked. She had heard of other parents doing the same thing. I just couldn't wrap my head around a parent doing that to their child.

My night's sleep was fretful, filled with sadness and nightmares. I woke crying. Pull it together, Bradley! The last thing you need is to start crying at school. Mom was her cheerful self when I entered the kitchen. Sarah and I scarfed down the breakfast that Mom had prepared before heading to school, Sarah in her car to Country Day and me in mine. As I neared the academy, I could see most of the boys lined up along the front of the school. Maybe it was a fire drill, but why were they there early? Had I missed an announcement? The closer I got to them, the louder their words became until I finally understood what they were saying.

"Fag, fag, fag, fag!" they yelled in unison. My heart pounded like it was going to explode out of my chest. A couple of the football players ran up to my car and kicked it, "Get out of here, queer. We don't want your kind. Get out, homo."

I couldn't get out of there fast enough. I sped home, barely able to see through my tears.

My mom had seen me pull up and was waiting for me to come in. When I didn't, she came out. Her eyes filled with tears as she watched me fall apart. "Brad, you're home, darling. Talk to me." I couldn't for the life of me say what had happened. Every time I tried to utter something, I broke down again.

"Let's go inside, honey," she said, wrapping her arm around me. She got me a Coke and must have called my dad.

Fifteen minutes later, he arrived. I was still crying, and my body trembled. I tried desperately to compose myself. Mom kept looking at Dad, looking for something to say.

"Bradley, did someone hurt you?" he asked. "Were you in an accident?"

I put my head in my hands, lurching with sobs. I told them what had happened at school. Before they asked, I said the answer was yes.

"I'm gay."

"Son, that's your personal business and no one else's. Is there a particular boy at school who knew before, like for sure?" Dad asked. I knew what he meant.

"No, sir. I've never had a relationship with anyone from school. The only thing I can think of is I saw one of the faculty at a gay hangout. But I never told anyone. I wouldn't have done that to him." My dad's face turned bright red, and he clenched his hands like he was ready to take down whoever had hurt me.

"Honey," he said to Mom, "stay with Bradley. I have some business to take care of. No one is going to treat my boy like this. How dare they! After all the support we've given that school."

I'd later come to know all the details of how well off my parents were. Even though they didn't drive a fancy car or own a luxurious house, they invested in our education and future.

"Tell me the name of the person who told everyone!" Dad demanded.

"I just don't feel right about telling who it was," I said, wiping my nose. I didn't want to, it wasn't my personality, plus I wasn't one hundred percent sure it had been the vice-principal, maybe ninety-nine point nine percent.

"Okay, I understand," he said. "I respect that because you're a man of character. I'm still going down there."

Soon after Dad left, I calmed down as Mom sat by me on the couch, holding my hand.

"Bradley, I always suspected that you were since you were a young boy," she said. "It doesn't change the fact that you are my little boy and so precious to me." She started to cry.

"I didn't know for sure," I said. "I always had felt different, but I didn't know until I met Berit."

"Berit is a lovely young man and a good friend. What your relationship involved is between the two of you and no one else." She hugged me like a mother bear protecting her cub. Mom didn't get pissed often, but I could tell she was livid.

I turned on the TV, and soon Dad called. All I heard Mom say was, "That's good. I'm glad to hear you said that. I agree. I'll be sure to tell him. Yes, dear, I love you."

When Mom came back in the living room, she sat next to me again. "I just talked with Dad. Bradley, he's pulled you from the Academy and was able to get you in school with Cindy, starting tomorrow. Heck, y'all have been doing things together since nursery school. It'll be a nice change for you. Just think you already have a built-in friend. Y'all can even ride to school together. How do you feel about that?"

I didn't give a shit where I went as long as it wasn't back to the Academy. I still couldn't believe my vice-principal for ratting me out to everyone at the school when he was also gay. What the hell!

"Mom, that's cool. Y'all are the best. Thank you so much for loving me the way you do. Not everyone has it like this." I told her about what happened to Berit and his parents and being thrown out. She was appalled and couldn't understand how someone could act in such a manner. She felt sorry for Berit and was pleased he had his grandmother. I looked up at the clock. It was now noon. I figured it was Berit's dinnertime, so I asked Mom if I could call. I promised I'd only stay on for five minutes, no more. She nodded and repeated only five minutes.

I dialed the number from the letter. Berit's gran, who spoke little English, answered the phone in Dutch. She called to him, and he answered in seconds.

"It's so good to hear your voice. I'm glad you called," he said. "Are you okay?"

I told him the whole horrible story, starting with the boys at school yelling fag, and I could feel my voice waver. I had never heard him curse as much as he did; he wanted to hurt someone.

"So, how did your parents react?"

"They told me that they loved me, and my sexuality was my business," I said. "I don't know what Dad did when he went to the school, but Mom and Dad said that I'd no longer be going there and am starting a new school tomorrow. I'll be going where Cindy goes. I know a few people there from riding."

"That's good to hear that you don't have to face those kids anymore."

"Yeah, oh, by the way, I wrote you a long letter after I got yours and included a picture of us for you. Even though she was a pain in the butt, I'm glad Sarah took so many pictures."

"I really miss and love you, Brad."

"I miss and love you too. And Berit, we'll get through this. I told you already I'm determined to make our long-distance relationship work because I don't care how long the distance is."

"Friends always?" he asked.

"Yes, friends always."

About an hour later, Dad returned home after he had caused a scene at the school and managed to pull all its proposed funding. He told the headmaster that I, his teenage son, had more class and character than the spineless weasel telling other people's personal stories, and he better get a handle on the issue because he had one hell of a lawsuit coming his way. The next person, the school, would hear from was his attorney. He said they had screwed with the wrong cadet.

Evidently, he had stopped by Cindy's dad's office and made all the arrangements for my new school before going to the Academy. Dad and Mr. Alan weren't just friends; he was also my dad's attorney.

"Come here, Bradley." He embraced me and kissed my head. "I'm so sorry that you had to go through such a thing, but I'm proud of you, and I love you."

He excused himself to his study, where Mom and I could hear strategizing with Mr. Alan. They talked for several minutes. Mom and I waited to hear what they had decided, but by the end of the conversation, whatever plan they'd made, I never found out about it.

Cindy and I had always been close as far as the horse world, but now that we were carpooling and going to the same school, I had the opportunity to get closer.

What better time than the drive to school. "I'm gay."

"Something must be in the water because three of my other friends recently told me the same thing," she said.

Little did I know, but the new school would be influential throughout my adult life. My art teacher spent more time with me and helped me develop my talent and style. I also became fascinated with books and made a point to read the classics. For every book I finished, I rewarded myself with a call to Berit. I used a payphone because I didn't want my parents to know when we spoke and for how long.

With the Fall Saddleseat Horseshow coming up, I had lots of work with Trumpet to get ready, and both Cindy and I were spending many hours at the barn.

"I want you to meet my other gay friends," she said one day.

What the hell, I thought.

Little did I know she had invited them to the barn to watch me that next day. Several people—barn hands, other riders, or family and friends of riders—were always watching, so I usually paid no attention to who was watching the horses train.

After a few hours, Trumpet was as exhausted as I was. I started to cool him down. Trumpet had heard every secret and detail of my life. We were having one of those heart-to-hearts when a head popped under Trumpet's head.

"Bradley?"

"Yes?" A young guy, dressed in khaki shorts and yellow oxford, definitely not dressed for horseshit and muck at the barn, stepped in my view. I'd never seen him before. He had dark hair, almost a military cut like former classmates, and his green eyes had a soft glow, but he oozed fake friendly with a way too practiced smile. I had no idea who he was, and I didn't care.

"Hi, I'm Anderson," he said. "I'm a friend of Cindy. Your horse is outstanding, and I just wanted to say hello. Cindy has told me a lot about you."

Then I guess you know I'm not up for grabs, I thought of saying, but instead, I said, "Good to meet you. Not to be rude, but I gotta groom Trumpet." I continued brushing him.

"He's beautiful."

"Thanks," I dismissed him and his comment. I was acting like a dick, and if Cindy had said nice things about me, I wasn't behaving the way she had touted me.

"Do you ride?" I asked.

"I have, but I don't now. Horses intimidate me." He giggled like a little girl. He was way too effeminate for me. Nelly boys, as Berit would call them, were ridiculous, in my opinion. Why not put a big sign on your head that says I'm gay, but I guess everyone had their own thing. Nelly just wasn't mine.

I heard Cindy and a couple of other voices heading our way.

"Y'all, this is Bradley, my riding buddy," she said. "I see you've already met Anderson. This is Matt and Spencer." She had told me they were a couple, but they looked more like brothers, both short and about the same height with wavy blond hair, summer tan skin, and light eyes. Even their outfits were similar—low-slung faded jeans, tie-dye T-shirts, and Jesus sandals.

We shook hands. They didn't hide their not-so-sly flirty glances at one another or how close they stood to each other. Anyone who couldn't tell they were a couple had to be headless.

"Dang, I didn't realize how tall you were," Matt said. "What are you, six-five?"

"No, six-three." How long was this pretense going to go on? I was losing patience.

"I think someone's tape measure isn't telling the truth," he said with a singsong to his voice. For fuck's sake, how long did I have to endure this torture? Cindy had crossed a line. We'd have to remedy the situation for the future.

"It was nice meeting y'all," I said. "I do not doubt that we'll run into each other again." I glared at Cindy. "Cindy, before y'all leave, I need to check something with you."

They walked away. A few minutes later, Cindy came back to my stall.

"Brad, you gotta get out of this Berit funk," she said. "Live a little. If you don't like Anderson, that's fine, but you need to come out of your hole." I knew she was trying to be helpful, but she was butting in where I didn't want her to go.

"Please stop and never say anything about Berit, especially something like a Berit funk," I said, giving her a dirty look. "He's a no-go zone."

"I'm sorry. I won't do it again."

"I know what you're trying to do, but I'm okay, really," I said. I tried to lighten the mood, so I changed the subject and talked about the show, our fears, and apprehensions. We knew who our competition was, and they were outstanding. Cindy left, and I was finishing up. I liked everything put away perfectly.

We had a week more training before the horses would leave with the trainers, and then we'd follow two days later.

Mark walked into the stall. "Can we talk?"

"What about?" I didn't look up, staying preoccupied with Trumpet. Mark wasn't a bad-looking guy—a little rough from working around the barn. His dark brown hair was feathered in a shag haircut like David Cassidy and hung a little past his shoulders. He was around five-ten with broad shoulders. Although he was friendly, I knew he was one of Pelim's buddies, which creeped me out.

"Pelim won't leave me alone, and I know you saw us go in the tackle room. I'm not gay. I only mess around with guys every once in a while. He wants to do things I don't want to do and won't do. He told me he saw you out. I wanted to let you know that your secret is safe with me. What do I do about Pelim?"

"What do you want to do?" He knew Pelim trained Trumpet. Was he asking me to have my parents fire Pelim? I often wondered anyway why we had Pelim. No one could work better with Trumpet than me. I knew *that* for damn sure, but there was no way we could fire him before the show.

"I want him gone," he said. "He's doing some of the women around here as well as trying to get his jollies with me. He's gross." I couldn't agree more, and after Berit's comment of not wanting even to shake his hand, I figured he was too sleazy for words.

"My family can't do anything about the situation at present, but I'll let them know what I think after the show. He trains other people's horses, so my parents won't have much say there. I could ask my parents to talk to the other people he works for, but I feel awkward trying to get someone fired. I'm sorry that you feel trapped, but you need to stand up and say no."

I had a feeling he was going to come on to me. While petting Trumpet, his little finger touched mine. I moved my hand quickly.

"Would you be interested in going to the tackle room with me?" What gall.

"Thanks for the offer, but no." Hell no. Was the whole conversation a setup so that he could hit on me? Shit, Berit was right. The gay world could be unsavory. There probably were just as many, if not more, people trolling in the straight community. But right then, I felt vulnerable with people coming on to me from every direction, and I wanted Berit.

Sarah never asked me if I was gay, even though she knew Berit was and knew we were tight. Did she want to ignore the obvious, or was she into the Sarah world so much that she was oblivious, I wondered. Sarah and I usually shared a room at horse shows, so maybe we could talk then. I wanted her to know for some reason, perhaps because she knew Berit and liked him almost as much as I did, but different. Sarah could talk the Berit lingo with me. She'd had the experience of him and his total cool. He was indescribable, and I missed him terribly.

His letters continued to pour in, and I, the dutiful friend, responded to each and every one. From what I could tell, he sounded more upbeat. He had a job selling cars, had taken his level tests, whatever that meant, and was going to attend college. He was excellent at selling cars. Of course, he was. Who wouldn't want to talk to Berit and buy a car from the coolest guy on the planet? If Berit thought a car was good, Lord knows he knew enough about them. It was gonna be great. He could talk automobiles. He was making enough selling that he hoped to come to New Orleans for Halloween.

I always liked being at the stable to see Trumpet off, silly as it sounded. I wasn't comfortable with him leaving without me. There were too many variables out there. Towing could be treacherous, but with live animals on board, it was even more complicated. I was always afraid of Trumpet getting injured. A mere slam of the brakes could be monumental.

We headed to the show a couple of days later and settled into our room. Mom and Dad were in their room and Sarah and I in another.

"I have hardly seen you. What's going on with you? Anything new?" I asked her after we had settled into the hotel.

"Well, a new boy at school reminds me of Berit, only he's straight, and he is so fine. All the girls like him, and I know he's been around a lot, but I think he digs me, too. I'm playing hard to get right now, hoping he's interested. So far, he hasn't asked me to go out, so I'm not sure my strategy is working." She plopped on the bed, teen magazine in hand.

"Be careful," I said. "Hearts can easily be broken." I sat there looking at her waiting for the right moment.

"So what the hell happened, and why did you transfer schools?" she asked out of the blue. "I'm sure it wasn't your fault because you *never* get in trouble. Those military-type schools are lame anyway."

It couldn't have been a better segue. I explained what had happened at school and the shouting and beating on the car. She was horrified.

"And by the way, if you're wondering, yes, I'm gay." It was like a lightbulb went off. "I can't believe you didn't put it all together." Oh Sarah, completely absorbed in Sarahland.

"Let me get this," she turned on the bed looking at me. "So you're telling me you like boys?" Her eyes were like saucers. "Ah, okay, I get it. You and Berit. Everything makes sense now. Are you like seeing any other guys, or are y'all like a couple?" Oh, my God, she could be spacey.

I explained how the whole thing had started with the car washing and him squirting me with the hose. Then I described the next day: how we got high and went to the lake and then back to his house.

"That's when he told me he thought I was gay," I said. "At first, I got pissed, but it all made sense to me, and no, I haven't been with any other guy. I love Berit."

"Bradley, that's so sweet. I'm happy for you. I wish I was in love with someone who loved me. Have you told Mom and Dad? "

"Yes, and they were cool," I said and compared them to Berit's.

"I'm glad Mom and Dad didn't flip out….If they haven't yet, they'll give you the talk they gave me about sexual discretion," she said. I guessed for being parents; they were pretty hip. They knew we had come to the age where things would start happening, not that Dad necessarily saw the whole gay thing coming.

We talked about the possibility of Berit coming for Halloween, and she said she wanted to hang with us. I didn't know if I wanted her there, so I said nothing. I had to get my head ready for the show the next day. Keeping my mind on Berit may have felt good, but it would do me no good in the competition.

I was a bundle of nerves the next morning, and Trumpet felt it. He was trying to say, be cool, fool, but I was nevertheless nervous.

"Bradley, you are too uptight," Pelim said, coming up behind me and startling me. "He feels your tension. I can help you relieve the tension." He put his hands on my shoulders. I looked down at him.

"Get your hands off me!"

"You, Bradley, are like a whiny girl," he said and walked off.

I was pissed. I no longer had one ounce of guilt for wanting to fire him as our trainer, but I didn't want to create a scene at the show in front of everyone.

The organ with its piercing sound refocused my attention, then the MC announced my name, and I was ready. I proudly entered the arena. Trumpet was at his best, gallant and noble as always. I felt confident— our presence, Trumpet's size combined with my height, made for a handsome picture like one on the cover of an equestrian magazine. I glanced at my competition and saw the new mare enter. She looked young and out of step. I felt for the rider because the high shrill of the organ spooked the filly. She was pretty, and a year from then would definitely be a contender. A few more shows and the organ wouldn't frighten her anymore.

Meanwhile, our trot was perfect. I sat high in the seat, my posture impeccable, and I couldn't have asked for a better walk to canter. Trumpet was on fire, and I felt it to my core. The only way I wouldn't take first would be if someone paid off a judge, which I knew happened frequently.

After the different riders entered the arena and made their passes, the judges were ready to line us up for presentation. They couldn't hide their nods or smiles when they came up to Trumpet and me. We were the jewel in the crown, and I knew it. The MC regaled the winner's beauty and majesty, bellowing for us to take our victory round. I held myself confidently as I made the round. After I dismounted, Mom, Dad, and Sarah greeted me with hugs and congratulations. As we walked through the sea of tents meandering to ours, numerous people stopped me to bestow compliment after compliment on our, Trumpet's and my accomplishment. The day couldn't have been better.

Pelim was all smiles. Although he creeped me out, I knew he loved my horse. Who wouldn't? One couldn't help but admire Trumpet's beauty, grace, and temperament. I watched Pelim as he approached Sarah, and I felt the heat rising on the back of my neck.

I barged through people to stand by her side and glared at Pelim to let him know she was off-limits. "This is my sister Sarah, Pelim." Then, I whispered, "Hands off."

"I *love* your accent," she swooned. "Where are you from?" She actually batted her eyes. "I never come to the barn; that's Bradley's world, but I might have to make an appearance from time to time now that I know there's more to see than just the horses." She giggled and fidgeted in a way I think she thought she was alluring. Puke. Puke.

"Bradley never told me he had such a lovely sister," Pelim said, taking her hand and kissing it. "Pleased to meet you, Sarah. I've been in America quite some time, but I'm *Turkish*." He gazed into her eyes. "Indeed, you must come. I teach you to ride. No charge."

I couldn't stand it one more second. "Sarah doesn't ride, Pelim." I took her by the shoulder and escorted her away.

"What on earth are you doing? I'm perfectly capable of taking care of myself. You're an ass, Bradley."

"No, you don't know him. He offered to do me this morning to 'calm my nerves.' He's a creep. He'll screw anything with a hole. Stay away from him!"

She wasn't happy with me, but I didn't care. No way was he gonna get my sister. He had to go.

Later that evening, after all the show activities had finished, we went to eat with some other show families. My dad ordered his cocktail, but I asked him if he and I could talk outside before it came. I knew that what I had to say wouldn't count if I hadn't spoken to him before the drink. I told him about Pelim's conversation with me in the morning and how he was diddling some of the stable guys and women, too. I wouldn't name any names, which he respected, but I felt pushed over the edge when I saw him coming onto Sarah. Up to the Sarah part, he had listened. When it came to his little girl, the gloves came off.

"Thank you for standing up for your sister," he said. "Sometimes, she can have the wool pulled over her eyes. Don't worry about Pelim. I'll find another trainer."

"Actually, Dad, we don't need a trainer," I said. "I can take care of Trumpet better than anyone. And if it's too much, I'll let you know. You can then hire another trainer, but don't expect it." Damn, I was on fire.

We headed back inside just in time to order dinner. Dad slugged down his waiting drink and tapped the glass with his finger to let the waitress know he wanted another. Being with the other horse families was like hanging with extended family. Like Sarah, some of the other brothers and sisters of riders came to dinner, including Lillian's older brother, Leonard, who I had never met before. Berit had been right. I could now spot like-minded people. No doubt about it, Leonard was gay, and he was charming. We were in on a secret that no one else at the table could tell. He knew I was gay. I could tell by the way he looked at me.

The guilt riddled me. How could I think anyone but Berit was charming? Why would charming even come to mind? I was gay, no doubt. My thought processes appeared to be changing. Never before had I described people or places as lovely, charming, and quaint. What the hell? I just want to be a teenage boy, I thought. So what if I like boys, it's only one boy? I just didn't want to feel like a fucking fag.

After I finished dinner, I excused myself. I used the excuse that I was tired and needed to rest for the next day's event. Leonard said he was beat as well and that he'd walk back with me to the hotel only a few blocks away. Isn't this lovely, I thought. There I go again with my new gay words. Truth be told, these new terms were far more mature and expressive. Talking like a stupid teenager didn't suit me anymore. What could I say? I very well couldn't say he couldn't walk back with me. Shit, he was charming, and I knew if I got to know him better, he'd probably be someone I'd like to hang out with but was that not being a friend to Berit? I'd have to be upfront with Leonard about Berit from the beginning. I didn't want him to get the wrong idea.

"You did great today," he said as we stepped outside the restaurant. "Trumpet is a magnificent creature. I never go to these shows. Dad and I usually stay home, and Mom and Lil go. I'm glad I decided to come this time. What grade are you in?"

"Tenth."

"Where do you go to school? I go to Country Day, and I'm a sophomore too. Your sister goes there, and she's a senior, right?" Sarah hadn't recognized him, par for the course for a senior.

I told him I went to the same school as Cindy, who also had been at dinner. She and I had been friends forever, and our parents were friends. We soon exhausted the small talk.

"So, are you involved with anyone?" he asked bluntly.

"Yes, his name is Berit," I said, telling him about Berit's situation with his parents and the move to Amsterdam.

"Man, that sucks," he said. "I'm dating a guy named Wayne, but the situation isn't good." He went on to tell me about cheating issues with Wayne.

"Do you smoke?" he asked, pulling out cigarettes. I told him I didn't.

We ended up sitting by the hotel pool and talking for a long time. It was a pleasant evening, the best I'd had since I last saw Berit.

The parents returned late, all more than tipsy, but Sarah wasn't with them. They said that she had already come back. I went into the room, but no Sarah, so I sat at the desk and wrote a letter to Berit about

my success at the horseshow and meeting Leonard. I told him it was
conversation only.

I sealed the envelope and watched TV for about an hour. Sarah still
hadn't returned, which worried me, so I decided to look for her. As I
scoured the hotel, I felt sick to my stomach, like I could throw up. I
knew where she was, dammit. She was with Pelim! I went to the front
desk and got his room number, went to the room, and knocked nicely on
the door. Although I wanted to pound on it, I didn't want to give him
any warning. He answered the door in his underwear, and I punched
him square in the face. As I forced my way in, Sarah was buttoning her
shirt. I grabbed her arm and dragged her out of there.

"Are you insane, Bradley?" she yelled. "You hit him. I think his nose
was bleeding. What the hell were you thinking? You're not Dad."

I didn't say two words to her and dragged her back to our room. I
was angry and went to bed, but my mind was on overdrive. What the
hell was I thinking? No, what the hell was she thinking? I had warned her
about him. I had also told the sleazeball that she was off-limits. I wanted
to tell Dad, but I didn't. I knew Pelim was soon to be a non-subject
anyway. I hoped the parents would spread the word, and he'd be long
gone from our barn for good. What a prick.

The next morning started awkwardly. Sarah and I didn't speak, the air so
thick with tension that I could have cut it with a knife.

I must have looked distracted at breakfast. "You okay, pal?" Dad
asked, patting me on the shoulder.

I nodded. "Yes, just meditating, getting into the right headspace."
What kinda bullshit was I trying to pass off? I couldn't believe it. He
bought it. I had become such a good liar.

Pelim was brushing Trumpet when I arrived. I wanted him to get his
vile hands off my horse. He saw me come in and lowered his head. When
he finally looked up, I regretted what I had done. His nose was bent, and
both eyes black. I had broken his nose. Shit. Was I gonna get in trouble,
and how would I explain the whole thing without outing Sarah?

He was silent.

"I didn't mean to break your nose," I said. "You knew my sister was off-limits."

"I know."

He knew what: the part about not meaning to break his nose or my sister being off-limits or both?

"I was wrong, and you were right."

I didn't know what to say, so I said, "As long as we're clear on the issue." What the hell? Who the hell had I become! I certainly didn't recognize myself.

Even though I was still angry at Pelim, I did well at the show and took blue in both classes. After the show, Dad told Pelim that we no longer required his services. Dad must have told Mom, and she spread the word to the other parents, and that was just how it was. The expression may have been something like railroaded out of town. The horse community was a close-knit group, and we stuck together.

Sarah asked me if I thought Pelim's firing was because of the situation with her. I knew it wasn't right, but I neither confirmed nor denied, at least not right away. She needed to respect herself more.

Chapter 7

As time passed, Berit's and my letters continued in a steady stream, keeping us updated with each other's life. At the beginning of October, a letter came with good news, bad news, and horrible, unthinkable news.

My dearest friend, I miss you.

I purchased my ticket for the Halloween festivities in New Orleans. I hope you're as excited as I am. On a sad note, my grootmoeder has lung cancer. I've been taking care of her as I can between work and college. Both of those are going very well.

My father is a total asshole. Nothing new there. I called to tell him about his mother and suggested he might want to visit her. He was cold, void of any emotion. He said the only way he would come to see her was if I wasn't in the house because I sickened him. For her, I agreed to be away for a week.

The day he was to arrive, I rented space at a hostel. It was a bed and a roof. The journey to work and college was longer because the closest hostel was city center Amsterdam, but I wanted her to see her son. She is a good woman. The only possession she has is her house, which isn't very nice, but she has given it to me. It's in my name as of now, as well as the contents, much ado about nothing on the furniture front. She knew if she left it to my father, I'd be out on the street. Having it in my name, he has no claim, and I actually could have told him he couldn't stay in my house, but I would never do that to her.

While at the hostel late one night, two men attacked me. After work, I stopped for a pint before going to bed, and they were drunk. They overpowered me, raped me, said I wouldn't mind, and that they were probably doing me a favor. Don't worry, Bradley; I'm okay. Maybe my pride is a bit battle-weary and my heart suspicious and loathing of humankind, but this too shall pass, my friend. Please don't cry, Bradley. From that point on, I have been on guard. I know I told you always to be aware of your surroundings. I wasn't. Maybe because of sheer exhaustion, I was careless but had I not had the pint. I may have been more aware.

Brad, I look forward to meeting Leonard in October. You make me smile with your words. What's the most important thing? Think, Bradley… friendship. I'm happy you have a new friend and am not concerned about anything else. Before you start worrying or wondering, I haven't been with any other that is consensual. Please know I am your friend whether you share intimacy with another or not. I only ask you to make sure they are your friend first. I love you and can't wait to see you.

Friends always,
Berit

My heart raced with anticipation when I read that he was coming to New Orleans. That feeling of euphoria lasted all of another second after reading about his gran. He had a lot of responsibility. He knew me all too well, and I was livid about his father. What a bastard! When I read of the rape, I threw up right then on the floor in my room, and I couldn't even cry. I wanted to hurt someone. I hurled again. He was still my cool Berit, but those assholes stole something from him. I felt his sadness and humiliation. All I wanted to do was hold him *and* beat the shit out of the two guys. I think I could've killed them. But, my Berit, he was putting on a brave front for me. I wanted to hold him. Kiss him. I wished I could make it all go away. How dare they.

I knew he'd be home and that his hell week had passed, so I asked Mom if I could call and told her about his gran. She nodded and asked I keep it short. I knew it was late there, probably around eleven, but I had to talk to him. He answered immediately, and I apologized for waking him.

"Bradley, no apology needed. Good to hear from you, man," he said. "So, what book did you finish this time?" He knew my call pattern— finish a book and then call him.

"I haven't finished a book. I just read your letter and had to call you." I paused for a moment. "I can't wait to see you. How is your gran?"

"She's not doing well. The doctors hadn't caught the cancer soon enough, and it had already spread. She doesn't have much time left."

My heart ached for him. I couldn't imagine being in his situation.

The elephant was still in the room. I was waiting for Berit to bring it up, and he seemed to be waiting for me.

"So, how are you, honestly?" I felt my bottom lip start to quiver. "I can't believe they attacked you. Oh God, are you really okay?" The first blubber came out. "Sorry, I'm so fucking mad. I wanna hurt someone, Berit."

"Calm down, Brad. Yes, I'm fine. Not to be gross, but they didn't pack much, thank God. I've started back to judo, only once a week. It's all the time I have now, but after, um, I'll have more time. I'll go at least three times a week. It will *never* happen again. Had I not been exhausted, and had I not drank a pint, it wouldn't have happened the way it did. Sadly, my friend, there is a lot of hate in this world. Be on your guard. Don't go places at night alone. Okay, no more sad talk, no more focusing on the past. Let's look forward to the future. Just think you'll always have a place to stay here. I own a freaking house, pretty impressive for an eighteen-year-old, I'd say. It's not great, but a coat of paint and some updated furniture will greatly improve the appearance."

I focused more on the eighteen. When was his birthday? Why didn't I know? Why had I never asked? Some kind of friend I was. "Did you say eighteen? When was your birthday, and why don't I know this?"

"Stop freakin' out," he said. "It was just another day."

The hell it was, I thought.

"It was September 28." He answered.

A sickening thought came over me. I wondered if his pint was a birthday treat to himself. I didn't have the heart to ask because if it had been the case, it was fucked up.

"Well, happy belated birthday," I said. Berit knew my birthday was January 2.

"You know, Bradley, yours will be here before you know it, and unless we get a little busy during Halloween, you'll be known as the sixteen-year-old virgin. Not saying there's anything wrong with that. I think it's sweet."

"I don't want to, but I have to get off the phone. You need to go back to sleep."

"I'll sleep much better now. Can't wait. About three weeks, right?" He sounded excited.

"Yep. Friends always."

"Friends always."

I hadn't asked my parents whether it was okay or not for Berit to come and stay a week. I wasn't concerned because they never had a problem with anyone spending the night. Our house was the place where kids were always welcomed, but I decided I better ask.

"Mom, is it okay for Berit to spend a week at our house the last week of October?" I asked in passing.

"Maybe it wouldn't be the best time because it's a school week," she said. How odd, I thought.

"Well, he already booked his ticket," I said. "It has to be okay."

She looked perplexed. "Well, I guess we'll work it out. Maybe we can put a cot of some sort in Dad's study."

I was confused. "Why wouldn't he stay like last time in my room?"

"Bradley, would Dad and I let one of Sarah's boyfriends stay overnight in her room?" she asked, cocking her head as she looked at me. A-ha, it was because I was gay. Wow, I was pissed, but I had never thought of this side of the equation. "I'll talk with Dad. I'm sure he'll let Berit stay in his study."

I wondered if Berit had considered the possibility of a change in sleeping arrangements. I checked the calendar, and Halloween was on a Friday; curfew wouldn't be an issue. I hoped Stuart and Leighton would put us up Halloween night, but I felt a little uncomfortable asking, so I called Leonard.

Leonard lived in the ritzy section of Old Metairie, and his family had a pool house. He had told me that other people had stayed in the pool house, and he'd see what he could do about us staying there. After we hung up, I mulled it over. Would my parents let Berit and me spend the night at Leonard's house? They'd probably want to talk to his parents about it. I called Leonard back and asked if his parents knew he was gay. They did. I posed the question, shit, like Sarah, with the what-if scenarios. I could tell he was annoyed like Sarah's questioning had annoyed me over the years. He was a nice guy, and I didn't want to aggravate him. He told me to relax, and he'd help me get it all worked out. I had no other choice but to trust him.

I then called Stuart and Leighton. Stuart answered. I told him Berit was coming in for Halloween.

"So, where are you guys staying Halloween night?" Stuart asked.

"We have a couple of options," I said. "I'm not sure, though."

What a liar, I thought.

"If it isn't in the Quarter, you'll never find a parking spot or at least a safe one," Stuart said. There was so much I didn't know about gay life.

While Stuart and I were talking, I could hear Leighton talking in the background.

"If they don't mind sleeping on a sofa bed in our living room, they can stay here," Leighton said. Stuart confirmed the invitation.

"Are you sure?"

"Of course, or else we wouldn't have offered, honey."

I had grown a set and taken care of the Halloween matter. I hoped Berit was cool with it and hoped my parents would allow us to stay out. There were more obstacles than I could ever have imagined. Being gay and a teenager was complicated.

I then called Leonard back.

"Yes, Bradley, what now?" he asked, his voice rising in annoyance. "I told you I would call you when I knew anything. Don't go all nelly on me. Child, you need to relax."

"Thanks, but we don't need to stay at your place," I told him about the new sleeping arrangements. And no, I wasn't going nelly on him.

Dad came home, and I could hear him and Mom talking in his study with the door shut. Shit, that's never a good sign, I thought. I remembered when a senior had asked Sarah, a freshman at the time, to Homecoming. They had a closed study door discussion. The result ended up being sorta okay for Sarah. She had to go on a double date with someone they knew. I remembered thinking maybe I might have the same luck.

"Bradley," Dad called up. Shit, I was a nervous wreck.

"Coming," I answered, trying not to seem nervous, and trotted down the steps.

"I would appreciate it in future if Berit didn't invest in an international flight without checking with us first," he said. "Things are a bit different now, and the same rules for Sarah apply for you. I hope you understand. We aren't trying to be unfair. Brad, you're only sixteen, and you have a long future ahead of you. Think out your decisions carefully because they could impact your adult life, and you'll be an adult a lot longer than you'll be a teenager."

I had heard that one before a la Berit.

"We're going to have Sarah sleep in your room and Berit in hers. Everything will be the same. He'll keep his things in your room; y'all will be able to come and go, as usual, nothing different there, just the sleeping. I'm sure you understand. As we would if it were Sarah, there is a level of respect we expect. Don't push the envelope." He seemed patient about the whole thing.

"Yes, sir," I said. I didn't think my knees were noticeably shaking. I cleared my throat. "About Halloween, there is an all-night huge, mammoth, unbelievable party I wanted to go to. Is it okay?" They looked at each other.

"Do we know anyone going?"

Right out of my ass, it came. "Sarah's going." As if they already knew that.

The relief on their faces was unmistakable.

"I suppose it's okay," Mom said.

Sarah had said she wanted to hang with us and go to the French Quarter Halloween event. I hoped she hadn't changed her mind. I'd have to hurry and give her the scoop. I knew she wasn't going to be thrilled sleeping in my room for a week.

I rushed to her room to explain everything, and she was as excited as I was about the Halloween thing. I had no idea what to expect. From my experience at the Parade, I knew there would be a lot of action. She might get upset by some of it, but Berit and I were never one for public display other than him marking his territory with a kiss.

Whew, dodged another bullet.

I called Berit via the payphone and explained all the new rules and the new lies. Not much bothered him, at least not to my ears.

Three weeks later, I was back at the airport, picking him up. In the short time since we had been with each other, he probably put on twenty pounds of solid muscle. He was my own personal Adonis. His shirt grabbed his arms tighter, so not only could I feel the difference, but I and everyone else in the airport could see the outline of his arms and chest. Rather than my relaxed, no-cares Berit, his face had sharpened. It almost seemed more angular. The love still emanated from his eyes, but he looked older, more serious. I hoped being with me that my playful pal would re-surface. As he embraced me, I could feel the tightness and strength of his embrace.

"Where the hell did this come from?" I asked, clutching his bicep.

He smiled at me. "Sheer determination, my friend. I've been working my balls off." He was still my cool Berit, but something was lying beneath the surface. I'm sure it was the amount of pressure on him with his gran, school, and work. He had been thrown from being a child of privilege to the working world, basically child to adult, in one swift kick. Fuck his parents.

"I'm jealous," I said, flexing my bicep. I, too, had been trying to improve, although nothing like Berit. Because of my equestrian achievement, my legs had always been developed. The first time in my bedroom, he had mentioned my thighs. Since Dad fired Pelim, I had been doing all of Trumpet's grooming, cleaning, and handling, which bulked my upper body and arms. Although I wasn't the skinny weakling from when we first met, I still didn't compare to him.

We talked about the upcoming week, and I reminded him I had school.

"I might be able to miss one day," I said.

"Do you think I could come to school and be your world history or geography project?" He warmed my soul. His accent had gotten thicker, but his English was still excellent. "So what am I supposed to know and not know?" he asked as we were pulling up to the house. "Do your parents think we are an item or merely friends, or have they stayed away from the question?"

"I'm sure Mom knows, and Dad's no dummy," I said. "However, the new sleeping arrangements might indicate everyone's in on the skinny."

I grabbed his suitcase, but he took it from me. "I'm not your nelly, Dorothy!" He could be such a smart ass.

When we entered, Mom was in the kitchen. She ran over to hug him. "How's your grandmother? I was sorry to hear she's ill. From what Bradley has told me, you've had a lot on your plate. Make sure you rest and relax while you're here. That's an order." How embarrassing! She could be such a mom. I rolled my eyes.

"Mrs. Stedman, thank you. There's nothing like a mother's hug. I'm sure you've heard the whole horrible story with my parents."

She took both of his hands in hers. "Berit, I don't understand many things, is all I can tell you, but you're welcome in our home. You've never been anything but the perfect gentleman, and I'm sorry. It must be painful. If ever you need to talk, I'm here for you." She was teary-eyed.

His eyes glossed over. "Thank you. You have no idea." His sincerity was heart-wrenching.

She nodded and told me to take the suitcase upstairs. He stayed in the kitchen for an extra few seconds and then followed me.

"I'm sorry for any awkwardness," I said.

"Don't apologize. You're lucky to have a mom like that. I understand where your parents are coming from with the sleeping arrangements." He stepped closer. "They don't want me molesting their son." He grinned and grabbed my crotch.

"By all means, molest away," I said, cupping his package and drawing him closer with the other hand. "I've missed you."

Berit leaned in to kiss me, and I kissed him back. This time was better. I didn't feel awkward; in fact, I felt loved. All I could think was I loved him. If I were a couple of years older, I'd moved to Amsterdam with him, I thought. I desired his naked body but knew it wasn't an option at the moment. I could tell he wanted it, too.

"I want to say hello to your dad and thank him, but things need to settle down," he said, looking down at his pants. We heard the kitchen door close and Sarah talking to Mom. She sounded excited to hear Berit had arrived and ran up the stairs. We were both back to normal, like jumping in an icy cold lake; otherwise, both of us with tented pants could have been awkward. She thrust her arms around his neck.

"Dammit, Berit, you're even better looking than last time. Not fair!" she said, kissing him on the lips. Although it was only a peck, it was on the lips. I didn't like it at all.

"Sarah, Sarah," he scolded, "that's part of the no-go zone, right Brad? A kiss on the cheek is fine, and you can do that all day, but not the lips. Those belong to someone else." He smiled broadly at her and winked. "Besides, think of it as kissing your brother. Does the complexion change? I should hope so."

"You're no fun," she said. "I didn't mean to offend. And *gross*, it's not at all like kissing my brother, thank you very much." She laughed.

"None was taken. Keep the image in your memory." He was patient to a fault with Sarah. "I'm going to say hi to your father right now, so he doesn't think I'm rude." She put her hands up and let us pass and then followed closely behind.

Dad was working in the backyard and looked up when the patio door slid open. "Hey, Berit. How was the flight?" Dad even hugged him, albeit briefly.

"It was good, no issues." He looked Dad straight in the eyes like a grown man would.

"Heard about the rough hand you were dealt. If you need an ear, son, I'm here. Since Brad will be in school, I thought you might want to come downtown with me. One of my business associates is going to Amsterdam in the spring, and I told him you might have some suggestions.

"Thank you. I'd love to, and I have many suggestions regarding where to go and what to do, especially where *not* to go and what *not* to do. Your associate will find it beautiful, but different from America. Very different."

We sat at the umbrella table, and Dad started to crank the umbrella up, but I took over for him. Brownie points. Everyone knew, including me, that I was no Berit. No matter how hard I tried. He had it all; he could talk to anyone, and he was like a grown-up, but not. He was worldly and spoke with the perfect amount of knowledge and confidence.

Even though he was only eighteen, he seemed so more experienced with life. Adults, both me and women, admired him and his coolness, like some kind of movie hero. Here I was jealous, again. What the hell is your problem, I asked myself. He was my best friend, and his situation was more than shitty. To him, I'm sure I looked like I had it all. Could things get more complicated? Compared to Berit, I'm sure I looked spoiled with parents who loved and accepted me. My life was easy for the most part, and yet, Berit seemed together even though he had to work his balls off, was taking care of his gran, and had to grow up overnight. Shame on me.

"I guess you'll want to relax and get your bearings on Monday. Bradley can confirm your visit to his school for Tuesday and then Wednesday plan on coming to my office. I suppose Thursday will be a hooky day for Brad. Friday is Halloween, right? Saturday y'all can recover from Friday and then S—anyway, we have a tentative plan, right guys?" Dad nodded for confirmation from me.

"Sounds good to me." Thanks, Dad, good catch, I thought. As Dad started the "S" on Sunday, Berit had begun to frown, and Dad noticed and stopped talking. My dad was a good guy, and the fact he was as laid back about my sexuality spoke volumes about his character as a man.

He asked Sarah to get him a beer inside. He also offered one to Berit, who said no but accepted the offer of lemonade. He asked her to bring out two lemonades. I noticed he didn't offer me a beer.

Sarah returned with the drinks. With my dad's first swig of the beer, he expressed, "Now, that's good."

"You'd enjoy the beer in Amsterdam. It's hearty with fullness," Berit said.

"Oh, I know. I get Heineken from time to time, but it's a bit pricey." Dad leaned back in his chair.

"That's good for America, but we don't drink it. There's much better beer, but Heineken is a big moneymaker for us, and I'm happy about that, but it depends on whether you want pale ale, witte, that's white, or triples, fruity, or bitters. My personal favorites are from Brouwerij T'IJ, the oldest brewery in Amsterdam. It's part of an old windmill." He looked at me and said, "One day, when you visit, I'll take you there." There was a gleam in his eyes.

"I've told Brad, when he graduates from high school, summer before university, with your permission, of course, Mr. Stedman, I want him to visit Amsterdam. All of you would be welcome. I have a small house by Dutch standards, which is much smaller than American standards, but it has two bedrooms."

My dad seemed impressed at his knowledge, and he asked about Berit's job and studies.

"Not to sound bitter because of my father, and perhaps I am, but I feel like I have a head start as far as knowledge about the automobile industry," Berit said. "I've grown up around engines and the automobile industry. Most people in Amsterdam ride bikes and scooters and don't even own autos because of the transit system, which has improved by leaps and bounds. Despite those factors, there is still a lot of business centered around automobiles. When you get outside the city, having an automobile is preferred. In my two months at the dealership, I've managed to become top sales because of my knowledge." I knew he wasn't bragging. He was just matter-of-fact. I noticed he had become franker. I wasn't sure if it was because of the situation and the responsibility or if it was the way of the Dutch.

"My ultimate desire is to head up the American division of one of the big European car manufacturers, not only for my own accomplishment but also as a big fuck you to my father. I'll make damn sure his company doesn't get the advertisement contract." I swallowed hard. He said the "f" word in front of my dad and didn't blink, nor did my dad.

"I can certainly understand," Dad said. "There's bound to be bad blood there with your dad."

We sat around the umbrella table like three men enjoying the afternoon. Dad seemed different, but I knew he liked Berit just from his facial expressions. "I'm not heartless. I very well could have been, but I allowed him to stay in my home to visit with his dying mother, my grandmother, who was ashamed of her son and his treatment of me, his only child. My father refused to stay under the same roof as me, so I stayed at a hostel for a week in Amsterdam, which added a good couple of hours to my day with travel. I still worked during the day and went to night college."

The conversation carried on another hour and a couple of beers for Dad until Mom interrupted us because she needed something at the store. Berit and I split, post-haste, and went straight to the store, both of us glancing at each other. We quickly purchased the items, almost ran back to the car, and then headed straight for the park and pulled in.

As if in sync, we were on the same page. We had to make the most of any alone time. I locked my lips on his. I was starving for him. The temperature in the car climbed as his dick got stiffer in my hand. I wanted to take care of him and moved my mouth from his lips to his awaiting cock. I had gotten the knack of a blowjob, not the whole swallowing part so far, but he told me it would come in time and not to make it a big deal. Time was of the essence, so I sucked hard and worked him with determination. I quickly backed away as his wad hit the console.

"I've thought of you being naked so many times," I said, coming up for air. "I've laid awake at night, remembering being in the same bed with you and how sorry I was things hadn't gone better for you in the sex department when we had the chance. I'm sorry. I made it all about me and my gratification, I guess, because of the novelty of it all. This trip is gonna be about you, not me."

"How about, let it be about us? I often think of a time in the future when you'd be able to visit me at my house, and we'd have the freedom to take things slow and enjoy each other, sex or no sex. Those thoughts help me get through the long lonely nights."

Since the attack, he told me the thought of anything sexual repulsed him until seeing me at the airport— it was like a heavy weight had been lifted off him. Now all he could think about was our bodies touching and being close. He opened up about the attack and cried, and my heart broke, although he didn't sob like I had when I first found out. I was right. It had been a birthday beer. My gut twisted in anger because I wanted revenge, and I hated his father for putting him in such a dire situation.

I was glad that I had my car washing kit with us, or we might have had some explaining to do regarding the mess we'd made. Blobs of semen, like beads thrown from a Mardi Gras float, were everywhere, dangling and dripping. Practically everything on the dash got a blast.

We returned to the house in a reasonable grocery amount of time. No one gave us any suspicious looks, and we laughed about the adventure. I asked Sarah if she had any film for her Polaroid because I wanted to document Berit's trip. She could be the photographer.

The first picture I had her take was of Berit and me standing next to his suitcase as though we had just arrived from the airport. Okay, a little dramatic, but whatever. She snapped away, catching us in all types of pictures. After dinner, we sat around and watched TV as a whole family. I could tell that Berit was getting into the family thing. He seemed to be starving for love. I excused myself and confirmed with Stuart that the plan was still on. We spoke briefly about costumes, and he said the barer, the better. Not the answer I was thinking. What happened to witches, vampires, and ghosts?

By about ten, everyone headed to bed. Berit went in to put his PJs on, and I waited outside the door. He took longer than I thought he should. I wondered what he was doing. He came out with a pillow off one of my beds. Sarah quickly grabbed a pillow of hers, and I went back into my bedroom and he to Sarah's. Something had gone on; I knew it but couldn't figure for the life of me what it could be until I climbed into bed.

Under the covers, I found a card that he had placed. I opened the card. It had a picture of two young boys kicking a can in the middle of an old-time street. The inside said "Friends," and he added "Always" after it. He expressed all the frustrations he had been having being away from me. Not that he wanted me to grow up fast, but he had sometimes wished I was older and that I lived in Amsterdam.

I must have read it ten times. I was miserable knowing he was next door. Had I not told my parents and had I not been such a head case, he'd be in my room right now, but no, I had to break down and tell my parents everything. Any human being who had experienced what I had would've reacted the same way. I wasn't positive, but I felt reasonably sure the old bastard outed me after seeing me at The Parade. Why? I would've never done it to him.

Sarah was tossing and turning and then sat up in bed. "Bradley, do y'all do it? Are you the guy or the girl?"

"What?" I had no idea what she was talking about.

"You know? Do you play the role of a girl or a guy when y'all do things?"

I couldn't believe she was asking such personal questions and ones that didn't apply. It wasn't like that, or was it? No, definitely not. We were two regular guys, just gay.

"First question none of your business, and second question, neither one of us is the girl. We're just two guys. What a strange question to even ask." It kinda pissed me off.

"I'm trying to imagine who sucks who or do both of you, and what about?"

"Sarah," I exclaimed in a throaty whisper, "it's not like that, and it's none of your business. Go to sleep."

As I rolled over, I realized that there wasn't an explanation I was comfortable with. Once again, the question came to mind, what am I? Why do I feel grossed out and bad when push came to shove? If I were truly into the gay scene and Berit's and my relationship, I should be happy to say what we did with each other and how sensational it felt. Shit, I wouldn't ask her such a question. I had absolutely no interest in my sister's sexual activities or anyone else, for that matter.

I read the card again and then grabbed a pen from my desk to write a response. I must have pissed her off because Sarah hadn't spoken again. I figured she'd want to know what I was doing getting up. Then it occurred to me. I could make her feel just as awkward. It may not have been nice, but it was funny, and it was my purpose in life as a younger brother, to annoy her, right?

"Sarah?"

"What?" Yeah, she was pissed.

"How often do you masturbate?" It took everything I had not to burst out laughing.

"Bradley, you're gross," she growled.

I was glad the lights were off. Otherwise, she would've seen me fighting the fit of hysteria. "Don't pretend you don't. I know everybody does, including you."

"I do not." I had hit a nerve.

"Perhaps I shouldn't have asked you such a personal question." I gave her something to consider since she had been so personal.

She was quiet for about five minutes, so I rolled over toward the wall.

"Sorry if I pried too much," she said. "I'm just curious. I don't get it. I'm not saying I'm against it, but I just don't understand, I suppose." She sounded sincere.

"I'm not sure I do either to tell you the truth. I only do what feels right. For Berit and me, it's all about friendship. Yes, we've touched each other, but not a lot. I'm a beginner." I smiled at the thought. Berit would've approved of my answer.

The next morning I felt terrible for Berit. He had to wake up so Sarah could get dressed for school. He was sleepy; he trudged into my room and headed straight for my bed. When he pulled back the covers, he looked at me and smiled. I had left the card he'd given me under the covers and made my own note saying I would miss him while I was at school and I loved him. He climbed into my bed.

"Thanks for the thought," he said, throwing back the covers quickly, exposing his engorged cock. He gave me a sly smile and pulled the covers back up.

"And I have to go to school, not fair." I pouted.

"Have I ever let you down? Be cool. I'll be thinking of you." His laugh was almost sinister.

Thankfully, Sarah had finished getting dressed in the bathroom, and I quickly ran in and locked the bathroom door. What a tease! I couldn't believe he was giving me a show.

I couldn't concentrate at school. All I could think about was wanting to be home with Berit. The teachers approved his visit the next day and, in fact, were excited. Then I started to contemplate all the attention he would be getting. How did I feel about it? I was selfish when it came to his attention. I felt like the odd man out even when he and my dad got on like long-lost friends. Shit, I'm screwed up, I thought. I have to grow up and stop acting like a child.

The day finally ended, and the traffic getting out of school was no more chaotic than usual, even though it felt like it. Cindy was already waiting in the car by the time I got to it.

After making small talk, she asked whether I would pick her up the following day.

"Yes, why wouldn't I?" I felt my face contort with a look that said, are you stupid. I was being a jerk, no doubt.

"Well, you'll have an extra passenger, and I thought you might want alone time."

"No, I want you to get to know him," I said. Besides, I wanted to stay clear from any suspicions. I didn't want to advertise our relationship to the whole world, so I would carpool as normal. Nobody at school, except Cindy, knew I was gay. Some people may have speculated, but no one *knew*. Even though there had been the big to-do at the other school, it hadn't hit the rest of the world.

After I dropped her off, I pulled into my driveway just as Berit was walking out to meet me with a huge smile. *What's the big smile about*, I wondered.

"I told your mom I was coming to meet you, and we were gonna get some pizza," he said, opening the door and telling me to drive. He pulled out a joint, took a couple of tokes, and handed it to me.

"What did you do today? I missed you. Where did you go?" Mostly I wanted to know what I missed. Grumble, grumble.

"Well, it was a tough day," he said. "I slept until eleven. I then changed and washed your sheets," he said, winking. "I hung out with your mom. She's great. We talked a lot about my grootmoeder, my parents, and my plans for the future. I also asked if she would consider you visiting me this summer. She raised an eyebrow and told me probably not, but she'd think about it." I looked at him in disbelief. I would've thought the answer might sound more like, Hell no. "I went on a long walk, got stoned, and hung out in the park reading one of your classics. I wrote another note and hid it in one of your books, so you'll find it one day when you need it."

I took the unlit joint from him and lit it. "Look what you drive me to do." I took a hit.

We drove around, but the munchies got the best of me, so we headed to the pizza place.

"Man, this pizza is so damn good," I said. The cheese was gooey and loaded with pepperoni. "Man, this is the best pizza I've ever had."

"Probably because you're stoned," he said. We started laughing uncontrollably. We were so loud that some of the other customers turned around and looked at us.

"People are starting to stare," he said.

"Right. Okay, let's talk about our costumes for Halloween," I said, holding back laughter.

"We have to dress up?" He raised his eyebrows with a look of shock.

"Duh, it is a Halloween party."

We tried to come up with anything of merit, but we couldn't concentrate well, so we left.

By the time we returned home, we had come down from our buzz enough to ask Mom about our costumes. I have to admit she came up with a clever idea. She must've done some research on the gay world.

"What about biker vampires, ya know, leather stuff, chaps, and vests, maybe a cap?" she asked. "You can powder your faces white and put in some vampire fangs with drips of blood and ta-da." I was glad I wasn't crazy stoned or would have busted a gut.

"What a great idea, Mrs. Stedman," Berit said with a smile. What an ass-kisser. I desperately wanted to ask her about the visiting Berit scenario but decided to wait until later.

Berit was a smash hit with the faculty, and he confirmed my suspicions about the kids at school who I had suspected were gay. He said my gaydar had gotten stronger.

"The older you get, the stronger your gaydar will get," he said. "Just don't *ever* assume you're right. Wait for them to come to you because America is still in the dark ages about homosexuality. Be as discreet as possible." Sometimes he talked to me like I would be doing things with other people. He didn't get the picture, no matter how hard I explained. There would be no one but him.

The day with Dad went well, and, par for the course, Berit made a great impression on all the people in his office. Shocking. Dad said he gave detailed dos and don'ts to the business associate. They came home early, about the time I was getting home from school. I couldn't help but think it had been good of my dad to think of me.

I couldn't believe my parents let me play hooky Thursday *and* Friday. All they expected was courteous behavior. Part of me felt guilty about Halloween in the French Quarter and sleeping at Stuart and Leighton's, but not enough to stop me from going. Mom had gone to the fabric store, bought some plastic stuff meant to look like leather, and constructed chaps with staples and glue to wear over our jeans and vesty kind of garments. They were a bit cheesy, but for last-minute costumes, I couldn't have asked for better. She made a skirt and vest for Sarah and an extra vest and chaps for her date.

Chapter 8

Sarah had invited her latest squeeze, Frankie. He was handsome in a classic kind of way. Frankie was the same height as Berit with dark hair, about my color, but his hair was straight and would swing back when he flicked his head. I could easily see what she saw in him, and he seemed to dig her.

When she went to try on the skirt, I went upstairs with her. "What did you tell Frankie?"

"About what? You? Berit? The party? What?" She could be impatient sometimes.

"Yes, to all of the above, Sarah. What is he cool with? What does he know? Is he freaked out over the gay thing? And what about pot?"

She exhaled. "Oh, my God, Brad, you're wound way too tight. He's cool with you being gay and Berit being your special friend, and he knows we're going to a gay thing. He was worried that someone might come on to him and that he'd say something rude because he would. He likes girls, period the end. I don't think he knows about me smoking pot, so don't mention it. We're not spending the night at your friend's place. His parents own a hotel downtown, and he can stay there anytime." She went into her room with the skirt.

"Cool." What else could I say? I wanted to ask her if they could get two rooms but figured it would be too pushy. I don't know why, but I was apprehensive about staying at Stuart's. I told Berit about it, and he said not to worry—he could take care of anyone who messed with us. I guess because I was younger than he was, and he had been the one to put me on the yellow brick road, as he said, he felt responsible for me.

Dressed in our costumes, we headed out the door, followed by a slew of comments from my parents. "Be careful. Stay together. Don't be foolish." Okay, we got it, I thought.

My stomach was a ball of knots. I wasn't sure what to expect or how the evening would play out. Berit could read my nerves. "Don't worry, my friend. It'll be cool, and if not, we'll leave. See how easy, so stop worrying," he whispered and winked at me. I instantly felt better. He was right. We could leave if it didn't feel right.

Stuart and Leighton's place, while in the French Quarter, was decorated with a modern flair. Stuart greeted us at the door. The entry was smoky from dry ice and made to look like a graveyard with Styrofoam headstones. The mood lighting washed the walls and decorations, completing the scene.

Stuart decorated their place with fake spider webs that stretched across the ceiling, complete with a host of glowing spiders of every size. A black-light in the dining room emphasized colors in the fluorescent-framed posters on the walls. Mostly men scantily clad were standing around talking in small groups. One of the couples wore genuine leather chaps and vests—their chests were bare, and their dicks and balls hung out for all to see.

"Aren't your costumes *adorable*? We need to fix this, though," Stuart said, grabbing my shirt collar. Berit had already begun to take off his shirt. I had hoped he wasn't taking it all off because I wasn't about to, and I sure as shit didn't want anyone looking at his frank n' beans. He only took off his shirt and left his jeans on. His chest was chiseled, each muscle perfectly cut. He was fucking gorgeous, and everyone in the place noticed when he entered.

Sarah seemed to be enjoying the view, although Frankie seemed uncomfortable, locking his gaze downward. I felt uneasy as well. It wasn't my scene either, the difference being I was gay, and he was straight. He must've whispered to Sarah that he wanted to leave, and she turned to him, "I have to pee, and then we can split." Both Frankie and I walked her to the bathroom while Berit grabbed me a drink. She turned the doorknob and swung the door open to find two guys, one with his hand up the other guy's ass.

"Oops, sorry," she said, quickly closing the door.

I don't know who looked sicker, Frankie or me. She raised her eyebrows like she had seen something she could have never imagined. We all felt the same.

"That was unnerving, to say the least." I wasn't kidding. I could feel the vomit coming up my throat. Berit came up behind me with a drink, and I gulped it down to stifle the nauseous feeling.

"Sarah, we'll find you somewhere else to pee," Frankie said, "That was something I'll never be able to unsee." He looked at me and sarcastically said, "Have fun, y'all. Not my scene."

"Be careful, and we'll see you in the morning," Sarah said.

Berit was confused. "Everything okay?"

"Just some weirdness. I'll tell you later, but Sarah's splitting, and I think I want to as well."

Berit and I found Stuart, "Hey, we're gonna hit the street party with my sister, Sarah. We'll be back later."

"Y'all be careful; it can get crazy out there. We've had a far bigger turnout than expected. Hopefully, it'll thin out with time. I do hope y'all make it back." He put his hand on my shoulder. "By all means, stick close to your sister because it can get rough out there."

Still with my shirt on and Berit bare-chested, we left Stuart's. As we meandered through the Quarter, I saw more dicks than I had in a locker room full of boys. Everybody was hanging loose.

Sarah looked like she was watching a tennis match, her head going from one side to the other, taking it all in. The lack of discretion was alarming.

"Bradley, don't you dare come back down this way," she said. "I hope you think this is as disgusting as I do. You know I don't judge you or Berit, but this is—"

"Appalling?" Berit finished her sentence. "Yes, it's quite decadent, no matter who you are. Sarah, have no fear; your brother is a class act."

Even though my mouth, like Frankie's, was agape at the display, I couldn't help but think of Berit and how our night would turn out. Given the new sleeping arrangement at home, we hadn't been able to spend as much quiet time together as I would have liked. I was hoping that would be more than made up later in the night, but it didn't look promising.

Further down the street, we encountered some of the most elaborate costumes I had ever seen. Men wore feathered headdresses in an array of colors, glittery dresses, and high heels like they were Vegas showgirls. We stopped in at a bar catching up on all of the sights.

"What in the hell happened at Stuart's?" Berit asked. "I missed whatever it was, but all of you looked like you were going to vomit." He leaned into the table, waiting for our answer.

"Sarah went to use the bathroom. When she opened the door, there was one guy with his fist up—"

Berit put his hand up. "I got the picture. That's hardcore. Okay, I can see why you looked like you did. Why the hell didn't they lock the door or go somewhere else? I'm guessing it was part of the thrill, ya know, a chance of getting caught. To each their own, I suppose. That's too raw for me, but I'm not judging, just not into that."

Frankie was ready to move on. He looked like he was gonna jump up any second. "When we get to my dad's hotel, we can go to the bar if y'all want and then watch the action from the balcony. Free drinks and food." Frankie seemed like a nice enough guy, and who could turn down free drinks and food?

Soon we arrived at the hotel, which was old-school New Orleans with polished brick floors, Oriental rugs, and dark antique furniture. A grand staircase led to the mezzanine, where a buzz of people talked. We jumped on a polished brass elevator to the second-floor bar and restaurant.

Everybody seemed to know Frankie and treated us like royalty. We headed to an area on the balcony to drink, and the waiter brought us French bread and butter, perfect to soak up the alcohol we had consumed up to that point. Frankie ordered hamburgers and stuffed potato skins as the four of us watched the stream of people passing below. The street wasn't as packed as during Mardi Gras, but not far off.

Frankie heard some of his friends calling to him from the street. They invited themselves up to the balcony and joined us. A couple of the drunk and pushy girls started coming on to Berit and me. We were squished together in our chairs with little room to maneuver. A brown-haired girl with cantaloupe-sized boobs came on strong to Berit, blabbering about his accent, until she slid her hand down toward his crotch.

"Um, excuse me, but he's not available," I said, moving her hand.

"Says who?" she asked.

"Let's go, Bradley," Berit said.

"Please tell me that you're not a fag! Are you a queer?" Her voice got louder.

Before any more drama could unfold, Frankie apologized and handed me a room key. Berit and I wasted no time and rushed off the balcony toward the elevator and up to the room. "That was intense!" Berit said. "What a total bitch!" I couldn't believe a girl would act in such a manner.

"Even if I were straight, I wouldn't have fucked her for anything. Pretty obvious she's been with everyone there," Berit said, locking the door behind him. The room had two queen beds with fluffy oversized pillows. The wallpaper looked like dark green silk with a gold scroll-like print. Gold curtains with dark green tassel cords lined the windows that overlooked the street.

The night hadn't gone as I had hoped. Rather than fun and laughter, I was pissed.

"Relax and come here," Berit said, putting his hand on my shoulder before taking off my vest. As he looked into my eyes and put his hand to my face, I felt at ease and loved. He was letting me know everything was okay. We didn't say a word, yet a million thoughts passed between us. We just knew. Although I was scared, scared of the pain I might feel, I decided to make myself available to him.

We undressed each other and lay naked face-to-face. Berit's eyes questioned if I was sure, and I nodded. We had held each other for several minutes, and then I turned face down. He straddled me and massaged my back. I started to relax as his warm hands rubbed my shoulders. He ran his tongue down my spine and didn't stop, and the picture from the magazine popped into my memory. As he moved down my body, I lifted onto my knees and elbows. I could feel his warm saliva on my balls. My stomach became queasy, and he must have felt me tense. He stopped and knelt behind me, softly kissing my back to relax me. I could feel his rock-hard cock rub against my body. Thinking of him penetrating me was frightening yet somehow exhilarating.

He slid a finger inside of me. "Brad, relax," he said. "You're in control. You say stop, and I stop. Just remember to breathe deep." As I exhaled, he added another finger, our breaths matching. My body relaxed more, and then he put in a third. He slid them in and out, and I continued to mimic his breathing. He then pulled his fingers out and slid them in again several times. At first, I tightened up, but then I gained confidence and relaxed again as we continued to breathe.

He deeply inhaled and audibly exhaled. I followed, and during the elongated exhalation, he put his dick inside me. Damn! It hurts, I thought. I felt like I was being split in two.

"Slow down," I gasped.

"Oh baby, I'm sorry if I hurt you." He pulled out and paused a few minutes, kissing my back and grasping my clenched fist. After my breathing returned to normal, he started again as gently as before. I knew what he was feeling from performing the same act on him several times, and I knew he was exhibiting maximum control. I was sure he wanted to move faster and with more force, but he took his time continuing to breathe aloud purposefully. I took the cue, which relaxed me, and he picked up his pace, and the sensation became less uncomfortable.

After several minutes, his breathing increased, and I could tell he was about to explode. He groaned like he did when I sucked him off. When the moment came, he moaned, "Oh, God, yes," and then pulled out, and we both collapsed on the bed.

"Brad, you okay?"

I had tears in my eyes and didn't want to look at him. The tears weren't from the pain, more from being overwhelmed. "Yeah, I'm good."

"Then look at me." I didn't want to. I tried to will my eyes dry. He pulled my face toward him before I could turn my head. His eyes looked sad, maybe even regretful. "Obviously, you aren't okay. I tried—"

"Yes, Berit, I'm fine, maybe overwhelmed a little, but not hurt."

"With time, it'll be more pleasurable, I promise." He kissed my forehead. "You know I love you."

Enough with being so emotional, I thought. Stop being such a girl. "Ah, but will you love me tomorrow?" Nothing better than relying on lyrics from a Carole King song.

"You want to lay back and relax or—"

"For withstanding the torture of your humongous dick, you better show some appreciation," I said, rolling over. "I gave you my cherry, after all."

"Humongous? Hardly the case. Believe me, my friend, there's a lot bigger out there."

I noticed the wry edges of his smile as he lowered his head. He gripped the base of my still-hard cock stroking the shaft as he took me in his mouth, cupping my balls and teasing me to the point I wanted to explode, but he backed off, tickling me with wispy touches of his tongue on the head of my dick. Sliding his hand down the shaft, it felt like he was feeding my dick down his throat. I felt my hips tighten, and he knew exactly what to do. My heart raced as the pulsing down below pounded harder.

"Yes, oh God. Now!" I nearly shouted. He was brilliant, total perfection as I came hard, the thrill moving throughout my whole body. He was in control, and I was the recipient of the pleasure. If anything, he was consistent. The pleasure had always been indescribable.

We lay there silent in each other's arms. I finally rose and bathed, per his suggestion. Although I wasn't usually one for a bath, I took his advice. After he showered, we fell asleep. A slight knock on the adjoining door woke me. The bedside clock said one A.M., so I tiptoed to the door. "Yes?"

"Open the door, Bradley," Sarah's voice said from the other side.

"Okay, give me a second." I grabbed a towel and put it around my waist before unlocking the door. She was drunk as a skunk, slurring her words, barely able to stand without losing her balance. She started to speak, and I quickly shushed her. "Berit is sleeping."

"Sleeping? Why's he sleeping? I figured y'all would be, ya know, doing it."

She infuriated me, but I couldn't say anything since Frankie and she had been nice enough to give us their room key. "For God's sake, is that all you think about? I told you we were friends, and it's not all about sex."

"All I can say, brother dear, is if he were mine, we'd be doing it all the time." She giggled ridiculously because of being so drunk.

"Where's Frankie, Sarah?"

"Who?" she asked and stumbled.

I called into the room and heard someone throwing up in the bathroom. "Is Frankie sick? You should be helping him." I fussed.

"Why? I'm not his girlfriend or anything. That's gross—" A loud thud like someone had fallen interrupted her.

"Berit, get up," I said. "We gotta help Frankie."

We threw on our jeans and found Frankie out cold in a puddle of blood next to the toilet. Berit wet a washcloth and started cleaning the blood from Frankie's face.

"Get a towel and roll it up so we can put pressure on his cut." He patted Frankie in the face and raised his head onto his thigh. "Come on, Frankie, wake up." Frankie stirred and groggily opened his eyes, confused. "You hit your head on the porcelain. You have quite a gash above your eyebrow."

Frankie turned over and puked again with some getting on Berit's jeans, but he didn't even register he had puke on his pants. "Frankie, we've got to get you some care. You need stitches, friend."

Frankie muttered a few obscenities while Berit continued to tend to him. We eventually got Frankie on his feet, and with one on each side, we escorted him to the bed. Berit called the front desk for a cab and explained Frankie had hit his head and required stitches. I told Sarah to watch him while I went into our room to put on my shirt. Berit was still bare-chested, but he put on his shoes. He didn't seem to care what anyone thought.

We left the costumes in the room. Thank God Sarah hadn't done anything, so she didn't require getting dressed, but she was slobbering drunk. On the other hand, Berit and I were sober. We managed to get Frankie to the lobby and into a cab. Sarah was useless, so Berit and I accompanied them to the hospital.

In the emergency room, I bought Sarah some coffee in hopes of sobering her up. Three and a half hours later, Frankie had stitches and was almost soberly coherent. Sarah had finally shut her trap. I, by this point, wasn't sure if I liked my sister. She was a selfish bitch and perhaps the most uncaring human being I had ever encountered. Frankie was her friend and maybe even a boyfriend, but when he needed her, she turned her back on him. Some friend! I thought girls came with a mothering nature. My sister apparently missed the message. Maybe I was a fag, but at least I was a nice guy. She was just cold-hearted.

After picking up our costumes from the room, we had the cab drop us off at Stuart and Leighton's. Stuart and Leighton were cleaning and sober. When Stuart saw Frankie's bandage, he went into a maternal role, and I wanted to tell Sarah to take notes, but I didn't.

"I've been worried about you guys, but I'm glad y'all left. We had a few rough party crashers. They caused a scandal in the bathroom at one point and then brought their crudeness into the living room. It ended up with shoving and then a full-on fight. When I think about all the time we put into planning, decorating, and cooking, it makes me sick that it ended as it did. We even had to call the police." With a trash bag in hand, he managed to remain animated.

"I think everybody had their fair share of drama last night," I said, peering to my still-not-right sister. "Overall, we had a good time." I was ready to get home and not hear the details about the party crashers.

"Just to let y'all know, our friends are good people, not like the riffraff that crashed the party," Leighton said. "We like to dance, sing, eat, and enjoy ourselves. Thank goodness our neighbor, Stan was here. He's a big strong guy, into lifting weights. When the ruckus began with pushing and then swinging, he stepped in. One of our close friends even had his nose broken, but Stan was wrapping it up before anything else happened. Then the police arrived. Some people couldn't get out of the way fast enough, and one even had his front tooth chipped. It makes me feel like I never want to open my home again. We've always been pretty loose about friends bringing friends, but it'll only be by invitation from now on. Lordy, what a night." He was still unsettled.

I guess our evening hadn't been that bad, even with the screaming girl on the balcony and Frankie's busted head, I thought. We spruced the best we could before retrieving the car. We dropped Frankie at his house and headed home.

My parents were delighted to see we were no worse for the wear, although Sarah had seen better days.

"Shower now and go to bed," Mom said to Sarah. "You smell like the bottom of a whiskey bottle." She turned to us. "So, how was the party, boys?"

We sugarcoated it to avoid giving her a panic attack, telling her about the party crashers and the police. In case the word got out about Frankie's stitches and emergency room visit, we told them about him falling and cracking his head, but we didn't mention the injury was due to his drunken stupor. I wondered if the hotel staff would tell Frankie's parents about the hotel rooms or if they'd tell my parents. If they did, I'd cross that bridge if and when it came.

For the rest of the day, we lazed watching TV in my room with the door open.

"How are you feeling?" he whispered.

"Truthfully, I'm fine." I grinned with a wink.

"Okay, I just wanted to make sure," he said. "You're the first virgin I've been with." He described the feeling he had in more detail than I wanted to hear. I was still a little uncomfortable talking about sex and being gay. The fooling around stuff was okay, better than okay, but I just didn't want to talk about it unless the thoughts crept into my mind without command. Since I didn't think about it on purpose, it didn't make me feel weird. The whole thing was a juxtaposition—none of me made sense. My identity still confused me. Yes, as Berit put it, I liked dick. I certainly wasn't into girls, but my sexuality was one big red flag of uncertainty. Was it a Berit thing? No one else had made me feel excited and certainly not in a way to give me a hard-on.

"Which book did you put the note in?" I asked. Because I had a ton of books, it would take forever to find it.

"Not gonna tell, Bradley," he said with a smirk. "One day, you'll want to re-read one of your books and stumble upon it. Things like secret hidden notes or gifts come at the perfect time. Oh, while I'm thinking of it, I need to get some of Sarah's pictures. Grootmoeder will be happy to see them." Sarah was still sleeping.

"What time do I need to—" I started to ask him about his flight.

"I'm not talking about it until tomorrow....I'm gonna hold onto this week and live it over and over to help me through the tough times. My life has zero pleasure at home. No friends. The ones I had before from childhood deserted me when they found out I was gay. Things back home are more sexually open; I figured I could tell my best mate, but nope. He wasn't mean and didn't try to beat me up or anything, but he stopped coming around and didn't want to hang out. It still hurts. I couldn't believe it. When we ran into each other, he was polite and friendly, but I knew. Last I heard, he got some girl pregnant."

I waited a few moments before talking. I could see Berit's mind ticking over, and I wanted to ask him what was wrong but fought the impulse. Saying it killed me, but I had people to hang with when he left and a family that loved me, and he had a dying gran, work, and school. "Berit, if you want to see other guys when you get home, I understand, and it's okay. I know how you feel about me. You need some support over there." I knew he needed companionship, but the thought of him with someone else, even only a friend, made me jealous.

I could tell he was mulling it over. "I told you how I tried to kill myself. What I didn't tell you was it hadn't been the first time; it had been my second time. When my so-called best mate turned his back on me after I learned about being gay, I took a handful of pills. All it did was make me sick, and I vomited for days."

He paused a bit. "Do you truly mean it that you won't mind if I make a friend back home? It might help with my loneliness and depression."

I hated hearing the words out of his mouth, but I loved him, and he deserved to have fun and support with all he was going through.

I felt my voice waver. "Only if you promise to still love me." He shot me a look of disbelief. I could tell he wanted to be closer, but my parents' rules had been crystal clear, and physical contact was off-limits.

"Wanna take a ride?" I asked.

"What kind of ride?" he guffawed as he got off the bed.

"Funny," I stood up. "In the car."

We headed out to the car, just two guys, driving to nowhere.

"I want a couple more hurrahs before you leave," I said.

"I love it! Your awkward sexual communication is so adorable." His smile was undeniable.

I wanted him just to know what I wanted without actually asking, but he was going to make me say it aloud. "You like embarrassing me, don't you?" I gave him a sideward glance.

"Why are you embarrassed?" he asked. "We can tell each other anything, Bradley. If I don't want to do it, I'll say no, but I can't imagine that happening. I want all of you anytime I can have you, so the sooner you tell me what you want, the sooner you'll have it, but you have to tell me. Blowjob? Hand job? After last night I wouldn't recommend a good fuck. You'd probably be sore."

"I wish we could go back to the hotel and relive last night. That's all." My voice sounded sad.

"No problem. Let's just go to the hotel." Upbeat and crazy Berit.

"But we can't stay all night, maybe just a few hours at most, and it'll be a lot of money for just a few hours." I reminded.

"That's okay with me. Let's go." He was gung-ho.

We were in luck because the hotel had a few rooms, so we checked to see if the room from the previous night was available, and it was. He was the most caring, considerate person I had ever met.

The afternoon opened my eyes to things I had never imagined. He showed me different positions where we could both have pleasure simultaneously. He was far more skilled and willing than I, but he seemed to enjoy what I did, based on the sounds he made. Although he said my skills had greatly improved, he assured me that he wouldn't break and that I could be rougher with him. We didn't waste one minute of our time in the room, but my heart ached, and I was still in his arms. I didn't want him to leave New Orleans. I held it together. I didn't want to cry and ruin it all. Before we left, he kissed me deeply.

"I love you, Bradley, and I always will."

Back at the house, we visited with my family and watched TV.

"So, do you have everything planned for the trip to the airport tomorrow?" Mom asked.

"Yes, but I still need to pack a few things," Berit said.

"We've enjoyed your visit, and you're welcome here anytime," Dad added.

I looked at my mom and dad. They cared about Berit and were more than understanding about our relationship.

After our conversation, they headed to bed, and Berit and I talked until midnight in the dining room, neither of us wanting to call it a night when Mom came down and told us to go to bed. She hugged and kissed us both on the forehead and wished us good night.

Sarah had been too stubborn to wake up from the night before, so Mom put us on the honor system and allowed us to sleep in my bedroom with the door open. My parents had nothing to worry about; we were both sexually spent.

The next afternoon I drove him to the airport. We didn't say goodbye, more like a see ya next time. I watched as he walked through the door. I stayed by the terminal window and watched as the plane taxied out and finally took off. It was as though all my inner peace and happiness went as the plane soared into the sky. Saying goodbye to him was like a kid giving up his security blanket. He made me feel loved, secure, and desired. The world crashed down on me—the emptiest I had ever felt. I walked to the car and broke down crying. I wondered whether Berit was also crying. If he wanted to cry, he would. He wouldn't have given two hearty shits what anyone thought. Part of me hoped he was crying, but the genuine friend part of me hoped he would return home with a bright vision for the future.

Chapter 9

Days turned into weeks and weeks into months. Berit's letters continued as usual—upbeat about work and school—but I sensed the sadness as his gran's health declined. From what I gathered, her death was close, and I felt his pain. When she died, no one would be there with him. The thought made my heart cry.

School for me was going well, and Leonard and I had become closer friends. I hadn't realized, but he was hurt because I hadn't included him in our Halloween plans, especially after I had asked him to help out before the Stuart decision. I had been so self-absorbed in my excitement that I hadn't considered his feelings. I realized that I was just like Sarah and how she had been with Frankie when he was sick.

Frankie and Sarah were still an item, and our families started to socialize. I feared that my parents would find out about Berit and me staying in the hotel on Halloween night. Frankie said that the staff knew better than to tell his dad about his escapades at the hotel. His dad had way too much to concern himself with than his son's goings-on; after all, Frankie would eventually be taking over the family business someday.

Thanksgiving came and went. Christmas, as always, was great, but I wished Berit could've been with me. We spent an hour on the phone, one of my presents from Mom and Dad. I don't know what an hour set them back, but it had to be expensive. Berit sent a card for my birthday and called the house; we spoke for about a half-hour, and I missed him terribly.

With spring break upcoming, some of the kids were planning a trip to Florida.

"Are you thinking of going?" Mom asked me one night at dinner.

"No, I'd rather continue saving for Amsterdam," I said.

The boom came crashing down. "We think that going to Amsterdam would be a good graduation present, but we don't think you should go before then." She was matter-of-fact.

I wanted to run away. I didn't want to talk to her or my dad. I just wanted to go to my room. They'd regret their decision. When I left for my graduation trip, I would never come back. They had screwed me, thinking the trip was possible. They should have just said no right from the beginning rather than giving me false hope. What chickenshit! I went to my room. I wanted to hit something more than just a pillow. Maybe throw something, but there wasn't anything other than my books, and that just didn't have any oomph. I kicked my bed but ended up stubbing my toe. Dammit! I fell back on my bed and grabbed my notepad.

Berit,

I'm so fucking pissed at my parents right now. They just decided to inform me that Amsterdam was out of the question for this summer, and I have to wait because it's gonna be my graduation present. That's two years away. I can't believe they're such assholes. To soften the blow, they dangled spring break in Florida with kids from school. They knew I wouldn't want to go. Spring break is where a group of high schoolers go, with a teacher chaperone. Everyone gets drunk and tries to cop a feel and get laid in the dunes. They feel okay about Florida because they know I'm not going to try to fuck any of the girls. It's all chickenshit if you ask me.

Now that I've subjected you to my whining, how are you? I miss you. Will you be able to come over for a couple of weeks this summer? I need something to look forward to. I gained another two pounds this week, making it a total of twenty-four. All muscle, my friend. How's your working-out going?

I wish I were there. I'd help you paint and clean out whatever you needed. I've been training Trumpet hard; we have a show coming up in the next few

weeks. I'm sorry. I have a bad attitude right now and probably shouldn't be writing. All I want to do is yell and punch something. Fuck. Fuck. Fuck.
 Friends always,
 Me

After taking the letter to the post office, I drove to the lakefront. I couldn't remember ever being this angry before. Granted, I'd been hurt, sad, mad, but not this mad in a long time. I knew Berit wouldn't get the letter for a week, and it'd be another week until I got a response. It wasn't good enough. I knew it was late, but I found a payphone at the picnic area and called him. It rang a few times until he picked up.

"Hi, I know it's late, Berit."

"No problem. I figured you'd call as soon as you got my letter."

"Your letter? Something I missed in it? No, I was calling you to tell you my parents aren't gonna let me come to Amsterdam this summer. I'm so pissed. I wrote you, but I had to tell you sooner. I'm warning you that the letter is pretty whiny."

I heard a voice in the background, and Berit answered the voice, "It's Bradley. Everything's fine."

"Who are you talking to?" I asked.

"I guess you *haven't* gotten my last letter." He sounded apologetic. "I've met someone. His name is Sven. You'd like him; he's a nice person. He knows all about you and how much I love you." That was the last thing I needed to hear. I was so pissed I couldn't even cry. My stomach twisted. I was a combination of angry, hurt, betrayed, the whole fucking gambit. Could this be any worse? I was in a fucking nightmare. Here I was calling the one person I loved to have him in bed with another man. I felt betrayed.

"No, I haven't gotten your last letter….I'll let you go….I'm happy for you."

"Brad, I'm here for you. *You* are the love of my life; you know that. You told me—"

"I know what I told you." I suddenly felt guilty for the way I was reacting. "I guess it's the timing. I'm broken right now, and to have you with another lover hurts. Let me go. I love you, Berit."

"Brad, I can't leave it like this. I feel dreadful. I love you too much to hurt you like this.”

"I'm okay, Berit, really. Go back to sleep." I hung up the phone.

I got back in the car, slammed my fists on the steering wheel, and took off. I felt like a crazy person. Fueled by my anger, I drove too fast and took the curve way beyond the speed limit. The last thing I remembered was my car losing control and seeing a light pole right before I crashed.

My next memory was fading in and out. I was in the emergency room with doctors and nurses rushing around me.

I don't know how long I was out, but I slowly woke to Mom sitting next to me, tears running down her face. I barely could make out Dad's figure on the other side of the room. I wasn't sure where I was or how much time had passed. Nothing made sense.

"Bradley, it's Mom. You've been in a car accident, but you're going to be okay sweet pea." She patted my hand.

I tried to talk but couldn't move my jaw. My eyes must have had a question wondering what was wrong.

Dad's voice cracked as he fought back the tears. "You just got out of surgery. Your jaw is wired shut, son. You broke it in the accident. You've also sustained other injuries, Brad. Besides breaking your jaw, you broke your nose and have stitches in your head and on your chin. You have a compound fracture in your right arm, and your pelvis has a slight fracture. The accident was bad. The good news is, you're going to be okay and back to normal." He cleared his throat to try and gain control, but he had to turn and walk away.

Mom gave me her best smile through tears. "It was bad, Brad. I'm grateful you're alive," she said and then lost it. "I'm sorry. I don't mean to cry, but I could've lost you. You did great in surgery, and you're going to be good as new."

I felt myself fading out. Now and then, I'd hear a familiar voice, but otherwise, I was unconscious. My body was in a fight for survival and slipped into a coma. Darkness.

A small sunbeam shone through the sliver of the blinds, warming my freezing body. Leonard was sitting next to me, reading. I must've moved because he stopped reading.

"Bradley, it's Leonard." He scooted towards me.

Something was jammed in my nose, and I tried to pull at it. Leonard jumped up and frantically pressed the call button. "Shh, Bradley. Don't touch it; they're coming." Just then, the nurse entered, followed by a doctor. Within seconds multiple medical personnel stood over me.

"Bradley, just relax and breathe calmly," the doctor said as he used a flashlight to examine my eyes. He then listened to my chest, but I was agitated. I wanted whatever was in my nose out right then. He had kind eyes, with a knowing look like Berit had with me. The doctor seemed to feel my pensiveness. He put his hand on my shoulder.

"Bradley, I'm Dr. Barnes. Now that you're awake, Jen, your nurse, and I are going to remove the tube. Relax your breathing and think happy thoughts, and we'll have it out in no time. This is teamwork, you, me, and Nurse Jen. Ready?" He was calming. An image of Berit telling me to breathe deeply popped into my mind, and I followed Berit's imaginary breaths as Dr. Barnes and Nurse Jen pulled the tube from my nose. As it came out, I felt like I was choking. "Relax, Bradley; it's almost out." Nurse Jen calmly said.

Reality was still an abstract concept to me.

"Don't speak," Dr. Barnes instructed as I started to open my mouth. "Just ease into it."

Just then, my parents bolted in the door.

As Nurse Jen ran small pieces of ice across my lips, she continually said, "Relax, breathe slowly," The ice felt good on my lips, and it made me thirsty. She glanced up at a screen above the bed.

I could only whisper a word or two, but nothing made any sense. I was confused like everyone was playing a big trick on me, and I was the only one out of the loop. Although my throat hurt, I thought I remembered not being able to speak because of something about a broken jaw, but I could move my jaw.

In a matter of a few days, the pieces started fitting together like a jigsaw puzzle. Until then, everything had been a mishmash of thought fragments and words without meaning. I found out that I had been in a coma for almost six months. All my injuries, one had been a broken jaw, were healed.

I learned that doctors hadn't detected the extent of my brain injury, which had caused the long coma. They didn't know whether I'd wake up until I did, and then the extent of long-term damage was another concern. The one consistent fact, which was huge, I always shied away from pain stimuli. They had said the opening and closing of my eyes and the twitching of my muscles didn't reflect my condition, but Dr. Barnes reassured my parents it appeared I was making steady improvement. Waking up was a slow process, not like a snap of the fingers as seen in the movies. To cover their ass, the doctors always followed up with some comment that anything was possible and said it could be weeks, months, or even years before returning to the person I was before the accident. The bad news: The longer the waking up took, the less likely of full recovery.

Some days my parents had thought I was awake, but the doctor said I wasn't. Dr. Barnes explained the stages of recovery, so it wasn't like poof, and I would wake up. I had caused many false alarms, so my poor parents were frazzled, but I was fully awake and somewhat cognizant now, of that I was sure, even though the lines of reality and imagination were still blurry. Dr. Barnes said it was normal.

After a couple of weeks, Mom brought a stack of letters from Berit.

"Does Berit know about me?" I asked.

"We finally reached him. Because of the time difference and our schedules, I found it nearly impossible. About a month after the accident, we finally connected," she said. "Since then, I've spoken with him a couple of days a week. I'm due to call him today, but I have to wait until our appointed time. He sobbed when he heard about the accident and thought you didn't want his friendship any longer because he hadn't heard from you. I explained you didn't write or call because you couldn't." Mom was compassionate.

I wanted to read the letters—every single one.

"I have them all in order, none opened," she said. I remembered being pissed at them, but I was unsure why. I did know that they were good people, and I had acted like a spoiled child. They had respected my privacy, and many parents wouldn't have been as respectful and gone the extra steps to get ahold of Berit.

During my coma, I had missed Sarah's graduation and a ton of horse shows. My school had promoted me to eleventh grade, even though I hadn't taken exams. School officials said I could make up eleventh-grade work at home while recovering. I had grown an inch taller but lost more than forty pounds, mostly muscle, but I knew it would come back.

"Is Leonard in the waiting room?" I asked. Mom nodded. "I would like to see him." Although visitation was one visitor at a time, the hospital let my parents come in together. They left to get Leonard.

He slowly cracked the door, and I signaled him to enter.

"Thank you," I said with a croak. Leonard was a chatterbox, and I could depend on him to keep the conversation going.

"I skipped spring break to stay here with you. I was afraid you were going to die." His eyes teared up. He blinked hard to hold the tears back.

"Thank you," I choked out. I then asked, because my parents couldn't be objective, how I looked—I could only imagine – broken nose and jaw, cuts on the head and face, and a significant drop in weight. My voice had not wholly returned, and words would come out oddly. I'm sure I looked like a frail skeleton.

"Bradley, you look great, skinny, really skinny, but great," Leonard said. "They did a good job on setting your nose. Your parents had a plastic surgeon stitch your face, and I think he was the one that set your nose. You look skinnier and a little older because your facial hair has gotten thick and grows like grass. I've actually shaved you a couple of times. And before you think or ask, I haven't touched you below the waist. Tempted as I was, I didn't." He laughed. "I'm just kidding, but I'm gonna get you a hand mirror so you can see for yourself." He left the room and came back in with a mirror.

I was afraid to look, but I knew Leonard wouldn't lie to me. I slowly lifted the mirror and stared. He was right. I was skinny, and my beard had come in pretty thick. The most shocking was my hair; it was long, so long that I pulled it from behind my back. It was almost as long as Gregg Allman's from The Allman Brothers. Last I remembered, it was a few inches past my shoulders. Leonard said he wouldn't let them cut it. Because of all the vitamins and supplements, it grew at twice the speed.

"I figured it was your call whether to cut or not, and I'm confident that you'd be well enough eventually to decide," Leonard said. My hair was a far cry from the military cut I had sported for years. The last time I remembered brushing it, my hair was shaggy, and Leonard admitted to brushing it. I nodded in thanks.

"I talked and read to you," he said. "I even would actually answer my questions pretending you had answered." He paused for a moment. "I know that I'm not Berit, but I can be your stand-in boyfriend until Berit comes, and I don't expect anything in return. I thought it was the right thing to do." He blinked hard again, and his voice cracked.

I was grateful for Leonard's loyalty and friendship and didn't feel so alone. "I know you need your rest right now, so I'll see you tomorrow after school."

I nodded.

My parents came in for a little while but wanted me to get rest and said they'd be back in the morning. Feeling my mom's kiss on my forehead felt like the world had stopped turning; it was with so much love and thankfulness. God, she loved me. Dad grabbed my toes and winked at me.

I grabbed the first letter and tore open the envelope. I remembered bits and pieces of a conversation with Berit, and my heart sank, so I knew the first letters might be something I didn't want to read, but I had to.

My sweet Bradley,

I miss you so much it hurts. I know what I'm about to tell you might not sit well at first, but please don't put down the letter. I had an interesting client buy a car from me last week. He's been in for repairs on his previous autos, but he decided he was sick of the repair stuff, and his car's warranty was almost up, so he bought a new car from me. His name is Sven, and he's in finance and investment. I think he's sixty-one.

He thanked me with lunch, and I just felt comfortable with him. I talked about everything—you, my parents, Han, the rape, my last visit to New Orleans, everything. He was a plethora of advice, not only in investments but also in love. My assumption about him being gay was correct. The love of his life for more than forty years recently died. I told you that commitment in our world is rare, especially when Sven discovered his sexuality. Being a homosexual back then was only whispered, even here. He's lonely and understands my loneliness. He misses human contact and conversation.

A few years back, he had prostate cancer, which should ease your mind. You can look that up in the encyclopedia and see the side effects. You're going to like him a lot. I know it.

Any word on the Amsterdam trip? I'm figuring no news isn't good news. Maybe I'll have to visit you this summer instead. I think of you all the time and miss you.

Friends always,
Berit

I'd have to look up prostate cancer, but I felt like a real heel for my anger. I remembered my rage clearly before my car slammed into the pole. That's about all I could remember.

Oh shit, Brad,
I figured since I hadn't heard about the trip, it was gonna be bad. Shit, well, I'll come to you. So, after reading about the cancer side effect of impotence and loss of bladder control, it must have relieved any infidelity or fooling around concerns. I have let Sven spend the night and hold me, but that's it. He understands commitment and respects ours.

Work is going well. I've made quite a few big sales and gotten a lease agreement with a pharmaceutical company, which is a big deal. That means a residual bonus. More money to spend in New Orleans, right? I bought you something special. I can't wait to give it to you this summer.

Need some sleep. Look forward to your next letter.
Friends always
Berit
P.S. Have you found my note yet? If not, you're not reading enough!

I was the biggest jerk on the planet. I knew the next one was gonna sting as well.

Brad,
The timing couldn't have been worse. Would you please answer my letter or at least the phone? I feel as guilty as hell. I love you. I know you hate when

I get sentimental, but I can't help it. Please talk to me. Did you even read my letter? Are you even reading this? Am I the biggest fool on the planet?

I feel like I can't breathe. Please call me, any time day or night. I won't let him spend the night again if that's what you want. I only want to be with you. Are you okay? Just send me a word, even if it's a fuck off. I need to hear from you.

I know how you hurt. You have to know that I would never hurt you on purpose. Remember all the great times we had. Don't ignore me.

I love you.
Friends always,
Berit

Just as I finished reading the letter, the phone in my room rang, which was a needed distraction because I didn't know if I could read any more letters. With each word, my guilt stabbed me until my heart was shredded. In my childish rage, I not only hurt myself, but I had hurt Berit, who was like the key to my existence. I knew I couldn't speak much because my voice was still pretty weak and hardly audible at times, but I tried.

In a whisper, I answered, "Hello?"

"Oh my God, Brad," Berit's voice began to break. "I didn't think I'd ever hear your voice again. Your mom called me and told me you woke up. Shit. There is so much I want to tell you, but mostly, I love you."

"I love you, and I'm so sorry, Berit. I hope you're still friends with Sven; he needs you." My voice's volume and quality sounded like Sarah's record player when I'd screw with the dials; only there was no controlling it. One minute the whisper was there, and then the next, it was gone. Clearing my throat did nothing for my voice and only scratched my already sore throat. There was no way he could understand my gibberish.

"Shhh. Don't talk anymore," he said. "Once your mom and I spoke, I lost it. The thought of anything happening to you was more than I could bear. I wanted to come right away, but your mom told me to wait. That's when we set our call time. Yes, I'm still friends with Sven, but I told him that he couldn't spend the night until I spoke with you. If it's okay, I want to see you. I miss you." He was talking a mile a minute.

I wanted to see him, but I didn't want him to waste money. I had no idea how long I would be in the hospital. "Me too" was all I could muster. I felt myself fading.

"I'll be there tomorrow evening if I can get a flight. And as far as money, there's no worry there, my friend, I'm flush. Go to sleep, get rest, and I'll see you as soon as possible. I love you."

He waited for me to hang up. Hearing his voice was better than I had expected. My stomach turned over with butterflies like the first time I met him. How was that even possible in my condition? I wondered what he would think of the way I looked. I was too exhausted to think, and I called the nurse.

So many questions would have to wait. I closed my eyes with thoughts rattling around my head: When would I be able to walk? How long was I gonna have to be in the hospital? I had done nothing but sleep for six months, so how could I possibly need more? Sleep scared me. What if I didn't wake up? I became agitated.

"What's wrong, Bradley?" Nurse Jen asked.

"Wake up?" I mumbled.

She understood my slurred words and assured me that I would wake up. She said I could look forward to clear liquids and to call if I needed anything. The nurse coming on shift, Linda, would be happy to get anything I needed. I fought to keep my eyes open long enough to acknowledge Jen, but it was a struggle. I lost the battle.

I woke up around two in the morning, trying to put the pieces of my life together. My internal clock was all askew. I was awake but not like myself. I was groggy, and my thoughts haunted me. Pictures in no particular order or reason flashed through my mind like a messed-up slideshow. I remembered pounding the steering wheel, enraged. I had lost my temper, and because of my tantrum, I had almost killed myself. Could I have subconsciously done it on purpose? I thought I was stronger, that I had it more together. Who had I become? Did I have to have Berit in my life to be okay? Dumb. Pathetic. The tears rolled down the sides of my face into my hair and on the pillow.

Linda came in to check on me. "Oh Bradley, Jen told me you're having a tough time. It's to be expected, sweetie. You've been through quite an ordeal," she said, taking my hand. "Slowly, answers will come. Don't expect things too fast, and don't get discouraged. You have a long road ahead of you. Don't make these thoughts of confusion consume you or become the reality because they're not." It was like she was looking into my head and could see the flashing pictures. "Do you need something to help you sleep?"

"No, ma'am, thank you." What little voice I had sounded weak and strange. I wasn't sure I wanted Berit to see me like this. As I tried to fall back asleep, the slideshow continued, but I focused on the flashes that felt better than the scarier ones.

I slowly drifted back to sleep. Mid-dream, I heard squeals, rattles, and a loud bang—my tires squealing, objects flying and rattling in my car, and a loud bang as I hit the light pole. The cement cracked, and in slow motion, crushed the roof of my car. I was watching this horrible accident from the sidelines. A voice echoed in my mind, "Bradley, Brad." Wait, the voice sounded real, I opened my eyes, and there stood Sarah. She looked different. I know I looked confused.

"Mom called me to let me know you had woken up," she said. "I'm sorry it's taken a few days to get here. My prayer group and I have been praying for you, and here you are awake." Who is this person, and where is my sister? This certainly wasn't the Sarah I had grown up with. Praying? Prayer group? She stroked my hair and looked at me like a mother comforting her sick child. Something was wrong with the picture. I pinched my arm. Wake up, Bradley. Was I having another nightmare?

She smiled. "I've been saved, Bradley, and it's been through your accident. God takes bad things and makes good. I guess it took something as horrific as your accident to make me hit rock bottom, but we'll talk about it at another time. Right now, you need to focus on getting better." She leaned in and kissed my forehead. She pulled up a chair, patted my hand, and began reading the Bible to me.

Thank God the nurse's aide brought in some food, gross—light-colored tea, and Jell-O. She asked if I wanted more Jell-O. I shook my head no but mouthed thank you. My voice hadn't woken up, or I was shocked, speechless by my sister's radical change.

"School?" Anything to stop her from reading the Bible.

"LSU. I was gonna rush, but I realized Greek life didn't offer the lifestyle I was comfortable with anymore. Instead, I joined a Christian group on campus, and it's been far more gratifying. I bet you're surprised by the change." All I could think was, No shit. "Brad, it's great." Her smile was sweet but simple. It didn't suit her, for sure. "Can I help feed you? Here," she held my cup of tea up to my lips. I took the cup and signaled okay. "I wasn't sure if you were strong enough. I'll stay while you eat, but then leave so you can get your rest." She sat and watched each bite of the Jell-O, babbling on as I contemplated this change about her. I guessed it was another one of her fads, like when she dyed her hair red or decided to get involved in the councilman's campaign.

Sure enough, I finished my Jell-O, and she split, promising to pray for me. I smiled. What else could I do? My sister was crazy.

I closed my eyes, but Linda interrupted my rest to take my temperature and check my vitals. She then picked up a bag from the side of the bed full of pee—my pee. The alarms sounded in my head. I lifted the sheets and noticed that I was wearing a fucking diaper. Upon further inspection, a tube was coming out of my dick. She saw my concern.

"As soon as we have you walking and stable to use the bathroom, all that goes away. Don't worry." What the hell was she saying? Don't worry? Seventeen with a diaper and pee bag! I couldn't deal with the thought of someone wiping my ass and washing my balls.

"Bradley, I'll see about when we can get you up. Physical therapy will be coming by in just a few. They'll be happy to see you awake," she said as she checked the monitors by my bed. "They've worked hard to keep you active. You've lost some of your muscle mass, but they have been working hard with you. I think your therapist has eyes for you," she said and winked.

Great, just great, some girl had been working my legs. Certainly, she knows I'm in a diaper with a pee bag. Things had to change and fast before Berit saw me. I pouted like a toddler, not getting his way.

"Well, what did you expect?" she asked. "You've been in a coma for almost six months. You should be glad your systems are all working. Many times coma patients end up with colostomies due to a lack of bowel function and permanent kidney problems." Basically, she was saying, Bradley, grow up and be grateful.

A tap interrupted our chat. A muscle guy who looked like a wrestler, maybe five-seven but built like a brick shithouse, walked in. He had wavy brown hair, brown eyes, and a smile that genuinely seemed happy to see me awake. "Finally, I've been waiting to meet you, sport. I'm Steve, and I've been working hard to keep you limber with a full range of motion. We're gonna have you up in no time. We'll set goals for your recovery. Warning, I can be a force to deal with. Bradley, you're gonna either love or hate me, but know it's all for your good."

"Goodbye and good luck!" Linda left laughing down the hall.

He was tough, for sure. He showed no mercy and didn't play into the pity the poor kid. No, he was demanding and made me work, but I felt alive even if I was just pushing my feet and legs against his hands and arms. We worked a little on my arms and hands, but he wanted me to walk as soon as possible. Because I could hold a cup and a spoon, I was ahead of the game. He was like a coach, pushing me to go more.

After a half-hour, I felt exhausted but good.

"You'll probably experience some cramping in your calves and quads," he said. "Good thing you had strong legs to start with."

I talked to him as much as I could, which wasn't lots of words, about Trumpet and riding.

"That makes sense with your legs," he said. "You've lost a bunch, but don't get upset. Your strength will come back."

I was the king of one-word answers. It took everything I had to concentrate on what people said to me. I had moments of clarity followed by moments of confusion. The more tired I was, the greater the confusion.

As Steve left, he told me another therapist would be coming later to help with my cognition.

"I'll see you tomorrow. Now make sure you take a nap before seeing the other therapist." He held his gaze at me a little longer than felt comfortable. The way he said he'd see me tomorrow sounded a bit too friendly. He was my therapist. Was he flirting with me, or did I imagine things through my exhaustion? I guess I should've felt complimented, but I didn't.

I slept for a couple of hours after Steve left and woke up about fifteen minutes before the next therapist, Andrea, arrived for our first session.

Now that I could communicate, she'd evaluate my memory, I guess. Time was a strange concept. Days and nights were mixed up, making time like an endless stream with no delineation.

I didn't realize how scrambled my mind was until she asked me a bunch of memory questions, called out a list of letters and numbers, and then asked me to recall them, not even in order, just say the ones I could remember. I struggled and jumbled everything, and I knew I was bombing. Bombing bad. She was patient and kept saying I was doing fine, but I knew I wasn't.

The common theme was, "Bradley, don't be hard on yourself." The nurses, Dr. Barnes, the nurse's aides, and Andrea all agreed I was doing well in my recovery. Steve was the only one who didn't treat me with kid gloves. He was all about progress. If there was a patient reassurance seminar, I felt he must've missed the class, but his tough attitude made me feel more normal if that made any sense.

Around three-thirty, Leonard arrived.

"Man, they sure are watching visitors like a hawk," he said. "We only get a ten-minute limit since you've woken up." I had learned that everyone but my parents had ten minutes. "Before you woke up, I could sit with you and read for hours, even though you could only have one visitor at a time like now. I hope this doesn't sound creepy, but I liked watching you sleep. You seemed so peaceful and beautiful.

"And, I have something to admit," he said with tears in his eyes. "I kissed you. Not on the lips because of the feeding tube in your nose, but I've felt guilty and wanted to confess."

I smiled. "It's okay," I said. "It was an emotional time for everyone, I suppose."

Although my voice was still shaky, I could tell it was getting stronger. I told Leonard about Steve and how hard he had been on me.

"Duh! He wants you; I can tell," he said. "What is it with you? Everyone wants to be a part of your life for just a chance to be close with you. What's the deal? And the only one you have eyes for is a million miles away. I admit it, Berit is gorgeous and a great guy, but Steve isn't a slouch. Have you seen his body?"

"Neither are you," I replied. "Who knows what tomorrow brings? Right now, I couldn't do anything with it even if I got it up because there's a big fucking tube—"

"I know, and thanks for the compliment. You really think I'm not a slouch?"

"Really." I could feel myself dropping off again and heard Leonard as he began to read aloud.

I don't know how long I slept, but I woke to Linda checking on me.

"Ready for food? On the menu today, you have," she picked up the lids on the tray. "Broth and pale ice tea. And for dessert, Jell-O." She rolled the tray to me and smiled. "No real food yet, champ." Shit, I wanted my toothbrush. If Berit was coming, I wanted fresh breath. Did I smell? Someone needed to do something to make me presentable. She noticed my panic.

"Bradley, what's wrong?"

"Company tonight. A bath, my teeth?" My voice squeaked. My skin felt like a film of ick coated it. I felt the same way I did after training on Trumpet, sweating my balls off, and then going into A/C. That was it, dried sweat. I probably stunk to high heavens. I certainly didn't want Berit seeing me like this.

"Don't worry. Reggie will be in to bathe you. You'll be spiffed up for your company. Somebody special coming?"

"Berit. More than ten minutes." I replied with my hoarse voice.

"Let me see what I can do." She winked at me.

She left the room, and moments later, a man with arms the size of my waist came in with towels. He reached in the drawer, pulled out a bowl, and prepared to bathe me.

"I can wash my own penis and butt," I said as he took the diaper off me.

"Not with the catheter," he said, pointing at the tube coming out of my dick. "You sure as hell don't want to tug on it." Okay, that made sense, but I didn't like it. "Seen one, seen them all, boy. Let me do my job. You might rather the pretty nurse bathe you, but it don't work like that in this hospital. Males wash males and females wash females."

Talk about embarrassing! He didn't seem bothered, but his bathing my junk was humiliating to me.

When he went to put a new diaper on, I stopped him.

"You don't want to have a BM in the bed," he said. "Trust me, and I sure don't want that."

"I will be getting up to go to the bathroom." I forced the words no matter how I sounded.

"You know, you may not have control yet. You probably don't."

I held my ground, and he eventually agreed and left. I felt as clean as I could've given the situation.

Around five, Mom popped in and said she'd been by a couple of times, but I had either been in therapy or asleep.

"You look fresh," she said. "I can always tell when they've just given you a bath." She rambled on about nothing I cared about, but I listened.

"Oh, by the way, your father is on the way to get Berit," she said. My stomach flipped with expectation. I wanted to ask how I looked and if she could put the pee bag out of sight, but I didn't want to waste my energy.

"Could you please ask the nurses to let him stay more than ten minutes since he's come all the way from Amsterdam?"

"I'll just say he's family. He's such a gem. I'll make sure he has the *carte-blanche pass.*" The family pass allowed for lengthier visits.

Chapter 10

About six-thirty, Dad walked into the room and kissed Mom. They briefly spoke—I guessed to discuss Berit's visitation with me but left to give us privacy, I guess. Before the door even opened, I could smell his cologne. I couldn't help myself. I started crying. When he opened the door, he, too, had tears rolling down his cheeks. He walked over and kissed me—not on my lips, but my forehead and the top of my head like a parent would a child.

"Oh God, it's you," he said. "I never thought I'd see you again. Brad, I've missed you so much. You're gorgeous." He stroked my hair. "Don't ever do this to me again." He pulled up a chair and sat as close to the bed as he possibly could. "Look at your hair! I'm jealous." Although his hair was much shorter, almost like an ordinary man's haircut, he was still as handsome as ever. He looked older, more mature. He saw the stack of letters and smiled. "Take your time with those. I was a basket case. I thought I'd lost you and begged for you to reconsider. I know, not very masculine or strong, but I didn't give a shit. I wanted you back. I can't begin to imagine how you felt calling me and hearing another man's voice in the background. I figured you were calling because you—"

"Shh. It's okay." I touched his hand.

He looked down. "That's when you got in the wreck, right?"

"Yes, my fault," I said. It was. I had been a child throwing a temper tantrum and did it to myself.

He began to cry again. "I'm sorry, so sorry I hurt you. I would never on purpose." After a few moments, he regained his composure and cleared his throat. "I love you."

"I know. I love you, Berit. I'm just so glad that you're here." I could feel weariness taking over, but I didn't want to fall asleep. I wanted to hear him talk to me more, even if I was too tired to respond. "Talk to me. I want to hear you." He held my hand and talked about Amsterdam and the sights and sounds. A picture of us walking down an Amsterdam street hand-in-hand formed in my mind as I faded to sleep. I faintly remembered his sweet kiss on my lips and my forehead.

Two o'clock in the morning seemed to be my magic hour. I woke with a start, for no reason. I decided to try and sit upright without support from pillows or the mattress. After sitting in the bed for a few minutes, I was ready to swing my legs off the bed. It should've been a no-brainer, but it was anything but simple. My legs felt glued to the bed. I fought and struggled to no avail. Oh shit, I thought, surely someone would've mentioned it if I had lost the use of my legs. I started bawling. I was going to be in a wheelchair for the rest of my life. Why hadn't anyone told me?

I pressed the call button and the graveyard shift nurse, Wendy, came immediately. "What's wrong, Bradley? Are you in pain?" She was almost panicked at my hysteria.

"No one told me," I sobbed.

"Told you what?" She wrinkled her brow in confusion.

I heaved out the words. "I'm paralyzed."

"What? No, you're not. You can move your legs. Remember in PT today? I heard you did great."

"Why won't they move now?" I *did* remember they moved fine during therapy.

She threw back the sheets. My legs were strapped to the bed.

"Sometimes, Bradley, patients forget about their condition and get up without assistance and fall. It's a precaution for your safety."

"I want to sit on the bed," I said. I couldn't think of the words to explain.

She unfastened the straps and stood in front of me, allowing me to turn. Having the straps off felt freeing. I wiggled my legs, and they were fine. I had been a buffoon. I was embarrassed, but they moved. She called in the night orderly, who brought in a belt. She then fastened the belt, with her on one side and the orderly on my other side.

"Try to stand, Bradley. We have you. Don't worry." I was scared but thrilled all at the same time. I slowly stood. I felt off-balance, but I was standing. "Do you want to sit in the chair?" she asked, and I nodded. "Okay, we have you. I promise we won't let you fall."

I slowly moved my leg and took a step. I felt weak but not too weak to take a second and third step. I then changed my mind. I wanted back in the bed. There was no point sitting in the chair. I'd be stuck until someone came and walked me back.

"Can I just get back in bed?" I turned around and slowly walked back to the bed, those three precious steps—six steps in total.

"Bradley, I have to strap your legs back to the bed." I nodded.

Those six steps exhausted me. I supposed the hysteria had taken a toll as well. I immediately fell back to sleep.

The rattle of the food cart had made its way into my psyche and woke me. I hoped there'd be something more than Jell-O and tea. As I opened my eyes, I saw Berit's smiling face. "Your mom dropped me off, and she'll be back. I hear you had a bit of a stroll last night."

"Yes." I beamed, unable to contain my enthusiasm.

"They said you're ahead of schedule with standing and walking. The nurse also told me I could walk you in the hall for a few minutes. Maybe after you eat your breakfast?"

I teared up again. Why was I so emotional? "I'd like that."

"The nurse will put a belt on you, and the IV and urine bags will have to take a walk with us."

How embarrassing, but if I could walk out of the room, even just a few steps, I didn't care what I looked like. Berit was undoubtedly strong enough to hold me up should the need arise.

I had a real breakfast with apple juice, a soft egg, and of course, Jell-O.

"I want more," I said, pointing to the empty tray.

"After your walk," he said.

They must've unstrapped my legs right before I had awoken. After the belt was on, I took a step and another with Berit by me. I walked to the door, out the door, and down the hall. I wanted to keep going.

"Big man, remember you need to walk all the way back," Berit said. "Let's turn around now, okay?" By the time I returned to the bed, I was starving. "Still want more food?"

I did, and the orderly brought me a bowl of watery oatmeal, saying it should jump-start my digestive tract. Controlled pooping was like a rite of passage in the hospital.

"Brad, you're doing great. I'm impressed. I thought it would take longer." He kissed the top of my head. "I'm gonna leave so you can rest."

Steve from PT was scheduled in a few hours, so I needed rest. I grabbed Berit's shirt, pulled him down, and kissed his lips, but he quickly pulled back. I heard someone clear their throat. He winked at me and grinned.

It was my mom, shit! "I hear my boy's been strolling the halls. How are you, honey?" She walked over and kissed my forehead. I now understood why he had only kissed the top of my head. Well, if it hadn't been out the bag before, it certainly was after the lip-lock, but Mom didn't say anything.

Physically, I grew stronger day by day, but my memory was a whole different matter. Dr. Barnes said it was part of the dance—all normal and to be expected.

Berit planned to stay until I was released. I felt guilty he'd spent a lot to be bored. The good news – we had lots of time to talk. I made sexual advances, but he declined, not out of lack of desire, but out of respect— no fooling around in the hospital, period.

Berit and I were chatting as usual, but thoughts hammered around in my head, causing a torrent of emotion. "What is it? Come clean," he said.

"I've gone over and over, in my mind, the accident. Thoughts have crept in like: Did I do it on purpose? Was I trying to kill myself, or was my rage that out of control? It's scary to think I could get so upset I'd lose all sense of reason." I toyed with a straw, knotting it and straightening it. I couldn't look Berit in the eyes.

He leaned forward with a look of intent. "Brad, as close as we are, I don't think you were trying to kill yourself. I think you were desperately hurt and felt I'd betrayed you. That's what I think, and the guilt is heavy on my heart. I should've waited until you had acknowledged my letter and knew before having Sven stay the night. You're too together and too smart to make a permanent decision for a temporary problem. Nothing is worth taking your life, but I don't think you did it on purpose; however, it wouldn't be a bad idea to run it by a doc."

I pondered what he suggested; his advice was sound even if I didn't take it. It was like Berit could look into the future, maybe from talking to Sven as much as he did. He compared us to Sven and Sven's partner, Luuk. Berit's concern was he was my first and only, and I may feel like I missed out one day, years down the road.

"Brad, I don't want you to resent me, ever." He continued with an intense attitude. I wanted my playful friend back and no more serious talk.

"Why would I? Do we have to talk about this now?" I knew I sounded whiny. Was I pouting?

"Yes, Brad. It's important. I've been with more men than I care to admit. I'm concerned that one day you'll feel like I robbed you of being with other people, having other experiences. I know you don't want to hear it, but please think about it. I want you to know for sure that I'm the one you want. It's a bit like trying on shoes: You don't pick the first pair. You try on a few and then go with the one that feels most comfortable or suits your needs." He turned my face towards him and made me look into his eyes.

"I will think about it, okay? So far, I haven't felt an attraction to anyone but you. If I find myself attracted to someone else, I'll let you know, deal? No more talking about it for now. I got your message loud and clear."

Sven was only a friend, a good friend, and that was it. Luuk had been twenty years older and was eighty when he died. Their relationship was a rarity indeed.

"Did he ever make any advances?" I asked.

He shook his head no with a slight upturn on one side of his mouth.

"Brad, if I wanted to get laid or whatever, all I have to do is go to Amsterdam," he said. "The district has plenty of opportunities. I've had more sex than you can shake a dick at." He laughed and then resumed. "Seriously, you need to take another step, Dorothy, and venture out. I know you love me, and when the time is right, we'll be together like Sven and Luuk. Even though the age difference between us isn't like theirs, the two relationships have staggering similarities. How do you know I'm the one you want when you haven't been with anybody else? I'm not saying I want to hear graphic details or blow by blow, but if you do, it won't affect our relationship." He batted his eyes and said, "What? I can't make you laugh anymore?" He got up and walked to the window.

"Berit, I still question who I am. Am I gay, or is it just that I'm in love with you and would be even if you were a girl? It's you I love, not you because you're a guy. Make sense?"

"I hear what you're saying," he turned and leaned against the window sill. "My gaydar went off the second I saw you. It's okay. You're gay. Deal with it. Had I been a girl, there's no way you would've turned your bike around. If you want, try it out, pick the most attractive girl you can and have sex or try to. You may not even get it up. I played all the bases with perhaps the most beautiful girl I'd seen. Did it all, my friend, everything." I couldn't imagine and what he was saying seemed crazy to me.

He paced the room like an expectant father. "First, I had to get drunk and work myself up for the task. I love women as friends but jerking off was as gratifying as sex with a girl. Maybe you'll be different, but one way or another, Brad, you need to venture out. I don't want you to have regrets or wonder." He stopped, looked at me, and pointed at me. "*That* would kill me."

The conversation was exhausting. I was having trouble keeping my eyes open, so he sat and held my hand until I fell asleep and left. My dream was strange, incorporating our conversation into the dream. In the dream, Leonard had come to see me, and I caught him looking under the sheet. He started to fondle me and put his mouth on me, and I didn't stop him. I woke up; shit, it ended as a wet dream. Since I had the catheter removed, my morning wood hadn't been as woody, but it certainly had woken up in the dream, complete with a climax. Wonderful! How am I going to explain the wet sheets? Of course, Jen walked in as I was trying to wipe up. I felt my face redden.

"Bradley, did you have an ejaculation?" I nodded. How fucking embarrassing!

"Good! That's great. All systems are functioning. I suspect you'll be leaving us sooner than later. I need to get it on your chart."

What? I could just see it— Patient had a wet dream today. Oh my God. If my leaving had been contingent on shooting my load, I would've solved that issue right after they took out the catheter.

Two days later, I was released. I was a week ahead of schedule. When we pulled up, the house seemed vacant. I didn't see my car in the driveway. My car had to have been fixed by then. I realized no one had talked about the accident or my car while I was in the hospital. I hadn't given my car any thought, but now I wondered where it was. I did, however, have nightmares of the accident, but nothing exact.

Once inside, I asked, "Where's my car?"

"Oh honey, we've waited to talk about it until you got home," Mom said. "Here, sit, you two." While sitting around the dining room table, she pulled some Polaroid pictures of the totaled car out of the drawer. Holy shit! I was lucky to be alive. The wreckage looked like one of those accidents drivers would stare at while driving by and think nobody made it out alive.

The ride home and seeing the pictures zapped any energy I had.

"I need to sleep," I said, standing up. Mom, Dad, and Berit followed me upstairs. I had practiced stairs in the hospital, but not as many. I was glad I had the entourage to support me.

Berit had been sleeping in the other bed in my room. Mine, still with the blue and white spread and perfectly positioned red pillows, seemed untouched. God, it was good to be home.

"Now, we want you to rest," Mom said. "I've put this bell on your side table. Just ring if you need anything." I wanted Berit to stay upstairs, but I needed to close my eyes, just for a minute.

When I woke, Berit was on the other bed reading one of my books.

I stirred, which startled him. "Hey, sleepyhead. Your mom has food prepared downstairs. They ran out for a few, but they should be back within the next couple of hours." He smiled.

"In that case, come here." I beckoned him to me. "It was your fault I had that damn dream in the hospital, but it worked out to my benefit because it was one of the things they were concerned about, which I find odd. Why would they give a crap if I could – whatever?"

He stood next to the bed, looking down at me. "You want to see if it will work again? Let me be the first to test its function." My pajama pants had an opening, and he pulled out my dick. I was hard, like throbbing hard, and his hand on me felt like heaven. I tugged on him so his crotch was closer to me and unzipped his jeans. He was ready. Holding him in my hand felt good, but I wanted one of the tricks he had taught me over Halloween.

"Remember the position you showed me at the hotel where you straddle me?" I asked as we stroked each other. "I want you to." So, we did.

He dismounted and washed me off, which made for another erection.

"Clean up your own mess," he said. "I dare not touch your wild thing."

"Hey, it's been out of action for a long time, at least to my knowledge." I wiped myself off and handed him the washcloth.

"Be right back," he said as he headed to the bathroom.

When he returned from the bathroom, he looked back to his perfect self. I moved over and patted the bed.

"Just for a minute, he said. "I've already broken house rules, but you looked too good—I couldn't help myself." He cuddled next to me, face-to-face. "I've missed you terribly. Something's gotta give. Maybe I can see if the company will relocate me over here. Closest would be Dallas, I think. I'm making enough to travel back and forth more frequently, though. And there's the matter of the house, which I guess I could rent. Do you see yourself ever moving to me? Truthfully?"

"Truthfully, I don't know what I see for my future. I know I'm not mentally right yet. Do I want to be with you always and forever? The answer is yes, no doubt. I know this probably sounds childish, but I don't know if I could move that far away from my parents." He stared into my eyes.

He had a peaceful look, his eyes twinkling in concert with a gentle smile. "Not childish, Bradley, you have great parents. They're gonna let me stay in here the rest of my stay."

"How long are you planning on staying?"

"Only three more days." He'd already been away from work for more than eighteen days and needed to get back. He paused and then asked, "What do you want me to do? Do you want me to move to America?" He moved a loose strand of my hair away from my face.

"We have so much to consider and talk about," I said, but I was still struggling in the communication department. "I have no idea when I'll be ready for school, and I can't think of anything permanent until I graduate. At the pace I'm going, who knows when that will happen? My doctor and parents speculate I might be able to return to school in November at the earliest."

"I understand. There's no rush." He acted so grown up, not like the wild kid he had been.

"Thanks, to something lighter; what were you reading?"

"*Of Mice and Men,* have you've read it?" He stood.

"I've read *every* book on the shelves." One win for the skinny kid.

He seemed impressed. "I have a couple of things to give you." He opened his suitcase, which was more like a trunk. He first handed me three magazines with naked pictures. "The articles are the best." He smiled and then gave me a small box, wrapped simply but with an expensive feel. "I told you I've been doing quite well, and upon Sven's financial advice, my money is making money. Pretty cool." I opened the box, and it was a Tag Heuer watch. I knew it was an expensive gift. I took a closer inspection: He had our initials engraved on the back with the date we first met when I was on the family vacation. Mom and Dad had given me neat gifts before, but this was the first time someone other than family had given me something so expensive. I couldn't believe he remembered the date. It seemed all so grown up, and a kind of special I had never felt before.

"I want you to enjoy it. Your dad probably won't want you to wear it, but I want you to. If anything, over the past months, I've learned 'don't wait for the right time because it may never come.' Have you had any realizations?"

To be a smartass or not, I thought. Okay, maybe a joke isn't appropriate right now. "Don't drive upset, ask questions, don't make assumptions, and I am loved." My eyes filled with tears as he started to cry.

"You are immensely loved by many. When I think of you, I feel like my insides are trying to explode through my skin." I understood what he was saying. I felt the same.

My stomach growled at the thought of real food, so we went downstairs and ate until we couldn't eat anymore. While we watched TV in the den, Mom and Dad walked in, and Dad tossed a set of keys my way. "It was a combined effort, and Berit got us an insanely good deal. Go see." I wanted to run, but I took my time to walk to the front door. In the driveway was an older Volvo. Granted, it wasn't a muscle car or even a fun car, but it was classy.

Because I wasn't physically or mentally capable, I couldn't take it for a spin, much like having a candy bar but unable to tear open the wrapper. I walked around the car, sat behind the wheel, and suddenly felt sick to my stomach. "This is great, Dad, thanks." I made the excuse that I was tired, so I got out of the car and walked inside. I had zero desire to drive again—maybe because I felt weak, or perhaps I had developed another hang-up. Great, just great.

I sat back on the sofa with Berit next to me. Dad made a drink, and Mom had a glass of wine. The room was silent except for the TV. While I stared at the TV, I could feel glances sparring around the room, Mom to Dad to Berit and back again. I think they were all dumbfounded. I don't know what they expected. I wasn't ungrateful. I was given the keys to a car I couldn't drive brought feelings of inadequacy and a reminder of my inability to have a life and independence.

"Mr. Stedman, would you mind if I took Bradley for a ride in his new car?" My guess is Berit hoped a ride would lift my spirits, but would it? Would it serve to emphasize how he was perfect, and I was back to loser status? Did I trust myself behind the wheel of a car ever again? My last adventure took more than six months off my life, fucked my memory and body, and took every bit of self-esteem I may have developed.

"Of course. A quick ride around the block, I'm sure, would be okay," Dad said, trying to sound upbeat.

"Maybe later, y'all; I'm tired." I was down and ridiculously sad. I got up to go back to bed, and Berit followed close behind.

"Brad, let me have it. What gives with the attitude? It's not your dad's fault you got in the accident, and what did you just say, you felt loved? Why the anger? You need to get your anger under control. I get it; you have a long road ahead of you, but your progress has been super. Take the little wins and run with them. Hold onto the good stuff and let the bad roll off you." He was supportive, but I felt condescending.

"What can I say? I'm down. It comes in waves. When just you and I sat on the sofa, I was good. Dad tossing the keys made me feel like he's happy to show me how incapable I am." I think I was pouting. I was jealous, jealous of everyone not in my condition. "How could anybody understand?" I ranted.

"I'm not listening to this shit anymore," he said. "Nobody has it perfect, and granted, your accident was substantial, but there is a light at the end of the tunnel. Not everyone gets that light, Dorothy, or the light they see is a fucking train ready to annihilate them. I've never thought of you as a spoiled brat, but this shit smacks of it. Come back down when you can act like a normal human being and not pity-boy Bradley." He walked out and headed downstairs.

I knew he was right, but who was I angry at? Him? Me? Dad? I felt as though I'd be this sack of crap the rest of my life. I took the corkboard with all my ribbons off the wall and threw it across the room. I wanted to hurt something, someone, anything to make this horrible, gut-wrenching feeling go away. I could hear shuffling around downstairs, and I knew what was happening. Mom wanted to come up and check on me, but the two men downstairs said to leave the whiny little boy upstairs to throw his temper tantrum. I swept the top of my desk with my arm, and everything went flying. I threw down two model planes I had made when

I was young and stomped them before collapsing in a heap on the floor in tears.

I cried for about thirty minutes before I started picking up the mess. I headed downstairs to get a broom to clean up the smashed models and went through the dining room because I didn't want to see my mom, dad, or Berit sitting in the den. I climbed the steps, feeling winded. At the top, I had to rest a second before I walked back into my room. Berit was back on the bed, reading the book. Part of me was angry, and part of me was embarrassed.

He ignored me until I cleaned up the mess. "Such a shame. Those were cool, Brad." I glared in his direction, Mr. Perfect. What was wrong with me? I didn't feel in control and would never have done what I had done before. "I suggested your dad put a punching bag in the garage before you broke everything in your room. It certainly has helped me."

"You?"

"Why the fuck do you think I'm doing martial arts? It's not only good for self-protection but also a great anger reliever. You're not the only person angry in this house, my friend. We can't begin to feel what your parents feel. I'm sure they'd like to bust your ass for being irresponsible and nearly killing yourself, but because you were hurt and are still on the road to recovery, they've cut you a break. Do you have any idea how much it must've cost them for six months in the hospital, three of those in intensive care, not to forget the months ahead of more therapy, and then a new car? I'm willing to bet their insurance went up. See, my friend, it's a chain reaction, but they've swallowed their anger and focused on you getting better. I get you're angry and must be frustrated as all hell, but channel it for good and not the momentary gratification of breaking something."

"Are you angry with me?" I sheepishly asked.

"Before I knew what had happened, I was angry with myself and confused," he said. "Then when I found out what happened, I felt guilty for the circumstance and then pissed as all hell at you. Brad, I thought you were smarter than to give into reckless abandon. Me, I've been more than guilty of recklessness on many occasions, but I'm not as smart as you. You're a thinker. Also, this is huge, so head trauma often changes personalities or anger triggers. If this is who you've become, you need to learn to control it and not let it control you. I'm sure your parents will tell your therapist, but you also need to. You're too fuckin' big to go out of control; you'll wind up hurting someone and going to prison."

I sat still and watched him. I wondered if my anger issue was from sadness or trauma. What if my personality had changed? "Do you think this is who I am now?"

"I don't know. You've seemed perfectly you up until this point. Can you pinpoint what started the outburst?"

"Yes," I said, embarrassed. "I felt like it was being flaunted in my face how incapable I was. I know it's not real and a wild story in my mind, but it felt real."

He looked sad. "And then I complicated it by offering to drive, something like that?"

I nodded, feeling even more childish. "And I know it wasn't like that, Berit. God, I hope this isn't me."

He knelt closely behind me and whispered, "I love you, and you're gonna be alright. If this is you, we'll deal, okay?"

I agreed, and we went downstairs. Mom had been crying, and Dad, I could tell, had belted a few down and was a little drunk. "I've decided to go for a ride in the new car. Thank you, Mom and Dad. I'm sorry for all the grief I've caused y'all."

Mom started to speak, but Dad cut her off. "They told us you might have some angry outbursts. I had no idea what they meant, but, son, you need to talk or go pound on something when you feel like this. I'm taking Berit's advice and putting up a punching bag in the garage. You can pound on it all day."

With Berit behind the wheel, we talked about when I might be able to drive. He shrugged and thought maybe getting the car was premature in hindsight. Then we changed the subject to him not moving to the States—it was my suggestion. He was doing great in college and work, and I didn't want to interfere. I hoped he could visit more frequently, as he'd said earlier.

"I bet the ticket here was a fortune with such short notice. I'm sorry." I felt sick.

"Brad, I'm pretty flush. Besides, the airlines have reasonable rates for family emergencies."

Over the next couple of days, I noticed a more significant difference between Berit and me. He was different, less like a boy and more like a man. He didn't say it, but I knew I came across juvenile. I could see him analyzing the situation. Because he was thrust into adulthood and responsibility, he had to grow up almost overnight. I was still in the cushy comforts of parents and little responsibility. I felt like we were drifting apart. Or was this my mind screwing with me?

I knew Berit and I wouldn't have a physical goodbye with Dad driving to the airport, so I asked Berit to take me on a ride a few hours to the lakefront before we had to go to the airport. As soon as we parked, the crotch groping began, but I wanted to be closer. I was the one to initiate the heavy kissing, but the car wasn't conducive to my desires. I wanted to feel him inside of me. The more his tongue explored my mouth, the greater my urges for more.

"Berit, I want you deep inside me, more than ever before." We couldn't get comfortable in the car as I wanted, so he slid a couple of fingers up my ass and blew me at the same time until I shot down his throat. He kissed me more, both of us breaking a sweat, so I took the opportunity and aggressively beat him off until we both felt fulfilled.

I wanted a chance to discuss us. "Berit, you still love me as before?" I asked. "You seem almost like a grownup, and I feel like we're not the same anymore. I mean, you've always been more mature and a lot cooler than I am, but I felt like we were equals. Are we?"

"Bradley, I don't know how many ways I can tell you I love you," he said. "Unfortunately, my friend, I had no choice when my parents threw me out. Maybe I seem older, but I'm still that same kid jazzed over swimming in the lake and exploring caves in the woods. I just had to change. I didn't want to, and you don't have to, so don't. We are as close as ever, and I think your trauma is putting all this doubt in your mind. Sorry to tell you, but it's your problem, mate, and I can't get in your head and control the thoughts. Wear your watch and look at it every time you have those thoughts, or you can always look at the magazines." He laughed, "Come on, Brad, laugh."

I stared at the ripples in the water. He was right; it was my problem. I needed to work through it all, and maybe the therapist could help. His leaving saddened me, but I knew I hadn't been a fun person to be around. I whined and moaned a lot. I had developed a real propensity for pity parties. Grow up, I thought. You have so much to be grateful for.

He leaned over, grabbed the back of my neck, and pulled me in for a kiss. He stared into my eyes with utmost sincerity. "I'm coming back in three months for a week, and whatever this shit is you got in your head, it better be gone. I'll give you a month to wallow, a month to turn around, and then a month to find yourself again."

"What if—"

"There is no what if….I love you and know you can do this. The therapists have given you goals, and now I'm giving you a goal. Three months, Brad," he kissed me again. His kiss still tasted like spunk.

We needed to get back, but I made him stop for a slush and peppermints. "You'd better get some, too, because you smell like sex."

The ride to the airport was downright depressing. My dad pulled up to the departures; he wasn't about to walk a grown man to the gate.

As I moved toward the front seat, Berit hugged me. "Three months, my friend." He took his suitcase, and I watched as he walked into the terminal.

"Get in the car, Bradley," Dad said. I slid in. "What was the three months about? I know he's coming back to the States for a meeting in Miami, right? He said he might stop over here for a few days." I agreed.

"He's a good guy and a damn hard worker. He holds a lot of bitterness toward his parents, not saying I blame him. I believe he'll achieve his plans, and his dad will come to regret his decision in time. I don't get why a man would act that way to his son." He stared ahead as we merged into traffic.

"Dad, when his dad realizes, if he ever does, it'll be too late." I was pretty sure that Berit and his dad would have little chance of ever making peace.

"I don't get it. Bradley, I don't approve of your lifestyle necessarily, but you are my son, and I love you no matter what. It's your life, not mine. So what're the three months about?"

"He wants me to get over my pity party," I said. "Berit didn't use those exact words, but that was the gist." My heart already ached for him.

Chapter 11

A few weeks later, Cindy started bringing me make-up work from school. I wanted to start living my life again, so Cindy took me to visit Trumpet. I hadn't seen him in more than seven months and missed him. I knew I couldn't ride yet, but I could be with him.

When I saw him, he started shaking his head back and forth, making an almost grunting noise. He couldn't keep still, his feet continually prancing. He was acting like I felt—excited. I wanted to cry because he remembered me. I put him on a lead line and went to the corral for exercise. I heard applause from behind me and turned around to see Leonard, who had come to the stable with Lillian, clapping. He had visited me at the house a few times, but I could tell he felt awkward.

"Fancy seeing you at the barn," I said with Trumpet behind me. "How goes it, Leonard? I can't thank you enough for all you did for me in the hospital." I stopped to talk but continued to pet my horse.

"You're my friend, Bradley, and that's what friends do." His smile lifted my spirits, and he was adorable with his baby face. One day while the rest of us were showing our age, his skin would still look flawless. "You think your parents would let you come hang at my house on the weekend sometime?" He leaned on the rail.

"I can't see why not. I mean, you were at the hospital every day. Shit, they better think it's okay. I can't drive yet; you'd have to come to get me, or they could drop me off." After weeks with just my parents, I was excited about being around a person close to my age. Even though Cindy brought me school stuff and was my ride to the barn, hanging out with a guy would be refreshing. How can the day be better, I asked myself. I couldn't wait until I could drive; the memory doctor or, technically, the cognition therapist had the final say on driving.

Mom and Dad were one hundred percent behind a visit with Leonard. I could tell they wanted a break and spend time with their friends. With Sarah in Baton Rouge, I could hang out with Leonard and give them some empty-nest time.

On Saturday morning, Leonard picked me up early. I was thrilled to go to his house because he had a pool and a billiards room with foosball and a couple of pinball machines. The drive wouldn't be boring. I could always depend on him for conversation—a regular chatty Cathy. He asked about Berit, and I confided in him how I felt about Berit being more mature and how I felt unsettled.

"What alternatives did Berit have? Besides, Bradley, Berit digs you, it's obvious, and it's just as evident you dig him. Jealous as I am, I have to say you two have a good thing. How many boyfriends have you had?" He looked in my direction.

"I thought you knew. Only Berit." I was confused because I thought I had told him.

"Oh." He nodded his head and had an in-the-know kind of look. Like he knew something I didn't. It bothered me a little.

After a momentary pause, I asked him the same. "How many have you had?" I had never given it much thought. Leonard always came across as level-headed and a good friend. I figured it was who he was – not quite, apparently.

He thought for a second. "Four, well five if you count my first time. I was at summer camp, and this older, cute guy was there, but it ended after four weeks. In those four weeks, we did it all, and I mean *all*."

"How sad," I said, or at least I thought it was.

"No, actually, it was great. I got all my mishaps with someone I'd never see again. He taught me a lot. He was one of the camp counselors. When I hit the market per se, I had a good idea of what I was doing and landed a great catch, Martin. He was older, handsome, rich, and had a cock the size of a bat. I couldn't take all of him, but he understood since I was new to the game. It was such a relief to be myself finally."

Hearing the description of Martin was more information than I needed. "How long were you together?" Since I was sorta new to the lifestyle, I was curious.

"Martin and I were together for six months, and then I met Teddy. What a great piece of ass. He was always willing to assume the position, but it only lasted a couple of months," he said. "Then there was Steven. What a stud." He halfway snickered. "We were together for a year, and then I met the love of my life, or so I thought, Wayne. I thought we'd be together forever, but he cheated on me after five months, and that was that. He broke my heart. I've had maybe six in-the-moment experiences, you know the kind where you get a first name and a number, but throw the number away knowing you'd never hook up again more than likely." He was so matter-of-fact.

I realized what Berit was referring to about fleeting romance and on-the-fly sex; it all sounded superficial. The friendship and emotional aspect seemed nondescript. The first-anniversary celebration of Stuart and Leighton was a big deal. Only then did I get it.

Berit and I had been friends for more than a year and four months, fighting a long-distance relationship filled with drama and trauma, and yet our friendship was as strong, if not stronger, than ever. Given my accident, childish temper tantrums, and insecurities, I could confidently say we were best friends.

I also understood what Berit was saying about me having other experiences. I couldn't fathom it, but I understood a bit better. Thinking about what he had said, friendship being the key as the most important thing, I couldn't help but feel a no-name quickie would be better. I wouldn't ever have to face them again—just my luck, it would be my neighbor or boss. No, for right now, I was staying in my Berit-and-only-Berit world.

I nixed the sex and partner conversation, and we watched TV, played foosball, talked about Trumpet and horseback riding in general, and drank wine coolers out of the pool house fridge. I only had a few sips because I was worried they would react funny with my mental condition and the meds I was still taking. Leonard was getting drunk and started saying things that made me uncomfortable.

"Bradley, since I met you at the horseshow, all I can think is what it would be like to give you a hand job or a blowjob," Leonard said. "You wouldn't have to do anything, just sit there on the couch. I wanna make you moan or just let me watch you do yourself." He dropped his pants and started stroking himself. "Watch me and tell me it doesn't turn you on. We're friends, and I know you're in love with Berit. Help me fulfill my fantasy. Here," he stepped closer, "jerk off on my cock. It's not like cheating."

I was hard as a rock watching him, but I was not sharing an experience like that with Leonard.

"You can just watch, and you don't have to touch me, but I do want to taste you," he begged.

What pressure. Hell, I had jerked off with the two Rickys, and this wasn't any different. I felt my manhood throbbing in my pants, and before I blew in them, I figured I could at least pull it out so I wouldn't have the mess in my pants. As soon as I pulled it out, I started stroking, and he watched.

"That's it, Brad, your cock is so hot and hard," he said. "I want to wrap my lips around it. Grip it, faster and faster, Brad. Yeah, that's it. I want you to fuck me, fuck me now. Please."

What can I say? I got caught up in the moment, and the next thing I knew, I was banging him.

"Faster, Brad. Deeper. Give it to me," he begged. I gave him what he wanted. "That's it, Bradley. I've been waiting for your hard cock up my ass. Fuck me hard," he murmured. "Yeah, that it's. Shoot inside me. That's it, harder, harder, harder." He grabbed the top of the sofa and held on with one hand. He was jerking off, and as I came, he came.

He collapsed on the couch out of breath. "Damn, you're good. I always knew it would be euphoric."

For me, it was strictly self-satisfying with no emotion, no desire to pleasure him, or no worry about his experience. I just wanted to get my rocks off. I obeyed Berit's rules, and he had been a friend. There wasn't any petting, cuddling, or any expressions of love. I fucked him, period, the end. Yeah, it felt good, but it wasn't like being with Berit. Then the guilt hit me while we were sitting in the hot tub.

He returned to Trumpet conversation. He got what he wanted, and we were back to friends instead of fuckers. We spoke about horses and how well Lillian had been doing. He asked when I'd be able to ride. Strange how he could turn it off so quickly as though nothing had happened.

I started rehearsing in my mind how I was going to tell Berit, what I was going to say to him, and whether I should tell him. Maybe I'd mention in passing that I'd ventured out, I thought. If he wanted more information, he'd ask; perhaps it would be less painful for him. I felt guilty as hell, but the experience was as non-descript to me as the days of jerking off with the Rickys. Being with Berit was a completely different experience. It was real.

After a couple more hours, I was ready for my own space away from Leonard.

"Do you wanna spend the night?" he asked.

"Thanks, but I need to get home to take my medicine. Thank you again for being a good friend while I was in the hospital."

"I have a thing for you, as I guess you've already figured out, but I get the Berit thing. I'm jealous. If y'all ever split up, I'm here. I hope you enjoyed our time together. I have a velvet tongue, so I'm told. Maybe you can confirm the rumor next time?"

"Food for thought, Leonard." I wanted to leave, not recap the activities. He seemed to like to hear sex talk, real or imaginary, which wasn't my thing. I didn't think Berit was into it either. Maybe he was if joking, but not as part of the interaction. I planned to gather that info at another time.

As we got in the car, Leonard didn't stop talking. "Did you like fucking me, feeling cocooned inside of me—"

"Not to worry. Of course, it was pleasurable." End of subject, or so I thought.

"But did it make your balls tingle?" He continued to press the point.

Why the hell couldn't he just shut up? "I'm not a good talker. I'm quiet for the most part, and I don't do sex talk. I do it, not talk about it." I was quick to respond.

"Okay, you're one of those. I get it." I couldn't help but think, get what? There was nothing to get.

Finally, we pulled into my driveway, thankfully. I jumped out and said I'd be in touch soon. I had his number.

"Bradley Stedman, you are the sexiest thing on two legs. Boy, you got it all," he said, glancing down at my crotch. I didn't want to hear anymore. I was ready to be inside and away from his nonstop talking, so I nodded and went inside.

I headed upstairs to the respite of my bedroom, away from Leonard. He was pleasant and a good friend, and Lord knows he tried to please me in any way he could, but he didn't know when to shut up. I grabbed my notepad.

Hoi Berit,

I miss you and wish you were here. I look forward to your visit; in fact, I'm marking the calendar because it makes the time go faster for me. My life consists of going to therapy, spending time at the barn, and making up schoolwork. I did as you told and ventured out. Sex is weird with no affection or emotion, like when I was younger with the two Rickys.

The parents are good, and Sarah is still into the Bible stuff. This fad of hers is lasting longer than usual. Any chance you could be here for New Year's Eve? I don't know the exact dates of your sales meeting. I thought bringing in the New Year together might be fun; the fireworks on the river can be spectacular. Maybe get our room at the hotel. Who knows?

Friends always,

Me

Okay, I told him. I may have glossed over it, not for any reason other than I didn't think it merited anything more than a gloss. I didn't tell him every time I masturbated. That's how much it meant to me. Nothing more.

Dad took me driving on Sunday to see my reaction time and if I was ready to start driving. Steve thought I was good to go. All I needed was the memory guru to sign off.

One more week and I'd be able to go to school. I was looking forward to school, odd as it sounded.

The Friday before returning to school, I got a letter from Berit. I was afraid to open it: What if he was mad or didn't want to be my friend anymore? I breathed deeply and opened it.

My dear Bradley,

I miss you too, and I see no reason why I can't start my trip before the sales meeting instead of after. I'll be in on 28 December, and the meeting begins on 6 January. I'll be there for your birthday. Have I got a present for you, and I'll tie a bow around it, too. I'll fly from New Orleans to Miami and then home after the meeting or maybe come back to you for two days.

About the venture out: M or F? You followed the friend rule, right? Your description sounds about right. For the F, friendship isn't required, and better if not, but don't have any money involved.

I am thinking of selling the house for something better. Not sure, though. Just think a year and a half until graduation. If they don't get you the trip for graduation, I will. You'll come for the whole summer before going to college. Getting excited just thinking about you. It's all about you, Brad.

Friends always,

Berit

One of the words was smeared slightly, and I held up the letter to the light. It made me laugh. He'd left a deposit on the letter, and I suspected it was a dribble of spunk. Only Berit…

He'd been more than okay about the whole venture thing. On the other hand, I would've probably become maniacal or suicidal if the shoes were on my feet. I continued to improve: the anger outbursts had lessened, and the depression was dissipating. Steve was due for his final home visit, and then I would work with a different therapist at the gym. I still hadn't cut my hair, and I knew Dad would demand a cut before I returned to school. I made a mental note to ask Leonard where I should go for a haircut. I knew where to get the high and tight military cut, but I wanted a hip style.

Steve arrived. "I have to get some measurements, so today's session is gonna last longer than usual, Mrs. Stedman."

"Not a problem," she said. "Do you mind if I run some errands?"

"Since Brad is a minor, protocol is to have a parent in the home, but I think as long as you sign off on it, we're fine. How long are you expecting to be away?" She signed whatever she needed to sign.

We went upstairs and started with the bands, which pulled the hair on my legs. He knelt behind me to adjust the band. He was more talkative than usual and pushed me harder, saying he had to make this session extraordinary.

"You and Leonard are close friends?" He asked.

"We're friends. Why?"

"I noticed he spent a lot of time at the hospital."

"So I hear. He's been a good friend." Pictures of the craziness at Leonard's house came to mind.

"He can be a wild child. Watch out for him." Steve warned.

"Oh, I'm well aware of Leonard and his impulsiveness." I laughed. Boy, did I know.

Steve was chatty. He talked about my body and how I wouldn't bulk like he did because of my long muscles. He'd always admired my strong thighs, even when I was in a coma. He was almost flirtatious, and I remembered Jen, the nurse, saying she thought the physical therapist had eyes for me. I had never felt anything of the sort until right then, and it was uncomfortable.

"You're a good kid, Bradley, and you've worked hard," he said.

"I'm trying to impress you," I said sarcastically.

"Your muscles have responded beautifully." He clutched my calf and then wrapped his arm around me to feel my quads. He began to slide his hand up my gym shorts, just shy of my balls. What is he doing? I thought. Shit, I was getting an erection. In all the times he had worked with me, I never once got an erection even when he was working my back and gluteal muscles, but now there it was bigger than day.

"Impressive," he said.

What was impressive? "Get a look at this." I figured he'd flash his massive leg muscles, but no, he was flashing his hard dick stroking it. "You want it?"

"Want what? Your dick? I didn't see that on the horizon. What are we talking about here?" He was sitting on his legs with his feet under him.

"Being a friend of Leonard's, I got your number." He yanked down my shorts, grabbed my hair, and pulled me down onto him. "I want to fuck you. I have since I saw you the first time. I saw your limp package but knew it would pack a punch when aroused. Come on. I'll give you a ride on my stallion; I ride hard, so hold on." He ramped up his strokes on me, and he came quickly. I felt his waves of jizz, and he threw me to the ground on my back. He was nowhere near as gentle as Berit had been, especially when he got close to shooting.

He straddled my knees and thighs. "Tell me what you want since it'll be our one and only time, sport. I give good head."

"Go for it, Steve. Let's see what you got." He performed and performed well. His self-assessment was correct.

"Maybe you won't be one and done," he said, flattering himself because as far as I was concerned, I hadn't given an invitation, although when I saw his hard cock, my mind went straight to having sex with him. Because he had been so rough, I figured he owed me the blowjob.

I wanted to see his reaction. "You know I was a virgin," I said.

His face turned pale as a sheet. "Shit, Bradley, I had no idea." I could see the guilt on his face. "I thought you were into—I saw Leonard and knew his history, and because he was at the hospital every day. I'm sorry, I assumed. I never do that."

"Steve, don't beat yourself up. I didn't tell you to stop, which forms a question in my mind. I'm in a committed relationship with Berit, my friend from—"

"The gorgeous European?"

"Yes. Berit's actually from Amsterdam. He told me since he was my one and only, I needed to venture out. I can tell him I ventured and call it a day. Thanks for getting me back to almost normal," I said. As he cleaned off and pulled up his pants, he still seemed upset. "I'm sorry, I shouldn't have pulled the virgin card. I've had sex another time with Berit. If I sent the wrong message to you, I didn't mean to. You are a stud indeed, Steve. Wait for my mom downstairs. Oh, and by the way, great head."

"Wish I could undo the whole thing, continue your exercises. I've signed off on driving. You have my number if you ever want to grab a drink or things don't work out with your friend."

I nodded in acknowledgment and got in the tub. Shit, I was more than sore. I felt ripped open. Was I curious? Why hadn't I told him to stop? It was more surprising than uninvited. It was nothing like what Berit went through, but the experience wasn't pleasant. Although the blowjob was incredible, my ass was throbbing in pain. I don't know why, but I felt terrible for him.

I now gathered Leonard was a bit of a whore. Perhaps Steve had been his Steven.

I decided to write to Berit to tell him what had happened.

Berit,

I miss you and look forward to our time together. I don't want to venture out anymore. I love what we have. My therapist, Steve, thought I was sending signals to him and took me off guard in our last session. I'm sore as hell. I think he ripped me or something. I've had more than enough of anyone but you. Don't ever ask me to venture out again.

How's work and school? Speaking of, guess who goes back to school this coming week? Sad as it may be, I'm excited. Life is starting to look a little more normal. Other than my ass, all is well.

Dad has started asking me about college. Where do I want to go? My first choice, no kidding, was Amsterdam. Big fat no. My next choice is MIT, but I doubt I'll have the scores to get in there, but I got the okay for Columbia in New York, which has cheap flights from New York to you. Locally, Tulane is good, but I want to get out of New Orleans. I'm sending out requests for applications this week. There's also a good college in Austin, Texas, but I'm leaning toward New York. Would you mind?

As you know, I'm thinking of architecture, but Dad wants me to do engineering. What do you think? I'd love to design skyscrapers. Can you imagine me saying, "Oh, that building there, yeah, that's my design?" You'd be able to tell people your boyfriend designs massive skyscrapers. Impressive, huh?

What do you want to do when you come here? Think.

Friends always,

Me

Life soon returned to normal when I headed back to school. I was driving my car, carpooling with Cindy, going to the barn, showing Trumpet, and still hanging out with Leonard now and then. Hearing his conquests grossed me out. Almost every time we were together, he'd ask to suck my dick. I wasn't interested, but he sure was persistent.

For Thanksgiving, Mom always invited the older neighbors to our house for dinner, and Gran would come down from New York. Mom hired the same two people every year to serve: a bartender and kitchen helper. Her cooking started days before Thursday. She was an excellent cook, and Gran would make mincemeat pies, whatever that was, and pumpkin. I wasn't a pumpkin pie eater and sure as shit wouldn't eat the other kind.

Sarah was home and wanted me to spend time with her. She still dated Frankie, which in itself was almost miraculous. He accepted her religious behavior; for how long he'd hang around was anyone's guess.

"Bradley, honey, can we talk?" Gran asked. I thought it could only be about one thing—the elephant in the room—me being gay. We sat at the breakfast table while she sipped her tea.

"How's your college search going?" she asked. "I hope you choose Columbia." I was wrong. "That way, I can visit on weekends, and we can catch a play and go to dinner." I was excited at the thought. She was hip for an old lady. "By the way, how is Berit?"

I wondered what she knew; fishing, I answered her question. "He's great and quite successful in college as well as his job. Have you by chance seen his parents around town?" I grabbed a bag of chips and a glass of iced tea.

"Yes, I have. Your aunt and uncle are friendly with them, but they turn my stomach, so I don't want anything to do with them. Did you know they kicked out Berit because of his sexuality? How parents could turn their backs on their blood is preposterous!"

Her response was forward-thinking, more so than I thought.

"I've known you were gay since you were a little boy, so I wasn't surprised to find out for sure. Your mother suspected since you were five or six." Her lips pursed after each sip of tea like she savored the taste.

"Why hadn't they told me?" I asked. "That news would've made my life easier. Instead, I always felt weird, like I didn't fit in. I still don't know where I fit." I was not too fond of the gay scene or what I had experienced in the French Quarter.

"Just have friends and enjoy their company," she said. "You don't have to be a part of any group. Variety is the spice of life." Her laugh was similar to a chuckle, and smoke puttered out her mouth in whiffs like a locomotive.

Talk about being blown away! I pondered our conversation for days, and I knew the inevitable conversation with Sarah was on the horizon. A few days later, she cornered me in my room, "Bradley, I pray for you every day. You realize being gay is a sin. You need to ignore those impulses and save your soul. Please, Bradley. Promise me." I knew she was serious for who she was now, but this too would change.

"God made me this way, Sarah, and He doesn't make mistakes, right? From what I know about Christianity, which isn't much, is Jesus died for my sins and came back to life defeating death. He's the only way." I said with confidence.

"Yes, that's true, but it clearly says in the Old Testament that a man shouldn't lay with another man." She argued.

"You're right, but then Jesus came as the new covenant, talking about clean and unclean and how what's important are his commands and not man's rules." Wow, I impressed myself with what I remembered from Sunday school.

I could see she was getting frustrated. She turned like she wanted to leave the room, but I, pissed as I was, pushed it. "Are you having sex with Frankie? You know, Jesus told the lady at the well, go and sin no more because she was having sex without being married." Mark one for the tall gay guy.

"No, Bradley, we aren't having intercourse to answer your question." Her face was getting pink. I knew she was lying; she and Frankie had been having sex, not that I cared, but she lied to me on top of trying to make me feel bad for who I was. Fuck her.

"Oh, only blowjobs, I get it. That's not intercourse, but it most definitely is sex. Sarah, I don't care what you're doing or not doing. I love you for who you are. Please love me for who I am. I'm a good person, and I don't sleep around. I've had one sexual friend and am still friends with him. I love him, Sarah. I don't think being gay makes me go to hell, and if that is what you think and what your friends at church have told you, then there's nothing I can do about that. Love me for me. And if you're not fooling around to some degree with Frankie, he's getting it somewhere, so be careful." I left her standing dumbfounded in my room.

Yes, I lied to her about only Berit. I had sex with Leonard and Steve, but only Berit counted as far as I was concerned. I knew she had been a bit easy, only from how I'd seen her act with Pelim and the things she had said to Berit. Maybe she had settled down; perhaps not, I didn't care. I loved her because she was my sister.

Chapter 12

Thanksgiving break finally ended, and Sarah returned to LSU. Thank heavens. She watched me like a hawk, but there was nothing to see. She could watch all she wanted. I warned Berit that she'd attack him about the gay hell thing over Christmas break.

School was going well, and Cindy continued trying to hook me up with her friend, who was nice but too limp wristed for my taste. One night in Valencia, after one too many Tom Collins cocktails, several of us piled on top of each other in the car with some people sitting on others' laps. I let one of the driver's friends sit on my lap—I think her name was Linda. I had no idea why I did it, but I slid my hand up her skirt, down her panties, and fingered her. She slid one hand and rubbed the outside of my jeans. My body responded, and I was up and ready to go.

When we reached our destination, she told me to stay by the car until everyone went in. We had parked down the block. We got back in the car, and she straddled me. At some point, she removed her underwear, and I unzipped my pants. She eased down on my stiffy and rocked up and down on me. It felt warm and wet but lacked any oomph. She locked lips with me as she rocked, which was the best part of the whole experience. Her kiss was soft and sweet with just the right amount of tongue. She jumped off me right before I came and wrapped her underwear around me to catch the load. I rather would've liked her mouth instead of her panties, but oh well. I thought, Okay, Berit, I had the girl. It wasn't bad; in fact, it was okay, but not like his hotness. I wasn't sure why it even had happened. I didn't ask for her phone number.

Dear Berit,

I tried the other side of the bread, okay, but not you. It wasn't bad or a turn-off. My worries right now are that I might be a Han. I don't know why it happened. We were in a car with a ton of people, and she was sitting on my lap. I don't know why, but I put my hand up her skirt and inside her underwear. When everyone got out, we hung back, and she straddled me in the car. Wham, bam, thank you, ma'am. She caught my jizz with her panties. Would've preferred she wrap her lips around to catch it, but that didn't happen. Sorry, this is short, but I don't have much time and had to confess.

I'm done, no more boys and no more girls— you and only you. I love you. I feel like a man whore.

Friends always,
Me

On Wednesday night at about seven, Mom called to me, "Brad, Berit's on the phone for you."

"Hoi," he said.

"Hoi, yourself, how are you?"

"Not as good as you evidently. You're far from a Han, friend. Warning: watch out because girls can get complicated, especially a fuck on the fly. She's gonna start with the questions: What's wrong with me? Didn't you enjoy it?

"Some girls don't get the in-the-moment stuff. Be kind and gentle with her. Make sure you apologize. Make up an excuse that you were drunk. It's your call, but whatever. If she cries, be nice and, don't under any circumstances, give her a condolence fuck."

"I won't. I've seen her and have hugged her. It seems cool."

"Keep it like that. Sorry, I should have told you to go for an experienced girl only looking for a hookup. You say you're done with venturing. Keep telling yourself that sport, and it'll end up being 'It was an accident. This really is the last one.' Been there. Sorry about the Steve thing, unprofessional if you ask me. I don't care how much he had the hots for you. I can't blame him there, but he crossed the line."

We talked about his visit and things he might want to do.

"Do you think you could come to Miami with me for a few days?" he asked.

"Whatever you've been smoking has clearly gone to your head," I said. "My parents will never let me go, but I'll still ask." What could I lose?

"Wait to ask until I get to your house, and I'll approach them."

He reiterated about the girl thing. I told him that I wasn't dumb and could handle it.

The weekend whirlwinds to Valencia continued under the disguise of hanging with other teens, but truly for the sake of drinking Tom Collins cocktails. One evening while I was hugging Linda hello, she asked if we could talk.

I was waiting for it. "Is there something wrong with me, Bradley? Did you not enjoy making love to me?" Red flag. Making love? We fucked in the car. That was it.

"No, there is absolutely nothing wrong with you. You're beautiful and smart. To tell you the truth, I hardly remember that evening. The last drink put me way over where I should've been. I'm sorry I did that to you. I want to be friends, and I know friends don't do those kinds of things. It was my first, and I guess I couldn't help myself. I'm sorry." Liar. Liar. Well, it had been my first with a girl, *so half liar.*

She lowered her head and sniffled. Oh shit. "It didn't feel like your first. It wasn't my first, but it was the most exciting. I can't believe it was your first. I guess I should feel happy." She smiled up at me through tears.

"I promise you there is no other girl I want to have sex with. I'm not ready for things like sex yet. Maybe one day." What a lying sack of shit I was. The girl was nice, cute, and funny, but a girl. The moment had been pleasant, but I didn't want a redo. "Can we still be friends?" My expressions could not have been sappier.

"I'd like that, and please don't tell anyone. I hope you haven't." Her head cocked to the side with begging eyes.

"I'd never tell. I hope you haven't." The thought had never crossed my mind, but it might not be a bad thing if she did, but then I'd have to deal with other questions. Never mind, I hoped she hadn't.

I hugged her tightly. "Friends?" she asked.

"Yes, friends."

And then she said the one word that no one was allowed to say. "Always."

I let go of the hug, smiled, and walked away. *Friends always* with me was reserved for one person and one person only.

I decided to discontinue going to Valencia for a while. It was a guaranteed way to avoid such conversations.

On the sexual front, more had happened that month against my vowed policies, yet, as Berit had predicted, I had been a more than willing participant than at any other time in my life. Never had I been such a hypocrite, all for the sake of getting off. It was par for the course for being a seventeen-year-old boy, but I thought I was more mature than my age. What an arrogant, hypocritical bastard I was.

Berit's visit finally arrived. The sleeping arrangement was the same: Berit in Sarah's room and Sarah in my room and all the same measures. Berit had told me to stop fretting over such crap. He had a soft spot for my parents and truly admired them, much to my annoyance.

After picking him up from the airport, we stopped for deep sexy kisses and petting at the lakefront. Touching him and having him touch me felt natural. His touch felt like no other; it had real love to back it up, and maybe that was the difference. He knew the perfect way to me with no fumbling or guessing. I was prepared and had all the necessary cleanup supplies.

After we finished, he reminded me about our hotel reservations for New Year's Eve and New Year's Day, which I'm sure was expensive.

Leonard agreed to vouch for us in a made-up pool house sleepover. If he chickened out, then I'd claim an all-night New Year's Eve party. Whatever it took, we'd make it happen. My parents were thrilled to see Berit. They asked all the typical questions about his flight, school, and work.

Later that night, Berit and I sat up long and talked about everything: all my ventures, his past escapades, and his mindset at the time of his promiscuity. After Han and the attempted suicide, he had a couple of encounters in the Red Light District in Amsterdam. Then moving to the States, he had found a few places in Manhattan where he could be entertained and eventually wined and dined.

"I'm telling you, Bradley, being seventeen up until the early twenties, you're a hot commodity, especially looking like you. I could've had all the sex I wanted and not even left the bar. You've got to be careful to watch around you wherever you go, and please remember the drink thing. Always hold it and make sure you buy your own. One night I went to the men's room and forgot my drink. When I came back, an older man was sitting at my table. He flirted, but I let him know I wasn't looking for any action. Thank God I had only taken a small sip of my drink. He must have thought I drank more because he told me soon I would be putty in his hands. I got up, put my finger down my throat, puked in the bathroom, and told the bartender to call a cab and what had just happened. It could've been bad, but it wasn't. I kinda decided then to slow down."

I told him all about Linda and the conversation we had.

"You got lucky there," he said. "She could have been a nut job. Girls can be more sentimental about sex." I felt him glance at me.

"She used the words, 'making love' when she brought it up," I said.

"Exactly my point….Also, be careful because some girls try to get pregnant, so if you're gonna do a girl, wear a rubber."

I changed the subject to Leonard, and Berit didn't seem surprised. "I thought he had a major crush on you when I talked with him at the hospital," he said.

We talked until way past midnight when I heard Mom coming down the stairs. "You boys need to get some rest. Bradley, be quiet going into your room because Sarah is asleep."

After I heard her go back to her room, I changed the subject to Sarah. "The whole thing is wacko, and no doubt she'll corner you. She's gonna want to save you. She's really big into faith right now." I explained what she had said to me. He agreed with me but said he knew sex outside of marriage was a sin. But because gay men couldn't get married, what was the alternative? To live celibate?

"Don't get hung up on it and cut Sarah some slack. Bradley, I love you way more than many men love their wives and would offer vows to you, but you aren't old enough or experienced enough, and neither am I, for that matter. We both have a whole life ahead. Do I see us together forever? Yes, I do, but our time is yet to come, my friend."

He kissed me goodnight, and I headed to bed.

The following day while eating breakfast, I read an article in the newspaper about a large New Year's Eve party on the Natchez riverboat.

What better timing! "Berit and I are going to this party," I announced to everyone, pointing to the article.

"Wow. Have you paid to go to the after-party?" Mom asked.

Me, the big liar, said, like she was stupid, yes.

"It won't be over until the very wee hours. Perhaps you should plan to have breakfast before coming home, in case you consume champagne for New Year's."

"Sounds like a plan," I responded.

After breakfast, Berit and I left the house, walking toward the park. "I can't believe you sat there and lied to your parents. Do you have any idea if they're going on the boat? You didn't even give anyone a chance to say shit. We're up a paddle if they have tickets or decide to go." He began to laugh. "Wheeler dealer. Size 13 right in the mouth?"

I didn't know what Sarah and Frankie's plans were or if they'd be at the hotel. I sucked at this double life thing. Berit didn't have to conjure stories or make up excuses or be a big liar; he had no one to answer to. I then felt guilty because Berit didn't have anyone who gave a damn about him in his family. My parents cared more about him than his own. We walked and talked for nearly two hours before going home.

Leonard called soon after we returned. He wanted us to come over, and Berit nodded yes. I told him that we could stop in for a few. After twelve, we headed over and went to the pool house, where he had already had a couple of drinks. He was overly huggy with Berit and me. While hugging me, he grabbed my ass. "I've been taking care of ya boy while you been away." He had a shit grin on his face.

"And I thank you for that, Leonard," Berit said. "He keeps me posted on all his invitations and exploits. Gotta love his package, matching his size 13 shoes. *Ooh!* I'm one lucky man to have such a great forever lover," he said, kissing me right in front of Leonard. I thought Leonard's mouth was gonna hit the floor. How dare fucking Leonard try to stir the shit between Berit and me! "I see you've started the party early today? Expecting a big crowd?" Berit could make a point with one question.

I didn't hide my aggravation. "Who's coming over?" I asked.

"A couple of guys that you don't know, but they're running late," Leonard answered me in a bitchy manner.

Berit pointed to the sofa and said, "Good, we can have time for a private conversation. First, I can't thank you enough for being attentive to Bradley during the accident and hospital stay. I understand you were there every day. What a good friend. Let me share some friendly advice I was given a few years back: Make sure you're friends with someone before sharing your body, and I know you and Brad are friends.

"Secondly, I can see on your face and in your glass that you're lonely, but sex won't make that loneliness go away. It only serves to make you feel cheapened and worse. I know you're a good guy at heart. Here's another friendly warning: Don't *ever* try to come between us," he said, pointing at himself and me. "You'll lose every damn time. You need to sober up if you have company coming over. I don't know what you thought would come from this little encounter. I don't play games, sir, and it's about time you stop trying to play them. Our world, as you well know, has too much drama. Don't add to it, mate. Take care." He held out his hand to shake it goodbye.

"I wasn't trying to be a dick," Leonard said.

Berit looked him dead in the eye. "Yes, you were. Own it. Bye for now. We can visit when you're sober."

I had never seen this side of Berit, who had been gentle but also firm and crystal clear. No doubt Leonard had been shot down and put in the corner.

"I can't believe he acted like that. I'm sorry."

"You shouldn't be. You didn't do anything wrong. Leonard's a troubled person, and if he doesn't get control, he's gonna be a dead person. The writing is on the wall, I'm afraid. I'm not sure what he was looking for today, but you can be assured it had something to do with him getting his rocks off. I feel sorry for him because I understand loneliness. Are his parents ever around?" We got in the car.

"No, they're into the social scene." I started the engine.

"You need to check on him now and then. Don't give in to his wiles, and always make sure you're on guard with him. He's trouble only because he's lonely. He's in that place where he'll fuck anything and call it love."

After eating a po-boy, we spent the rest of the day outside on the patio talking about the future and life.

"That's so cool you're thinking about going to Columbia University," he said. "The flights to New York are so much cheaper. You know living in the city will be more expensive, but if your parents are cool with it, then great." He rested his feet on the corner of my chair.

He also told me that he wasn't getting high as much, which was fine with me. Somehow his boyhood was disappearing before my eyes; he was more man than boy.

"I'm glad to be with you," he added. "I feel like myself. I'm not complaining because I've been successful, but I'm tired of always having to be an adult. By the way, I was thrilled to get your birthday card." He nudged my knee.

"Crap, I nearly forgot. I have a present for you," I said. "Guess I'll give it to you on New Year's Eve unless you want it now." I had an ID bracelet made for him but didn't trust it to get to Amsterdam.

"A present for me? Shit, I want it now....No, I'll wait. The card was all I needed, and it came at the perfect time. Sven was taken back by the card because Luuk always gave him cards. He thought it was the most thoughtful gift. I can't wait for you to meet him." He was excited like a little kid, and for a moment, we were the same two boys from the summer on the lake.

The afternoon of New Year's Eve, I packed his gift along with our toothbrushes and a comb in my car. My parents would have noticed if we came home in the morning wearing different clothes.

We got to the hotel, and I was a bundle of excitement.

"Ready for your present?" I smiled minutes after getting in the room.

"Hell, yes. I've been most curious." We sat on the bed. He untied the ribbon, opened the box, and his eyes filled with tears. "Brad, this is too cool. It matches the new ring I bought." Copying his idea with my watch, I had Friends Always and the date engraved on the back of it. He kept flipping it front to back. His name was in stylish manly block letters. He playfully pounced on me, "You're too much. I love you." He kissed me sweetly and started undoing my shirt. "Before we get to business, I want to order room service. Some champagne for midnight, yes? And what do you want to eat?" His youthfulness was vibrant.

I raised my eyebrows, "Oh, food, gotcha!" He tossed a pillow at me.

"All in good time, Dorothy. I'll get you, my pretty!" I loved his wicked witch impersonation. He was fun and silly. He was my Berit. I could've gone for burgers, but he wanted steak and lobster. And so we acted like kids and ate like grown-ups.

We took the night slow, undressing each other, which led to kisses. The chemistry had always been hot, but New Year's Eve added an extra dimension. I kissed his lips and made my way down his body, working my way along his happy trail. He tried to pull me up, but I wanted to pleasure him.

He smiled at me and rolled over. I lay next to him and pulled him onto his side, my stomach against his back. After a few minutes, he was ready to go again. Our bodies tangled as I guided myself into him, kissing his shoulder and neck while our bodies connected. He rolled back onto his stomach, raising his hips, and I took him with all I had. I knew he'd enjoyed it as his movements and groans intensified with each thrust. The sex had been outstanding, but nothing compared to snuggling naked and watching TV as the ball dropped at midnight. Simultaneous fireworks explosions from the river lit up the sky with huge bursts, whistles, and bangs.

The next morning we scrambled out of the hotel on time. Funny, we met Miss Holy Roller in the lobby. She was full of the it's-not-like-it-looks comments.

"Too bad, Sarah, was for us and better." I had to comment. She scowled, and I wondered where the sweet Bible Sarah had gone. Her bitchy attitude felt way more like my sister than the other person who told me I would burn in hell.

New Year's Eve with Berit was all I had hoped it would be, and we were more in love with each visit. He surprised me with a ring to match his for my birthday. It was a heavy sterling puzzle knot ring. He told me not to take it off because it was near impossible to put it back together. Not a chance in hell was it coming off my finger. It hurt when it was time for him to go to his sales meeting in Miami. The more we were together, the harder it was to say, see ya soon. He wouldn't say goodbye.

The more I learned about being gay, the more I realized it wouldn't be easy. My parents had always told me the things I wanted most, I had to work hard for, and nothing worthwhile came easily. Berit was one of those things. Our relationship was strong, but the distance was a problem, and the more time passed, the more I could see why people said long-distance romances didn't last. My feelings hadn't diminished; if anything, they were more mature.

I loved him deep in my core, which is precisely where it hurt when I thought of life without him or when I missed him more than usual. I wanted boy Berit back in the most desperate kind of way. I wanted the lake and the cave, lying naked on the rock, drying off in the sun, and giggling at the pizza joint. The unfortunate thing was he wanted it back, too. Fuck his parents. Throwing him out when he was only a teenager was cruel. I admired him because he lived his life honestly. He could well have played the game and pretended to be straight. What the hell would I have done if the shoe had been on the other foot?

Before I realized it, my junior year was over. I guess missing the first half may have had something to do with it, but then I was faced with all the critical college decisions my senior year. Instead of Halloween or New Year's, Berit came to New Orleans for Mardi Gras. I had been doing Mardi Gras since I was a baby, but I had never experienced the gay side.

Thanks to the Frankie connection, we managed a room, not our room, but a hotel room. He was full-fledged into his family's business, and Sarah had changed her major four times but decided on nursing. She and Frankie were still together, but I got the distinct impression they had both strayed from a committed relationship. None of my business. I just didn't want Sarah to get hurt.

The rest of my senior year flew by, and I wondered whether my parents would remember the Amsterdam promise. I was eighteen and could make my own decisions but having their credit card made life a hell of a lot easier. I had hoped Berit would make it for graduation, but work got in the way. He was upset, but we both talked about the Amsterdam possibility. He told me if my parents didn't come through, he would, and I would have my ass in Amsterdam before going to college.

Graduation night finally arrived. By this time, even though I hadn't discussed it, most of the students in my class knew I was gay and didn't judge me. I supposed the guys were just as happy because it was one less guy to get in the way of the girls. Although I didn't think of myself as handsome, others would've disagreed. According to my dad, I still had some filling out, but we suspected my growth in the height department was done and left me standing a full six-five. I tipped the scale in the two-teen neighborhood. My dad said I'd end up around two twenty-five. Even though I was a big guy, I still had a slim-ish build, and I was religious about working out. My muscle definition was proof. My hair was just past my shoulders. The girls in the class loved to touch it, saying they wished theirs had been as shiny and thick. Even Dad was okay with it. Soon enough, after college, he knew I would be joining the workforce and forced into a grown man's haircut.

Despite missing as much school as I had my junior year, I graduated salutatorian, earning a full-ride scholarship to Columbia to earn an architecture degree. Dad was disappointed I didn't go into engineering, and I think he would've liked me to stay closer to home. Mom was far less trepidatious since she had family only a few hours from Columbia.

The pomp and circumstance of graduation felt similar to horse shows. Being the center of attention and every move scrutinized was no big deal because I had been showing since I was little. Although my classmates were cool with the gay thing, their parents may have been on a different page. When the dean announced my name, the applause had been light except for someone whistling loudly. I had to look even though I knew never to look at an audience. I'm glad I did. Berit was standing on a chair, hooting and hollering. He and my parents had surprised me. I had to fight the lump in my throat. I was gonna have the sexiest and most handsome date at graduation. He was drop-dead gorgeous. I smiled from ear to ear. God, I loved him, and my parents were the coolest.

After all the to-do, I met up with Berit, Sarah, Frankie, and my parents. I first hugged Mom and Dad and thanked them for Berit being there. I then hugged Sarah, shook hands with Frankie, and embraced Berit. He smelled so good. Mom and Dad told me to "skedaddle" because we had the graduation party to attend.

"You might want to forego the after-party party because you both have to be at the airport no later than nine in the morning," Dad said.

Huh? I'm sure I looked confused.

"Your graduation present, remember? Amsterdam," Dad said with a huge smile.

I may have squealed like a little girl, then hugged Mom and Dad. I was on cloud nine.

As Berit and I said our goodbyes and headed to the assembly for the graduation party, he said, "I have been dying to tell you. I'm proud of myself for holding the secret as hard as it was." He was beaming.

I wanted to hold his hand but decided to choose the wiser decision and just walk side-by-side. "When were the arrangements made? How long have you known?" I couldn't believe it was happening. Pinch me.

"We finalized everything over Mardi Gras. You have no idea how much I wanted to tell you. But here it is, and tomorrow we'll be on the plane and on our way to Amsterdam. Sven is picking us up at the airport. I think he's just as excited as you are. He's been dying to meet you." He smiled ear to ear with his dazzling white teeth. God, he was gorgeous.

My feathers didn't ruffle. I, too, *was* excited to meet Sven. What a night it was! I felt like I grew up in a matter of seconds. Graduation, Amsterdam, total trust.

Chapter 13

We flew through New York to Amsterdam, my first international flight. "I never gave the flight much attention," I said during the flight. "Shit, it's long! You've done it how many times?

"Too many to count," he said. "We'll rest when we arrive."

My parents had given me an open-ended ticket and one of their credit cards with strict instructions to go easy. Berit had a week off, but then he had to return to work and school. He had only a year left to get his business management degree. Damn, he'd been busting his balls, I thought. At work, he was moving up the ladder at a fast pace. He'd obtain a hefty raise as soon as he received his degree.

I must've passed out because I awoke to Berit shaking the heck out of me. "Come on, sleeping beauty, we just landed. Get yourself together. Your hair is a mess, and you have dried drool on your cheek."

I would've died if anyone else told me I had drool on my face. I felt like most of the Americans on the flight looked—in a stupor, bleary-eyed and disheveled. He gave me a mint. By the time we made it to the gate, I was alert and ready to meet Sven.

The airport was massive, bigger than any I had seen. It took forever to get to the customs agent. The announcements were in English and Dutch, which I thought was cool. I could feel I was somewhere foreign; it even smelled different. People didn't seem near as uptight.

Men walked with their arms around each other in friendship, which was liberating. "Berit, I can't believe I'm here." He took my hand and smiled.

"This is my dream come true, Bradley." He pointed ahead to a booth, "The customs agent is going to need to see your passport and ask you some questions. Don't worry, it's normal; it happens to me every visit to America." He led me along.

When I presented my passport, the agent smiled at me, "And the purpose of your visit, Mr. Stedman?"

"Um, here on vacation." I stammered.

"Ah, where are you staying on holiday?"

Berit put his passport on the counter. "He's a guest of mine. First time international, that's why I'm checking in here." The man nodded, smiled, and shrugged but told me to enjoy.

When we walked out into the terminal, I saw a sharply dressed man's face light up when he saw us, so I figured he was Sven. His graying hair and icy blue eyes made him appear sophisticated, and the little pudge around his midsection let me know he liked to eat. He stood up straight and confident.

I extended my hand to shake Sven's, who pulled me into a hug, "As much as Berit speaks of you, Bradley, I feel as though you are a long-time friend. Welcome to the Netherlands." Speaking to both of us, "I trust your flight was good, long but good?" He didn't have any hint of an accent.

"Long, indeed, sir." He looked at me strangely. "No offense. I'm a Southern boy, and calling sir comes with the territory. I'll get a handle on the sir, sorry."

He laughed. "You, my friend, be who you are, no other way. Sir is fine. I just hadn't heard it in some time, that's all, at least in conversation. It's refreshing, my young friend."

Schiphol, Amsterdam's airport, was one of the busiest airports in Europe. Even though it was only five or six miles outside of Amsterdam, I felt like we were in the middle of nowhere. During the drive to Berit's house, I noticed the rolling green pastures, and everything looked like a picture book.

I felt like Sarah on Bourbon Street, looking from side to side and taking in everything for the first time. Sven and Berit were covering some investment matters; all I wanted to do was look out the window. Watching them interact reminded me of a father-son relationship. Because Berit's dad had been such an asshole, I imagined Sven came along at the right time to be a father-figure friend.

One of them asked me a question every few sentences, and I assured them I was fine and enjoying the new surroundings. The farther we drove in the countryside, the more colorful it was.

"Now is the perfect time to visit because of the tulips," Sven said, pointing to the endless fields of flowers.

"I've never seen anything like it. The fields are endless. How long is it like this?"

"They start blooming mid-April through mid to end of May, but some gardens bloom in July and August."

"It's like a postcard, only real. I can't say I'm a flowery person, but this is fantastic. Mom would just die if she saw them. It's like a multicolored carpet that goes on forever."

After about an hour, we pulled up to a small two-story house, something from a fairy tale. The house was outside the city in a cluster of small houses all alike, tiny but quaint. Quaint? Why on earth did that word ever come to mind, I thought. But it had, nonetheless.

"The house may look charming, but most of the residents in the village are on a pension, and the others pretty much work in the tulip business." Sven was most informative.

We ducked through the low doorway, and the rooms were minuscule. As we sat, we took up most of the sitting room. Berit told me he had replaced the older windows with newer ones and added a fresh coat of paint on the walls. He was proud of the changes he'd made.

"Let me show you upstairs and my room," Berit said while Sven stayed downstairs. His room was big enough for a double bed, bedside table, and a small dresser.

"Nothing special, but it's home for now," he said. "My huis is yours for as long as you want to stay, but I won't let you miss college registration," he said. "Your parents gave me all the information. Now that you've seen some things, what do you think?" He beamed with pride.

"Words can't do it justice. Windmills, flowers, and beautiful rolling countryside, it's all so great. I can't believe I'm actually in your bedroom in your home. It's not at all what I pictured; it's far more beautiful. It smells like you. These past couple of days have been unbelievable, and I can't wait to see the places you've always talked about." I hugged him. Our touch didn't have any feeling of urgency. We just relaxed in each other's embrace.

When we went back downstairs, we discovered Sven had made some hot tea. I had never had hot tea, and the thought of it turned my stomach. When in Rome, right? I thanked Sven and drank it. I must've made a face before sipping it because Sven asked if I'd prefer coffee. I went with the tea. Grow up, Bradley.

"I want to make sure you see everything," Sven said. "You two need to spend a weekend in Brussels. While Berit is at work and school, I want to make sure you see anything of architectural or historic interest. You two can spend some nights at my house in Amsterdam." I looked forward to it. Berit had told me about Sven's art collection and his home being something to see.

"After your tea, you lads need to rest," he said, bringing out a tray of koekjes, basically shortbread cookies, grainy crackers, and cheese. "I have to take care of a few things, but dinner will be on me." He smiled at us, patting Berit on the shoulder.

I hadn't noticed any restaurants or anything commercial during the drive. The place Sven planned on taking us had been around since the early 1600s, called De Druif or The Grape in English.

Berit had been right. Sven was fascinating, and his knowledge of European history was vast. He would expand upon any comment with history or some other related fact. I could tell Berit was exhausted. He had made the long flight twice in three days just to see me graduate. Berit slipped into Dutch a few times, but Sven always answered in English.

After finishing our tea, Sven sent us off to bed and left. We crawled into Berit's bed and crashed as soon as our heads hit the pillow.

"Boys, you need to wake, or you won't sleep tonight," Sven's baritone voice said. "We need to get your internal clocks reset. Shower up. Time to go for dinner. I'm starving." We had slept a few hours, and it was past eight o'clock, but still light outside. Sven reminded me of a teacher, exceptionally bossy but in a good kind of way. He took his father role with Berit seriously. I didn't have anything to worry about him. Clearly, he didn't have an ounce of sexual attraction for Berit.

As Berit showered, Sven and I chatted in the sitting room.

"Do you have any idea how much you mean to Berit?" he asked, confiding how worried he had been about Berit after my car accident and during my convalescence.

"I'm the lucky one," I said. "I'm concerned because Berit was robbed of his last teenage years and has been thrust into adulthood too early. It blows me away how well he's accepted life, but I know it has to sting." Sven agreed.

Sven sat comfortably, legs crossed, shoulders relaxed with a pleasant smile on his face. "Back in the day, Bradley, I hope you don't mind my candor, one with *our* preference was ostracized should it be found out. There were just as many homosexuals then as there are today, but sex—any kind of sex—wasn't even spoken about in the home. Gay men were bachelors, and lesbians were old maids, such a horrible reference. Then came the sixties, and it was a sexual revolution. People—that is, boys and girls—were far more blatant. We, unfortunately, were still very much hush, hush." He was most animated with his hands as he spoke.

"I didn't move in with Luuk until my parents passed away. Sad, but true. We were two *bachelors* who hadn't found the right woman, wink, wink. We bought a place and finally could live together even though we had already been together for fifteen years. The families living around us referred to us as the uncle and nephew. Luuk was twenty years older than I." He opened his wallet to show me a picture of them together. Luuk was strikingly handsome in a Paul Newman kind of way. Sven was maybe an inch or two taller. They made a handsome couple, and given the darker hair and bright blue eyes, I could see why people might think they were related.

"Luuk was a good-looking man. Berit has told me about y'all

and what a great relationship y'all had." He nodded toward me in acknowledgment. "I'm sorry for your loss," I added.

"Me too. I prayed to die, but we always knew it would probably be the outcome given the age difference. Until he became ill, he was far more agile and stronger than I could have hoped to be, my Luuk." He sighed as though transporting back in time. " Luuk was a good man, and I miss him. When you come to our home, you'll see pictures galore. Berit playfully teases me and says I have a Luuk shrine. One thing while you're here, we'll get a professional picture of the two of you together. It will be my graduation present to you. In years to come, you'll be happy to have it. Every few years, make sure to have one taken. I'm glad we did. We traveled the world and had a picture from every holiday." I watched as memories played through his thoughts.

Berit bounced down the stairs. "I hear you two getting all sentimental in here. We need to go out and have a great dinner, no melancholy from either of you. My two favorite people in one room, lucky me." His smile melted me.

We walked about fifteen minutes to a small train stop. To call it a station would be overkill. Stairs led up to a platform that had two benches, and that was it. There was a brick cubicle like a toll booth where you could buy a ticket at certain times of the day. Berit said always to remember the train was his competition.

Amsterdam was a unique city. The city had old buildings and new buildings. I guess a bit like comparing downtown New Orleans and the French Quarter, with a mix of antiquity, charm, and style. The canals running through the city looked like a movie scene. Watching couples nestled in boats triggered thoughts of Berit and me riding together— the picture was far more sophisticated than our Sunfish sailing in Lake Ponchartrain, but that boat ride did have its perks.

Dinner at De Druff was unlike any meal that I've ever eaten. I ordered a beer, or as he called it, a pint, and for the most part, everyone spoke English. The food was different than any I'd ever had with such bizarre names I couldn't pronounce, like frikandel, kaassouffle, and geitenkaasdip. The Dutch must secretly worship a dairy god because most of the food had cheese of some sort. I devoured dinner like I hadn't eaten for days. Shit, I thought, I was eating in Amsterdam having a pint. Pinch me.

After dinner, we ended up walking around the Red Light District, where every doorway had a glowing red light. Each storefront window housed scantily clad people dancing suggestively, enticing the people in the street to come inside. I was a duck out of water.

"You *have* to experience a live sex show," Berit said, tickling my ribs.

"Eh, are you sure?" I unassuredly asked.

"Yes, anyone who comes to Amsterdam should!" Sven was quick to respond.

He grabbed my hand and pulled me into a nearby building that resembled a theater, although dark and not inviting inside.

It was awkward for me, and we didn't stay long. It was lifeless. I had no desire to watch people having sex, no matter what kind of sex it was, nor ogle naked people. If I hadn't seen it or imagined it before, it was on display. Berit had been right; whatever the pleasure one might fancy, it was ripe for the picking. I felt like I needed to shower again. It all made me feel dirty.

Sven talked about the Anne Frank house on the walk back to the train, but I was too jet-lagged to comprehend what he said and just smiled. I appreciated Sven, but I wanted to be with Berit, only the two of us. We agreed to meet Sven at his home for an afternoon lunch the next day. Berit and I talked the entire train ride back to his house, although the train's rhythmic swaying back and forth could have lulled me to sleep.

As soon as we returned home, we settled into bed, and having him next to me was the best feeling ever.

"You don't know how often I have dreamt of this exact situation," he said. "Nothing rushed, all on our time. Is Amsterdam all I said it was? And Sven?" He put his arm around me and stroked my hair.

"The city is spectacular. From what I've seen, I love the architecture. Sven seems terrific—never a dull moment. He's talkative, to say the least, but everything he says is interesting." I tried my best not to say I wished he could play the silent game sometimes, but I'd never hurt Berit with such a comment.

"Sometimes I have to tell him I need less distraction. He's lonely, and he means well, and he is, if anything, a great friend and a walking encyclopedia with some fascinating facts and some not so much." Our speech started to slur from exhaustion. We lost the battle, and sleep won.

When I awoke, I instantly felt trapped, like I couldn't move. Berit wrapped around me, almost in a death grip. He was sound asleep, holding me for dear life. I squirmed and tried to loosen the hold, but I couldn't budge free. I then had to laugh at the situation, which woke him.

"Well, at least you can tell how much I want you close to me." He smiled.

We got out of bed with far more energy and put it to use. We savored each touch and took our time. I still wasn't confident, but knowing I was giving him pleasure was enough for me. He took his time, and I knew what he was feeling and admired his ability to control. On the other hand, I had little control, which was good because he liked it rough and wasn't the ninny I was.

"We'd better get going to Sven's," he said after we were both spent.

I still felt like I was in the twilight zone during the train ride. Berit frequently checked in with me as he tried to read my reactions. The lifestyle was most different from New Orleans, and we, as Southerners, were known to have a slower pace of life. Berit's stomping grounds were even slower, and people seemed to savor everything.

Sven's place was in an elegant chic section of the city. I could feel the wealth around me. As I walked in the front door, there was no doubt about Sven's sexuality. Everything was classy, yet a bit ornate for my taste.

"Do you want to see upstairs?" Sven asked, even though the only answer was yes.

Upstairs and at eye level with the chandelier, I looked through it like a prism and noticed the diamond-shaped tiles formed a giant "O." Sven told me he had legally changed his last name to Ogden, Luuk's last name after his parents died. Taking his lover's last name was unheard of, or at least to my ears. Although marriage between two men would never be legal, I thought at the time; they figured a way around it. To them, they were married. Everything Luuk had was in Sven's name and vice versa. In hindsight, it had been most progressive.

As he spoke of their relationship, Sven teared up. I wanted to ask but dared not if Sven had been with anyone other than Luuk or if he'd been with a woman before. I was nosy. Who knows why my mind went there?

We toured three bedrooms, all fitted with matching everything and pillows galore. Sven proudly showed me his bedroom, complete with a lit painting of Sven and Luuk naked above the headboard. Judging from the picture, Luuk was packing. I didn't want to look, but how could I not? Berit smiled his shit grin, waiting for my reaction, I'm sure. Sven looked like he was in his twenties in the painting, which put Luuk in his forties. Dang, he had a great body. Sven's body was nice too, similar to his body now, without the midsection. How could he sleep with it over his head every night, I wondered.

"Go ahead and say it," Sven said. "Everybody does. No, the picture wasn't embellished. It was all his."

"Wow" was all I said. I think I might've blushed. After seeing the portrait, everything else in the house paled. Berit and I will never have a portrait of the sort, I thought.

We went back downstairs, and Sven served beer, cheese, and a type of French bread, but it was coarser, grittier, and a bit nuttier than what we had for dinner the previous night.

"So, what's your initial impressions of Amsterdam, the village, the RLD, and the coffeehouses?"

I told him what I had told Berit and that I hadn't been to a coffeehouse yet.

"Jesus, Sven, he's only been here a day," Berit said defensively. "Give me a break."

Sven seemed to ignore Berit's outburst. "I think we'll start away from the city and move our way in. I'm thinking Keukenhof, Edam, Volendar. We might do a windmill tour, maybe the Zaanse Schans; my gosh, it's been years since I was last there. We'll dedicate one day to the Jewish Quarter and Anne Frank's house. We can meet up with Berit at a quaint tavern there. Then there's Van Gogh, which is a must. A canal cruise would be lovely as well." The man could talk. I repeated to myself how lonely he was and how this was a fun opportunity for him as well. I didn't need to be an impatient jerk.

Over the next few days, Berit and I didn't do anything too strenuous.

My body was getting used to Dutch time, and the chilly mornings and evenings were intoxicating. The days were far from hot by Louisiana standards. On the fourth day, we didn't have anything planned—a nothing- to-do-kind-of day. We lounged in bed late and had a breakfast of oatmeal. He gave me some bread, and we headed out to where I hadn't a clue.

We walked through the village to a fenced field and through the gate.

"We aren't trespassing?"

"No, it's a public footpath." I could relate it to some of the trails we hiked in Gatlinburg, but we didn't have anything like it in New Orleans. I guess we had the lakefront to walk along or the levees, but it was different. I breathed in the crisp, clean air and took in the view: Greenfields turned into a fantastic color palette of flowers. We walked for two hours until we eventually came to a pub for locals. I bought us each a pint, and he ordered some bread and cheese. He didn't speak English except to me. We sat at a table on a patio or, as he called it, the garden.

"Man, the look on your face when you saw the portrait above Sven's bed was priceless," Berit said, laughing. "You wouldn't believe this, but it isn't the first male nude over-the-bed portrait I've seen. I saw quite a few when I was in Italy, but Sven's was the first portrait of lovers in the nude over a master bed."

"Let's agree on one thing," I said. "We don't want it on our to-do list, okay?"

"Deal," and we clinked our pints.

We decided to head back to the house two pints later, and both stumbled here and there. After about thirty minutes, he plopped down to the side of the path.

"Tired?" I asked through a laugh.

"No, I want to soak it up with you," he said, leaning back in between two rows of flowers. I sat on the row next to him. He grabbed my arm and turned to me. "I don't want you to go back."

"I wasn't planning on going back just yet. You got me for six weeks. By then, you'll be ready for me to go."

"No, Bradley, it'll be even harder." His eyes didn't have the Berit sparkle to them. They had a pleading look as tears welled in his eyes.

"Are you going all nelly on me? And who called who sentimental?" I poked his ribs. "I know how to turn that into a smile." I reached over between the flowers and unbuttoned his fly, slipped my hand in for a couple of quick strokes, and then stopped. "To be continued later…and I got the smile from you, mister sad face." I made a pouty babyface.

"Tease, Bradley, that's not nice. Finish what you started." He pulled himself out of his fly.

"Anybody could walk up at any time. Are you nuts?" What if someone were to come along the path? What an eyeful for them!

"Come on, Brad." He started talking in a whiny voice, "Do me, do me, do me. I'll never tell, I promise. We're boys; let's be bad!"

I'm sure the flower farmers, or whatever they were called, wouldn't have appreciated us squirting their flowers with our seed. Yes, we were those young boys swimming in the lake, acting crazy, and having a great time. I loved when boy Berit came out to play. The fact of the matter, I wasn't the boy I had been back then. I wasn't as grown-up as Berit, but I had grown a lot from being the gangly kid on my cousin's bike. What if Berit hadn't been gay? Would I still have wanted to turn around and talk to him? Hell, I didn't even know back then what side of the bread I buttered.

I still had some squashed bread in my pocket. "Come on, you bad boy. Let's go. This bread might subside the hunger for the walk back, but I'm hungry."

"Now you tell me, it's a shame you wasted me on the flowers. I could've filled your growling stomach." He was the boy, and I was acting more sensible for the first time. He reached out, and I pulled him up. It took another hour and fifteen minutes to get to his house. He didn't have much in the way of food, but I ate whatever I could.

"What we need to do is go to the grocery. You have little to nothing left to eat in your house. I want chips, maybe pizza to cook here. Fuck I don't know…food." I was used to having a fridge full of food.

He feigned yawning. "Markets are closed now. Let's go to the city, get some dinner, go to a coffeehouse." He tried a Southern accent but failed miserably with "go git me some grub." He had to laugh at himself.

"You must be drunk or, I know, delirious from hunger. When the fuck have you heard me say grub? Let's get some dinner. It'll be on my dad, and I can take some photos. Since Sven loaned me a camera, Dad got off the hook for a new camera." I splashed water on my face and flicked water at him, which brought back the memory of him getting me wet with the hose on the day we met.

I'm sure we smelled like boys just off the playground, but I didn't care. I was starving. Good thing the train pulled up as we purchased our tickets. My stomach made wild animal sounds the entire train ride. Berit tried to distract me and was cutting up. At one point, a couple of passengers turned and stared. Although I was a bit embarrassed, I dug it. We were just two boys riding to the city. Maybe the wind wasn't blowing in our hair, and we weren't traversing the countryside alone, but the flavor of another time was in the air.

By the time we pulled into the station, Berit had settled down, and we hit the first café. "I can't believe it. I can read the menu, and I'm having an American cheeseburger." I told Berit excitedly.

"You're going to be disappointed; it's not a real American cheeseburger." He warned.

"How can someone screw up a cheeseburger? Bun, burger, cheese, what's to screw up?"

"Do it your way, Brad, but don't say I didn't warn you," he said with a shit-eating grin.

The waitress came to the table, all smiles, giggles, and boobs. "Wat wil je drinken –"

Berit interrupted and asked her to speak English.

"Sorry, what pint you have tonight?" Berit gave me a crash course on the beers. I wanted something not too light and not too dark; I sounded like something out of Goldilocks and the Three Bears. He raised his eyebrow at me and ordered.

She was flirting like crazy with Berit, and he worked it. Nobody could've guessed he was gay. Then he told her I was from America, and she was all over me.

"My name is Mila," she pointed to her name tag. "Mr. American, you are?"

"Bradley. I'll have a cheeseburger dressed, Mila."

She found the dressed part funny, but Berit explained lettuce, tomato, and onion. She seemed perplexed.

"Where you go after? I meet you and have some pints? Have fun? I hear everything big in America. Yes?" Maybe my gay sign was turned off over my head.

Berit ordered his food, told her we had plans, maybe some other time, and smiled.

He had been right about the cheeseburger. I don't know what the hell it was, but it wasn't an American cheeseburger, that's for damn sure.

We bid good night to Mila and took off to a coffee shop. It should have been called pot central. Berit explained smoking establishments had a marijuana leaf and Jamaican flag or indicator of some kind.

What a strange setting to experience, and I smoked probably more than ever before. Everyone was chilled, smiling, and laughing.

"Okay, Brad, now that you're sufficiently fucked up, it's time to go see one of the shows. You're going to laugh your ass off."

I rolled my eyes. "You're the boss."

Berit had been right, and the show was hilarious. Rude and crass but funny, nonetheless.

After it was over, we headed for the train and his place. "My stomach hurts from laughing so much." I was in wonderland.

"Didn't I say you'd like it! I was right." It was good to get on the train and head back.

There were hardly any people on the train – the only ones in our car were us.

Berit whispered, "All night, I've been thinking about being alone with you at home. It's been fun, but I want you, now."

"We're on a freakin' train. There's no privacy." I leaned away from him.

"Isn't it thrilling! Come on, Dorothy, I want it now. Don't play hard to get with me." His laughter was contagious, and he was too gorgeous to refuse.

"Berit, are you crazy?"

"Getting blown on a train is something else. Now bring out your bad boy before I do it."

I got my first blowjob on a train. I don't know if it had been the movement of the train or the fear of getting caught. Afterward, I didn't want to move, only savor the sensation.

He looked up at me and smiled. "We must take a trip on a train, and we'll get accommodations in the sleeper car. The train jerking and swaying back and forth will add to the thrill of it all. Just thinking about it, feel how hard I am. Finish me, Bradley."

Finish him I did. It must've been good because he started with his moaning and heavy breathing and running his hands in my hair. When we finished, we sat and acted as nothing scandalous had happened.

After a week, Berit had to return to work and school, and as promised, Sven became my tour guide. I learned more in those weeks about European history, the customs of different countries, politics, world economics, and relationship ups and downs.

He first took me on a guided windmill tour, and he was more knowledgeable than the tour guide who rambled. Our outings gave him purpose in those weeks, and he got a spring in his step.

"You should be a tour guide. Didn't you see how all those tourists leaned in to hear whatever you had to say?" I put my arm around his shoulder.

"Thank you for the compliment—Bradley, you're full of beans, but you've given me food for thought." He patted my shoulder. "What is troubling you, my young friend?"

"It's a problem I have. Berit's pointed out to me I need to get over it."

"Get over what exactly?" He stopped and looked at me.

"Sven, I get jealous—all the time. I don't like Berit giving his attention to anyone but me. Even my father. Shit, I got jealous when he and my dad had a conversation. Everyone and yes, at first you, too— but not now." I realized how awful I sounded. "Berit is so much more worldly than I am. He knows a lot about a lot. Me, I don't know shit from shinola." I felt my brow furrow with concern.

Sven began to chuckle, "I know just how you're feeling. Luuk was twenty years my senior, and when he would converse with men of his age, I'd get upset. He'd tell me I was being pouty, which pissed me off even more. I had never loved someone like I did Luuk. I had a few friends before him, but they were more for pleasure only. Luuk showed me real love. We had a wonderful relationship, but I was haunted by jealousy like you. Time will take care of that, or it did for me. It waned with the years." He patted me again. He was calm, sensible, and it worked on me like a tranquilizer dart gun.

We strolled as I tried to explain myself. His words made sense, but he didn't understand my insecurity, or maybe he did. "When I met Berit, he was the coolest person I'd ever met. He was beautiful, had no hang-ups, and rolled with the flow. On the other hand, I wasn't the one to turn heads, had more hang-ups than a telephone operator, and went every way but with the flow. All I could think was why would someone like him want to be with me." We sat on a sidewalk bench.

"Your friend, Berit, may have seemed as such, but I assure you he wasn't. He had the world by the balls on the surface, but Bradley, he never had a true friend until you. I know you know about his mates and Han, then his dad. Everyone had always left him or hurt him when he was true to himself. You're a constant and stability for him. He was afraid of losing you because of distance. I told him to tell you to try on different pairs of shoes, and I was pretty sure you'd select the first pair you loved so much. He was afraid. My philosophy is it's better to be a knowing part of something than an uninformed bystander. So, if you had found someone you loved more, it would have been on Berit's terms. I knew you wouldn't; he had told me so much about you. I knew you were his Luuk."

I looked at my watch. It was time to meet Berit, who would meet us after work and school for dinner. "Berit time!" I beamed.

We met at a local pub a few minutes later and ordered pints.

"How was your day?" I gave Berit a bear hug. "What do you think of me going with you to work like you did with Dad and school with me?"

"If you want to go to class with me, that'd be okay. Work is a different story."

The following day Sven and I resumed our tour in his car through the countryside with Sven rambling about life in general. Closer to lunch, we stopped by Berit's work.

"Berit was one of the wide-eyed lads with dreams of rising up the ranks, but he was different than the others," Sven said. "He was determined as though it were a mission. He was impressive, your friend. He had a wealth of knowledge about automobiles from the inside out. Later he told me he built his engine for some old muscle car he bought whilst in America. It explained his understanding of automotive. The dealership owner came in one day—he owns quite a few and spends a good amount of time in Brussels and Munich—and I watched him watch Berit in action. I could see Berit had won favor. The next time I came in, Berit had become assistant to the manager. One thing about him, he's always one to look you in the eye when he shakes your hand, and to me, it spoke volumes given his youth."

Berit was with a client, excused himself, and came over to us. "Goedenmiddag, Mr. Ogden."

"Good afternoon to you too. My friend is American, so can you speak English, please."

"Certainly, I will be with you momentarily, but if you have time constraints, I'll have one of my associates at your ready."

I told him we'd wait, so he returned to his client. He had timed his greeting with us to make us feel important, and it gave the other client a moment to digest anything Berit had told him. How clever.

Sven cleared his throat and whispered, "I'm not sure if Berit's sexuality is known here or not," and winked at me. I heard the message loud and clear.

After he finished, he returned to us, shaking Sven's hand and putting his hand on my shoulder in a casual but professional way. I smiled. Okay, I understood. Every time he had come clean with his identity, it had cut him off at the legs. He wasn't chopping them off now, and it was sensible business. He showed us a couple of new cars in the showroom.

I pointed to the red sports model with its sleek lines and downright coolness. It screamed speed like a Corvette, only better. I sat in it, and it had plenty of room to sprawl my long body. "One day, this will be mine," I spoke perhaps too loudly because one of his associates stepped close enough to hear our conversation. Rabbit ears, my dad would have called him.

"What brings you to our fair country: the beer, the tulips, or the more feminine attraction?" He winked at me. I smiled big. My, oh so charming Berit, who wouldn't buy an outrageously expensive car from those dazzling eyes and Pepsodent smile?

"The problem is, you see, shipping it back home alone would break the bank, but thanks for letting me dream a moment." I slid out of the dream car.

"Mr. Ogden, is there anything I can do for you today? It appears your young friend has excellent taste. It's okay," he looked at me, "in a few more years, you can buy a car from me; I too shall be in America with a dealership of my own."

"Do tell?" I asked, my heart racing.

"I found out just today. Do you know New Orleans? The dealership will be a stone's throw from New Orleans in Metairie." He looked like he'd bust his buttons.

Sven nodded with a warm smile. "That's excellent news! I shall miss you, Berit, but you have my sincerest congratulations," Sven said. "We shall bid adieu now."

As he walked us to the car, Sven said, "Unbelievable, my boy. You did it! You'll get your chance at the big fuck you." Sven was exuberant. I, on the other hand, was utterly speechless. Part of me didn't want to stay in New Orleans. I had visions of moving to some cosmopolitan place with lots of skyscrapers and big money and mostly, where I could be me, and we could be us.

We got in Sven's car. Through the open window, Berit grabbed my shoulder, "Dinner, same place, same time?" He looked straight in my eyes and leaned in as though he were reaching to shake Sven's hand across the car. He was close enough I could feel his breath on my neck, raising my temperature a few degrees. He whispered, "I love you. See you in a bit."

"You bet." I wanted to hug him but knew I couldn't. In truth, I was happy for him, happy for us. My parents would be thrilled. Playing with a timeline in my head, I figured three years at Columbia and then Tulane, if it was possible. Whoa. Calm down, I told myself. You can worry about that later.

"I knew it wouldn't be too long before the opportunity came up for Berit," Sven said as we drove away. "I'll miss him tremendously."

"I'm certain we'll be back to visit," I said. Besides, who knew what three years would bring?

The Van Gogh museum was fantastic, and once again, Sven came up with some tidbits of info that I didn't know about Vincent, who he referred to as the master. All the greats were someway sideways, alcoholics and drug users. Maybe they couldn't handle the world as it was and preferred it through their eyes. Gazing at famous paintings seemed to stir something in my soul like I felt a deep connection and found something I had been missing my entire life.

Berit was waiting for us with his ever-present smile when we arrived at the tavern.

"Isn't it the coolest? It came out of nowhere. The owner and a couple of men from the company were visiting, and they called me into the manager's office. It was just me with them. My manager wasn't even there. I thought, oh shit, something wrong is coming down. They complimented me on my sales and management abilities and told me something that blew me away. I'm number one in sales for the entire company. Can you believe that? I had no idea. Even more, I was having a good time selling cars, so it was quite a shock. They sacked the manager, and I will take over as manager until they open the two new dealerships in the U.S.: one outside San Francisco and the other outside New Orleans. I wished it would've been outside Manhattan in some ritzy area, but the bosses had already made the decision.

"They then asked me if I had ever considered being an owner. I didn't even think. I just said, 'Who hadn't? I just don't have pockets deep enough to back up my dream.' One of the men told me he could make it work for me because he was so confident in me and my success. He just expected a good return on his money—no stress there! I might be able to buy him out in time, so was I game? Of course, I said yes!"

"I am so proud of you!" I embraced him. "I'll give you a proper congratulations gift when we get home tonight," and winked at him.

"Well done, my boy, well done!" Sven said. "You are young, and yet it looks like the stars are aligning. You two," he looked over at me and then back at Berit, "seem to have a glorious path ahead of you. Did it ever cross your mind to let them know you might want to work for the company instead of the dealership end? Not saying there's anything wrong with it. Do the different dealerships have different ad agents, or is it a company decision? Do you know?"

"I don't know, but I'm guessing, wildly mind you, it's the discretion of the owners. I may be wrong, but I've seen for myself Dutch ad agents approach the manager—I know *exactly* where you're going with this line of thought." He ordered three pints, one of them being witte for me.

We celebrated and didn't speak of my impending departure. It had been, by this time, seven weeks. I already had stayed a week longer than I had planned. Each time I'd bring up going back, he became sad, which broke my heart, so we kept putting off the discussion until the following day.

As we readied for bed, he started to plot the plans for our lives—where we might live, maybe have a place like Stuart and Leighton or buy a house in Leonard's neighborhood, of course, not as extravagant. No point in bursting the bubble with practicality, I thought. Now was all about celebration and excitement.

By the weekend, I still didn't have the guts to talk to him about needing to leave. Sven had prepared my departure and had all the photos developed and organized in three sleeves: one to show family and friends, one for color photos, and one for personal, sentimental pictures. None were that scandalous, but a few had our arms around each other with affectionate glances. Better to keep those separate, I had told Sven. He also made and hung a portrait of the two of us at the top of Berit's stairwell. Anyone going up the stairs of treachery, as I called them, would see it. If I fell down the stairs once, I fell twenty times. The treads were tiny, and my feet merely balanced either on my toes or heels. Me coming down the stairs was enough to wake the dead. I don't know how many times Berit laughed when I tumbled down them. So much for my caring, doting lover.

While enjoying breakfast at a quaint café, Sven was applying jam to his pastry and asked, "What day did you two decide for your bon voyage? I wanted to have a lovely dinner the night before with you two."

Berit's expression was clear that he didn't want to think about it. "We haven't even thought about it. I don't think anytime too soon. He's not been here very long. " He sounded like a petulant boy on the verge of pouting.

"Bradley, have you spoken to your parents recently, and what are their feelings on the matter? When does school start?" Berit asked, giving Sven a dirty look. I had to nix the moment before he said something he couldn't take back.

"Funny, you ask. They called me on Friday. So much was going on Berit that I forgot to tell you." I was such a liar. "Classes don't start for four weeks, but they reminded me that I had to register and settle in before classes started. Berit, how long do you think it'll take me to get organized enough to feel comfortable about Columbia? You know me better than I do when it comes to things of the sort." I had spent way too much time with Sven. I was starting to sound like a sixty-year-old gay man.

"It never entered my mind. Bradley, I don't want you to go, but putting it like that, you're going to need a shitload of time—it takes you an hour to get ready for dinner. I can't imagine you packing up your life and moving to New York—hey, I have a brilliant idea. I'll help you. We can leave in a couple of days. Make sure it's okay with your parents first. I'll fly back from New York—unless you want some alone time with your family? I just can't be gone for more than ten days." I could see the cogs churning in his head; he was going a million miles an hour.

The next day I called home. My parents were glad that Berit would help me settle in New York. Classes started in a couple of weeks after he'd leave, so I had enough time to learn the area, discover campus, and try to be a big boy on my own—no parents or Berit to guide me.

Chapter 14

Taping my last box, the excitement of going to college started to flood over me. My bare room with just the bed, dresser, and nightstand looked abandoned like no one lived there. Mom had purchased everything an incoming first-year student would need and a bit more.

Berit loved my mom and dad, and the feeling seemed mutual. Mom and Dad were over the moon about the American dealership and the prospect of Berit living close. I wanted to say *we* would be living close, but I thought it better to leave the discussion until the actual time. There was no need to push points—they knew Berit and I were together. It was something no one verbalized, just as well.

Although I still loved Trumpet, I realized I had moved on and decided to sell him to a family with a twelve-year-old boy who had recently begun showing. When I said goodbye to my friend, I cried even though I knew it was for the best. I wished the boy good luck and told him Trumpet's likes and dislikes. The boy and Trumpet seemed like a good fit. Mom and Dad had other things to pay for, and the money saved from no Trumpet went toward college expenses not covered by the scholarship.

Mom, Dad, Berit, and I flew to New York. Columbia wasn't as homey as Loyola or Tulane, but it wasn't as barren as LSU-New Orleans. Even though the school technically wasn't open yet for the fall, I could get into my dorm room—probably because many students were coming from abroad and needed to move in early.

At first, I was concerned because I wouldn't have my car, but Dad assured me that I wouldn't need it and most people wouldn't have a car, and he was right.

After moving all my shit into the dorm, we decided to go sightseeing. I could tell Mom and Dad wanted to spend time with me more than anything. Mom must've said a hundred times that her sisters and Gran were very close if I got lonely or felt sick. If it was too bad, she and Dad were a phone call away, and they'd be on the next available flight. Mom and Dad stayed for four days and then left with all their warnings and advice. For having been as protective and coddling for most of my life, they seemed not to have a problem with cutting me loose. They didn't shed many tears when they left, but I still felt their love. I knew I could call them, and they'd be there.

Berit stayed with me in the dorm for a couple more days, at night, both of us squeezing on the twin bed. During the day, we explored the city and rode subways. He would assign a place and give me the address, and then I had to get there by subway. At first, I fumbled and felt uncomfortable, but I was almost as good as a New Yorker by the time he left. I noticed that New Yorkers kept to themselves. My natural instinct to smile at people as they passed did inspire a few curious looks.

The last night he booked a room at a swanky hotel across from Central Park, and we dined at a hard-to-get-in restaurant. Even though the drinking age in New York was eighteen at that time, some of the fancier restaurants had theirs at twenty-one, and they carded everyone, including my sweet Berit, who was twenty-one. He liked either wine or beer with his meals, not necessarily American beer, though. He had wine with dinner, and I had a Coke, precisely what I wanted.

We then took a carriage ride through Central Park. I felt a bit embarrassed riding in the carriage with Berit because most others were couples.

"We're just the same as the other couples," Berit said, noticing my discomfort. "The only difference is we each have a dick. Relax. I've always wanted to ride in one, so enjoy." He did the tennis-match thing as the carriage rode along.

"I know what I prefer, and it has to do with being together in the hotel."

"Don't worry," he said and laughed. "We have plenty of time for mischief."

After the ride, we headed back to the hotel and made love like never before. He had been right; certain things did get better with time. We consumed every minute. The next day we didn't say goodbye, only see you soon.

Mom must've given Gran my number because out of the blue, my phone rang the same afternoon that Berit left.

"Hi, Bradley. Would it be an inconvenience to come see you this weekend before classes start?" I hadn't seen her for a long time, and classes didn't start for five days.

"That'd be great," I said. The visit would be good for my soul.

I ventured out and walked block after block during my time alone, trying to shake off some of the Southern boy and take on a more New Yorker appearance. Shit, the Southern was too ingrained. The sirs and ma'ams flew out uncontrollably, as did holding doors open. I still smiled at people as we passed. They probably thought I was deranged; they'd walk around me. Everyone looked to be on a mission.

Gran called Friday before leaving her house. "Do you need anything?" she asked. "Soft drinks, chips, cookies, nuts? I also have rolls of quarters for the laundry."

Laundry? What did she mean laundry? Well fuck me, I was going to have to do my own laundry, and I had no idea where to go. Did the dorm have a laundry room, or did I have to go to one of those laundry places? Certainly, the machines would have directions. My mission that day was to find the laundry location and read the instructions on the machines so I'd be in like Flint. How hard could it be?

I wasn't too worried because I didn't have a ton of clothes to wash in the first place. My wardrobe consisted of black jeans, blue jeans (I know not the New York look), black T-shirts, a few button-ups (primarily white, but I did have a black one), a couple of black sweaters, underwear, and socks. I had a pair of dress shoes and my Adidas.

My room wasn't anything special, but I looked forward to showing it to my Gran. A twin bed was against one wall. A few drawers were in a decent-sized closet, and the desk had shelves above it. The other side of the room was identical. Four guys shared the bathroom. My roommate hadn't arrived yet, but some of the students had, so there was a buzz of voices in the hallway like in a theater before a movie would start.

After searching for a few minutes, I managed to find the laundry and read the directions on using the machines. Not too tricky, I thought. People had posted all types of notes on the bulletin board looking for things and selling things. Some had left just their phone numbers. That's peculiar.

I set a plan. I would pick a day, the same day every week, bring my books down with my laundry, and study while washing my clothes. Reasonable? Yes. Thoughtful? Yes. Mature? Yes. Realistic? Uh, who would've known I'd be washing not only my laundry but also laundry from some of the people on my floor. Did I have sucker written on my forehead? Nah, I was Southern, and as a Southern boy, I had manners drilled in my head. Since I was going to be doing laundry anyway, what harm, right? Wrong. Can you say doormat, people pleaser?

Gran arrived the next day with a rolling cart of grocery bags jammed with Cokes, chips, nuts—any kind of snack I could imagine. She also had bottles of aspirin and meds for diarrhea, constipation, and antacids. Shit, I wasn't seventy years old. Okay, aspirins I got. Band-aids and ointments? Reasonable. Crap, she brought a drug store. I thanked her and stocked everything in the closet in one of my suitcases, per her recommendation. She said not to let them hang out because people would steal them. Just as I was stashing away the pharmacy, my roommate arrived with his parents.

His name was Ken Decker, an engineering major from Dallas. Another Southern boy. I could deal with that, maybe. His dad wore a cowboy hat and boots and looked like he came right off Bonanza.

My Gran was a remarkable woman. She dressed with style and held herself with poise like I'd imagine the Kennedys or Rockefellers. Although from a different generation, she rolled with the times and didn't fight the change. She embraced the world as it marched on. She had retired from a bank where she was vice president, a position not common for women. My grandfather had died when Mom was a little girl, throwing Gran into the role of breadwinner. She had worked her way up, smart old gal. She was pretty hip; not much, if anything, ruffled her panties. Maybe that's why Berit's parents disgusted her.

We left Ken and his parents in the room. Gran had already checked into a hotel near campus and had the concierge get her tickets to a Broadway play for the next night. A feat I thought and banked on being impossible. Wasn't that just great! I thought sarcastic shit that I was. Of course, I would never have said anything but thank you, but the thought of a play was like watching my sister's awful dance recitals when she was young. During dinner, she had two scotch on the rocks. She offered me a sip, and I soon learned I was not a fan. She seemed to be having a good time, and I was glad to spend some one-on-one time with her. She, like Sven, was an encyclopedia of knowledge, sharing stories about the Upper Westside.

"So, how was your Amsterdam adventure? I went there years ago and loved it."

"Incredible. I loved my time there." We talked extensively about everything I had seen—except Sven and Luuk's portrait. Although she was cool, I didn't know how she would have handled that news. I discovered that we had more in common than I knew. The things I particularly loved about Amsterdam, so did she.

"Do you have pictures?" she asked.

"Yes, they're back in my room." I had the photos locked in the suitcase with the pharmacy.

"Do you mind bringing them to breakfast tomorrow? I would very much like to see them; all of them, not just the sightseeing touristy photos. I'd like to get to know Berit better, and I'm sure the photos can help."

I told her everything I knew about Berit, his family, work, school, promotion, and the dealership.

"Sounds like he is one hell of a man. He seems to have a strong intestinal fortitude and will go places. Do you two get along well? Your personalities on a par?" At first, I wasn't sure what she was asking, but I figured out she wanted to make sure it was an equal partnership.

"Sometime in the future, when he visits, we'll make the trip to you," I said. "I'm sure we can stay at a nearby hotel, but I don't have a car."

"You're in New York, dear. You don't need a car. You two are welcome to use my car when you visit and don't even think about a hotel room. I have a perfectly good guest room." I didn't see that one coming. Surprise, surprise, as Gomer Pyle would say.

"What else did you see in Amsterdam?" she asked. "I loved the museums the most. Did you have a chance to go to the museum in the Red Light District?"

"No, we missed that one."

"How about shows?" she asked.

"Certainly," I answered meekly. I wasn't sure at first what kind of show Gran meant. "I went to a show in the district, but it wasn't my favorite, but the architecture there was incredible."

"Dear, I understand. Some people aren't voyeuristic. To each their own, I always say." How Sven, I thought. "I don't know if you noticed their faces. There's no life behind their eyes. Truly a shame." She sipped on her cocktail.

"Yes, ma'am, I did notice and even mentioned to Berit. It's just not my thing. I find it almost depressing."

When I stepped onto my dorm floor, I could hear loud music blaring from what ended up being my room. The door was wide open, and Ken lounged on the bed in boxer shorts. His boots and his discarded clothes were at the foot of his bed. He was holding a framed picture and staring at it.

"Have a nice dinner?" he asked.

"Yeah, I did. I see you've settled in." I had never shared a room with one guy, except Berit. Living with a perfect stranger was like a semi-permanent blind date, neither party knowing anything about the other.

"You have a girlfriend?" he asked, handing me the picture. "That's Bonnie. We're gonna get married when I get out of school. I didn't want to come here. I wanted to stay in Texas. My dad's in the oil business; that's what I'm gonna do, but he said I needed time away from Bonnie. I think they knew we were doing it." He rambled on about his exploits with Bonnie, sharing all their juicy private details— things I had no interest in hearing.

"You have a girlfriend?" he asked again.

"No, not at present." This questioning line was a bit more personal than I was used to with a stranger.

"So, who was your last screw?"

I felt dirty talking about the subject, but I had to play the game. I told Ken, now known to me as Dallas, about Linda and the car incident and quickly changed the subject. I asked about his dad's oil business, but the topic seemed to bore him.

"My Gran is here for the weekend and expects me bright and early for breakfast, so I better call it a night." I undressed, donned some gym shorts, and went to bed. He kept his bed light on, so I rolled in the other direction, but I could hear him. He was jerking off to the picture of his girlfriend. Wonderful. I played a game with myself on guessing about people. If I were to say, I bet he'd be chasing some other girl within the first week of class. Maybe I was wrong, and he was in love with this Bonnie girl.

The next morning I met Gran and shared the photos with her over breakfast.

"These are great," she said, flipping through them. "You two make a handsome couple. I can see the mutual admiration in both of you."

As she was paying for breakfast, we discussed what we would do for the day.

"Do you have a heavy coat? What about a muffler, hat, and gloves?" she asked.

"Yes, I have a heavy coat, but no to the other items."

"Well then, that's a perfect reason to go shopping." She took me to Macy's and bought me two mufflers, some hats, and two pairs of gloves.

I don't know why, but I told her about the carriage ride in Central Park.

"That's lovely," she said. A great word coming from her. Me, not so much.

We had a good time. Her sense of humor was dry and amused me. We explored different parts of the city on foot and in cabs. Even though I had done and seen most of the sites, thanks to Berit, she presented things differently—how the city used to be and how grand some places were that weren't so grand any longer. She said the next time she visited, we would go to Tavern on the Green. I felt guilty about her spending money on me because I knew many older people were on limited money unless someone was insanely rich like Sven. I had my dad's emergency credit card—maybe I could take her to dinner. I'd call Mom before dinner to make sure it was okay.

She wanted to go back to her room to get ready for the evening, and I hoped Dallas wasn't in the room because I needed some alone time. Even after just a day, Dallas had a way of grating on my nerves.

Thankfully no music was coming from our room, but I realized our door was wide open. Crap, I didn't want to be the whiny roommate complaining about an open door, but I'd do it if I had to. I wasn't too worried because I didn't have much to steal, although he had a stereo system in plain view. There was a note stuck to the phone with chewing gum. Gross. My cousin Berit had called. Call back collect.

I called him pronto. It would've been eight there. Why wasn't he out to eat with Sven? He picked up after a few rings. He was loaded, really loaded. I didn't think I'd ever heard him as fucked up. "You okay?"

I could hear the quake in his voice. "Sven's had a heart attack. We were at dinner when he grabbed his arm and could hardly breathe. He had this horrible look of pain on his face, and now he's at hospital in a cardiac unit. They won't let me in because I'm not family. He doesn't have any family, and he's alone. Bradley, there was nothing I could do to help him. What if he dies?"

"Berit, listen to me. He's gonna be okay," I said. "He's where he needs to be. Thank goodness you were with him when it happened, and he wasn't home alone. If I know you, you can sweet-talk some nurse. I don't care if you have to go to bed with her and work your way in to see him. Say or do whatever you have to. I'm confident that you can win your way into anyone's heart. Do you want me to come be with you?" My heart was heavy for him.

"No, I'm just in shock and scared," he said. " I needed to hear your voice; you always have the right words. In the morning, I'll call you to give an update on his condition and let you know how well I do in talking my way in to see him. Eight o'clock your time, too early?"

I stayed calm. "Perfect. Be brave and do what you gotta do. It's going to be okay, believe it." I looked around to make sure no one was within earshot. "I love you. Talk tomorrow." I should've told him to put the bottle down. He was evidently past his limit.

I shut the door, undressed, wrapped a towel around me, and went for a shower. I wanted to lock the door, but I was afraid Dallas would be back and not have his key. Dumb shit. All sorts of thoughts rolled around in my head. I wondered if Sven would make a full recovery. A kid in my sophomore class in high school's dad had a heart attack, had serious surgery, and was never the same again. Sven was a healthy guy and in good shape, so I felt sure he'd be fine. When I went back into the room, the door was wide open, and the music was blaring. Wonderful.

Dallas had returned with a blonde, doe-eyed ditz hanging on his arm. Shit, it hadn't even been twenty-four hours since he was jerking off to the girl he was gonna marry—what a schmo.

"Glad you didn't lock the door, sport," he said. "I'd have been shit out of luck. I lost my key moving my stuff in. They're gonna charge my parents a couple of smackers to get me another one. I'm gonna be up shit's creek." He was sitting on the bed cozied up to the girl.

The girl sitting next to him giggled. "Isn't he just the cutest?" Let me puke now.

"Hey sport, can I talk to you mano e mano," he twitched his head to the side. "Little filly, we gotta talk some man talk. Scuse us while we step outside a moment. Don't you go nowhere, ya hear?"

Fuck me. This is my roommate, man of no couth. Neanderthal. No wonder people thought poorly of Southerners. I stepped out into the hallway, in my towel, mind you, and knew what he was gonna say. Some stupid drivel about a sock on the door. Mindless excuse for a man.

"Hey, sport, me and this little filly got some sheet dancing to do if you catch my drift. Now we need a signal to let each other know when it's cool to come in or when we're entertaining." He rocked from one foot to the other like he had to pee or something.

"How bout we put a sock on the door?" I suggested, the sarcasm dripping from my mouth. He was too dense even to realize. "That'll be the signal, but I gotta get dressed. She needs to step outside the room for a moment."

"You shy or something, sport? She ain't gonna be looking at you," he said and chuckled.

I had enough. "No, *you* shouldn't want her looking at me, or she'll be knocking on the door asking for me."

He seemed flustered but laughed it off. They stepped out, and I changed, opened the door, had my things, key included, and headed out. As I walked down the hall, I heard the door squeak open. I looked back, and the sock was on the doorknob. I wondered what Miss Bonnie would think about her man stepping out before going to one class. Another bet came to mind: He wasn't gonna make it past the first semester; he was too damn full of himself.

I didn't get a chance to call my parents, but I figured they wouldn't be upset with me treating Gran to dinner. After all, she was taking me to a play. We met in the hotel lobby, and she looked smashing in a black and cream tailored dress with jacket to match. She had her black cashmere coat draped over her arm. She had made reservations at a place called Raoul's.

Meanwhile, I looked like every other man in New York—black jeans, black shirt, black jacket, and black dress shoes. Following dinner, she had tickets to see *The Wiz*. I had heard of it but knew nothing about it and figured I'd politely enjoy the performance.

My dinner and adventure with Gran were memorable, and *The Wiz* fucking blew my mind. I choked with everyone else in the theatre. Gran was completely up with the times. I told her that I loved my weekend with her. She was touched that I had paid for dinner, argued at first, but gave in, making me feel like a grown man. I felt sophisticated, almost worldly, even though I hadn't started my first day of college. Being with Berit over the summer, away from my parents, I finally cut the cord and went from coddled boy to independent man. Maybe not all the way, man, but damn close. I'm sure spending so much time with Sven played a role in my coming of age.

The first semester of school went as well as I could have hoped. My grades were near perfect, and as I had suspected, my roommate shipped home toward the end of October, his dad had paid for four lost keys. I found them all and wondered if they could be redeemed for cash, but I turned them in just because. I loved New York and had managed to get a phone call routine with Berit and Mom and Dad. I felt informed and connected but independent in the city. Sven made a full recovery, as predicted. Berit put his place on the market and moved in with Sven in his guest room. The heart attack had opened everyone's eyes. Had he been alone at home, he wouldn't have recovered and maybe even died.

Berit's place sold quickly, and he invested the money per Sven's instruction. He didn't have any furniture to move to speak of, but he hung the portrait of the two of us over his bed.

I wanted to take something home for everyone for Thanksgiving, so I went shopping at Lord and Taylor, Macy's, and Saks. Coming out of Saks, I literally ran into Berit's mom.

"Bradley Stedman?" She looked like she had seen a ghost.

"Yes, ma'am," I coldly responded.

She pulled us to the side out of the way of other shoppers. "Can we speak a moment?"

Still aloof and cold, I uttered, "Yes, ma'am. What about?"

"Do you ever speak to Berit?" she asked. She genuinely looked concerned.

"I do." I was gonna answer the questions and nothing more.

"How is he?"

"Extremely successful." I looked her straight in the eyes and wanted to say, No thanks to you and your asshole husband. What kind of fucking parent are you to kick out a child? Instead, I stayed quiet.

"I miss him terribly." Her eyes teared.

"Is that so?" Yeah, I was going to be a hard ass. "Lady, those tears mean nothing to me. Y'all hurt and almost broke the most precious thing in my life because he didn't live by y'all's expectations." This was an extremely sore point, and she was getting little to no sympathy from me.

"You must think we are horrible people. If you could only understand –" Okay, she opened the door. Sorry, Mom and Dad, I wasn't going to be the caring, loving Southern gentleman you raised me to be. No, this cold-hearted bitch was gonna hear it. She started it.

I kept my voice calm and low. "Yes, ma'am, I think what y'all did to your only son is appalling. I don't know your reasoning, and it's not my business. I imagine it's something you'll have to answer for one day. Personally, I don't know how y'all slept at night. Oh, and as a footnote, when your husband went to visit his dying mother, he was staying in *Berit's* home. She had already given her house to him because she knew exactly how your husband would respond when she passed. Berit is far more gracious and kind than your husband will ever be, ma'am. He's made his way in the world, has educated himself at the university, and has made a career for himself, earning a more than handsome salary. I do suspect one day your husband and your son will meet again. If you have nothing else to say, ma'am, good day." I turned to walk away.

She called to me. "Tell Berit I love him and never meant to hurt him."

I spun around. I probably looked like evil incarnate. "I highly doubt it," I said and continued walking. I could hear her cry aloud, but I wasn't having any of it. I hadn't been rude. I hadn't raised my voice. I was as cold and uncaring as she had been when I called after Berit's first visit to New Orleans. I merely returned the tone. Fuck her and her asshole husband.

I felt a tug on my arm and turned around. Mrs. Jensen had run up to me with tears flowing down her face and handed me a business card with a phone number. "Please give this to Berit and ask him to call me."

I took the card from her and walked away. Would I give it to Berit or not? I felt I had to, but it went against every instinct I had. I wasn't going to tell him on the phone. I'd wait until I saw him for New Year's Eve in New York. He could decide what to do with the phone number.

Thoughts raced through my head. Am I acting like a good or bad friend? Am I deciding out of love for him or hate for them? I needed help, so I called Gran.

"It's so good to hear from you. Are you okay?"

"I'm fine. Everything is okay." I said. "I just wanted to talk. Are you, by chance going to New Orleans for Thanksgiving? If so, can we fly together?" I knew she would stay longer than I, but we could be together on the same flight there.

"That would be a splendid idea. I'll make the arrangements."

"Gran, while I have you on the phone, I need your advice."

"Certainly, dear, what is it?"

"I ran into Berit's mother today at Saks."

"And?"

"She asked about Berit. I wasn't rude to her, but I must admit I was cold. I told her he was well and quite successful. She at one point said I probably thought she and her husband were horrible people."

"And did you say yes? Not only do you think it, but they *are* horrible people!"

"No, Gran, well, yes. I told her I thought what they did was appalling, and it was none of my business, and I said more, but bottom line, I left. She ran after me, crying, and asked me to tell Berit she loved him. She gave me a phone number to give him to call her. I took the card, didn't say a word, and came straight here to call you. I have questions galore going through my head. I'm just trying to understand my motives for what I'm feeling. Should I give him the card? Should I tell him that she loves him? Should I even tell him I ran into her? I don't want to hurt him. It took a long time for him to get over how they treated him, and I don't want to rip open any scars. What would a friend do? Wait until New Year's when I see him or tell him over the phone?"

"I see your dilemma, Brad. What would *you* expect of a friend if the roles were reversed?" Shit, she threw it right back at me.

"Tell me what to do, Gran."

"Bradley, I can't do that. I don't know what your heart is telling you, but if it were me and someone, let's say a friend, kept possibly important information from me to protect me, then I would think my friend, while intentions were admirable, didn't think too highly of me. You, dear, are a mere messenger. It's Berit's decision what he does with the information, wouldn't you say?" She had the answer without telling me I was acting like a controlling son of a bitch.

"You're right. I'll call Berit, even though it isn't our call night."

Because it was a school phone, I had to call collect. It rang twice until Sven answered.

"Everything okay, Bradley?" he asked after accepting the call. He hit me with a barrage of questions. As much as I wanted to get Sven's feedback on the subject, I had decided to talk to Berit.

Sven handed the phone to Berit. "I've missed you so much. You couldn't wait a couple of days? I'm flattered. Seriously, what gives, my friend?"

I hemmed and hawed until I spit it out. "Berit, I've been debating this call for more than an hour, and I don't know if it's the right thing or not, but I'm a mere messenger, as Gran pointed out." I could hear him tapping with a pen, like saying, get on with it, Bradley. "I ran into your mother at Saks today." Silence. I cleared my throat. "I was civil—nothing to embarrass you or my parents—you know how strong my feelings are, but I was cold. She wanted to know about you and if you were well. I said yes, and you were at the university and were making good money. Before you ask, I didn't say what kind of career. She mentioned something like I must think she was horrible, blah, blah, blah. I said I thought what they did was appalling blah, blah, blah. Then I walked away, but she ran after me, upset, and handed me a card to give you with a message. The card has a phone number on it. It's the reason I called on an off day. It wasn't my decision to make."

"Interesting," he said. "I'm curious about the blah blah blahs and what her message was."

"In the conversation, I said something like I didn't know how they slept at night after treating you like they did, and I also told her you were far more gracious than her husband. I mentioned how you had let him stay at the house when it was your house. Pretty much it. I was rattled at the time and trying hard to be someone you would be proud to know."

"I'm always proud to know you. The message, nelly?"

"She said to tell you that she loved you and for you to give her a call at the number on the card."

Silence again. I could hear the tap, tap, tap of the pen. I could tell he was thinking. "I see the dilemma you had, and you did the right thing. It's my decision to make—"

"I sorta thought telling you in person over New Year's Eve might be better than a phone call, but—"

"No, you did the right thing. I'm not going to get the number from you until then unless curiosity gets the better of me. I doubt it, though. It's what? Six weeks from now? Fuck them. She knew you'd call me and probably thought I would call right away. I have my life, and frankly, they no longer fit in. I wish no harm to either one, but a family rekindled isn't in the cards. They made their bed and now must lie in it. You realize they've had many opportunities to call me. They knew where I was living and the phone number. He didn't even want to see me when his mother was dying and didn't come to the funeral because I would be there. He broke her heart, and for that alone, fuck him and fuck them and the horse they rode in on. If I call, it'll be when I want, but I don't see it happening, my friend. You, Bradley, did the right thing calling me. I promise. I can see why you were nervous, but never, ever be nervous talking to me about anything, ever. I love you." We spoke for another minute or two, and I chatted with Sven for a few minutes before hanging up.

Chapter 15

Butterflies were dancing in my stomach as I packed for Thanksgiving. I was excited to see my parents and Sarah and curious whether Frankie was still in the picture. The last time I saw them, things seemed to be waning.

I locked up the room neat and tidy. I loved having a single all to myself.

Gran pulled up in the backseat of a town car. Taking a car to and from LaGuardia was more convenient. I had one bag compared to her three—one small, one medium, and one huge—and they matched. Of course, why wouldn't they?

The driver weaved in and out of traffic like an Indy 500 driver and knew how to use his horn. Something about driving in New York and horns could be alarming. While riding to the airport, I was amused at how things had come around. A girl on the second floor would flirt with me in the laundry room—heavy flirting—the kind that made me feel awkward. Berit called it fuck-me flirting.

One day while sitting on the washing machine, she asked, "Do you know why I sit on the washer?"

I had no idea.

"It's for the spin cycle; it gets me off."

Too much information. I just nodded. What would someone say to such a comment?

"Come here, Bradley." She wanted me to stand between her legs.

Not gonna happen. "I appreciate any offer you're making, but I play for the other team."

She stuck her bottom lip out. "What a waste," she said, which charged my ego and then some. "I bet I could change your mind." She then ran her tongue across her teeth.

"Thanks. If I'm ever in the mood for a blowjob and my boyfriend isn't around, I'll let you know."

"You'd really rather get a blowjob from a boy than a girl?"

Her question amused me. "You bet—every damn day of the week and twice on Sunday."

"Now I feel challenged, Bradley. I'm told I give an excellent blowjob."

Crap, a challenge; it had gone in the wrong direction. "I'm sure you do, and I know there are plenty guys who would take you up on it, but, to be blunt, not trying to be crude, just a fact, I like dick, but I'd love to have you as a friend to hang around now you know the rules."

It was such a Sarah-Berit moment and made me smile.

"What's on your mind, Bradley?" Gran asked. Do I tell her minus the graphic details? I thought. Why not!

"Gran, I was doing laundry, and this girl came on pretty strong," I said. "You know girls can be quite, um, pushy. I thanked her for the compliment, but I told her I played for the other team. She was insistent I hadn't been with the right girl."

"What a tart!" She guffawed. "People don't get we're all wired differently, whether it's talents, likes, dislikes, and especially sexuality. Goodness me." She thought for a minute and then added, "Have you ever been with a girl? I'm just curious, and you can say none of my business, too. I won't be offended."

I felt like I could tell her anything within good taste. "Yes, ma'am, I wanted to make sure I wasn't hung up on the person regardless of male or female. I did once with a beautiful girl and sweet as the day is long. It wasn't the same, is the best way I can describe it. It's no better than—"

"Masturbation? Right. I understand. I couldn't fathom being with a woman sexually. It was brave of you to give it a whirl." She smiled at me. I think she respected our candor. I couldn't imagine speaking to anyone else like this about my adventures. Neither of us seemed to care whether the driver could hear us or not. I bet he was getting enough details to amuse his fellow drivers in the break room.

The airport was a zoo, but we were up in the air and headed to New Orleans before long. I had a bourbon and coke with my peanuts, and Gran went a scotch on the rocks. The day was perfect for flying: bright blue sky with only a few fluffy white clouds. I looked forward to seeing Mom and Dad

Mom and Dad were at the airport waiting as we deplaned. Their eyes lit up when they saw me, even though we spoke regularly; in person was the deal.

Brushing past a few people, Mom hugged me. "Look at you. It's good to have you home. I've missed you so much, Brad." She then hugged Gran and said something along the lines of welcome and happy to see her.

Dad was all smiles and gave me a tight bear hug. "Bradley, you look great. Let's get the bags and get home." Mom and Gran trailed behind as Dad and I headed for the luggage.

Pulling in the driveway was good to be home, but somehow I was on the outside looking in. Even though Columbia was merely a means to an end, it was where I fit in as of now. In time, that too would change.

Mom came in and closed the door as I began to settle in. "Bradley, you've been such a blessing. I've been worried sick about Gran. Until you went to New York, she sounded like she was declining, but she's her usual vibrant self. I can't express how grateful I am for you reaching out. She has always loved going into the city, attending plays, dining, but now most of her friends have passed on, and it's not the same. Part of her had given up, but she's vibrant again. Thank you."

Sarah and I had our own special visit. She asked about New York and Amsterdam, and I showed her both sets of pictures. After I told her everything I thought worthwhile, I changed the subject to her and what'd she been doing.

"Are you still seeing Frankie?" I was curious.

"It's been off and on, more on, but things recently have gotten serious." She started choking up, her eyes filling with tears and her voice cracking.

"Is it a good thing, the closeness? If it's not, you're in control of the situation."

"It's not that easy," she said. "It's complicated." She looked down.

"What kind of complications could there be? Is he manhandling you because I can put a kibosh on that—" I felt my face flush in anger.

"Absolutely not. Nothing like—I'm pregnant, and Frankie's the father." I stared at her like a deer in the headlights. My mind started racing: What should I say not to offend, congratulations or condolences?

After a few deep breaths, I grabbed her hand. "It's not the end of the world. I'm sure you'll have everyone's support. Does Frankie know?

"Sorta."

"Huh? What does sorta mean?" I asked. "It's yes or no, not sorta."

"Well, I told him that I thought I was, but I never made the confirmation."

"So, have you had confirmation?" I tilted my head, wondering if this was a made-up Sarah move, but suspected not, and I was right. Yes, she had confirmed one hundred percent. Baby was on the way.

"I want you with me when I tell Mom and Dad and when I tell Frankie," she added.

What the hell? Where did I fit into a conversation like pregnancy or babies? I wanted to be the supportive brother, so I agreed to sit in the room but merely for silent moral support, emphasis on the silent. She was worried about Gran, but I told her not to worry about Gran. She'd seen or heard it all.

While Dad was sipping a cold beer to unwind, he and I had a chance to talk one-on-one.

"Your mom and I couldn't be prouder of how well you're doing at school and acclimating to New York," he said. "You've grown up over this summer and fall, and I love the man you've become," I swore; I saw him wipe away a tear.

Shit, I told him all about the idiot roommate, including him jerking off to the picture of his future bride only to have, wink, wink, nudge,

nudge, a filly in the room. I told him about what I said about dropping my towel, and he laughed heartedly.

"He really said filly? What a pompous asshole! It's a shame because every guy I know from Texas is standup. *Filly*, get the fuck out." I held back, laughing. Yes, I'd heard Berit use the word in front of my dad, but with me? He'd occasionally say things like shit, asshole, but never, ever the big F.

Enough time had passed, my laugh seemed to coincide with thoughts of filly, "Yep, Dad, I pegged it. I gave it a week before he was scouting the local talent, but I gave him too much credit. Being his roommate was painful. He never locked the door and sometimes left it wide-open. He dropped his clothes all over, and he was a pig. I knew he'd either flunk out or drop out. I think he left mid-October."

Since I was bearing most of what had happened at school, I told him about Miss Washing Machine.

"I thought the spin cycle was a myth," he said with a chuckle.

"Nope, that's what she said. She's a cute girl but forward, to say the least. When I told her I played for the other team, she said she could change my mind." I stretched my legs out and clasped my hands behind my head.

"The other team? I never heard it put like that. It does bring up the question, and if this is getting too personal, just tell me, have you experienced being with a girl?"

I nodded. "Valencia, bet you didn't know all the benefits I got with the membership you paid for." I grinned.

"Well, I'll be. Valencia. Live and learn. Not wanting detail or any specifics, and certainly not wanting to push past a comfortable boundary, but are you sexually active with many people, or is it like one or two?" I could tell he was uncomfortable but concerned with V.D. and the like.

"One, Dad, I've had a couple of experiences, if you will, but the answer is one. Berit and I have an extraordinary friendship. I know it's disappointing to you and Mom. For lack of a better word, it's a healthy relationship filled with respect and trust. I'm sure you've heard horror stories about the gay community, and for the most part, I'd like to say it's not true, but I'd be lying. I think monogamy is rare, and you see a lot of the fuck on the fly. I know it's crude, but it's an in-the-moment thing. Some of it is because the lifestyle isn't accepted, and emotions get pent up, so it's hidden in the dark as though it's something horrible. Sad, really."

He got up, poured a couple of drinks, and sat back down. "Bourbon and coke, okay?" I nodded and smiled.

"I always knew something was different about me, but I didn't know what it was and felt weird. I was insecure and withdrawn because I hadn't identified my feelings. The first time Berit told me I was gay, I got pissed off, but he told me as a friend. We talked then, and we still talk a lot about it. I have moments where certain words make me feel awkward. I call them, mind you in my head, queer words. I cringe when I think the word and shit when I say them, I almost come unglued." We both chuckled.

His eyes showed an understanding I'd never seen him have before. He was looking at me with love as his son, but also as a man. It moved my heart. "What words make you cringe, mere curiosity?"

"Try charming, quaint, delightful…those are the usual suspects. They just roll right off my tongue. Truthfully, when's the last time you walked in somewhere and said, isn't this charming?"

"I see your point, but you've been exposed to those all your life by Mom. Give yourself a break. Shit, be who you are, Bradley. You're a delightful person, and I'm proud to call you my son." We both had a good laugh at him using a word from my list.

We talked more in one conversation about my sexuality than we had spoken since my coming out on that hysterical morning. Dad jumped in when I mentioned that experience. He told me the school had been officially closed down, and a few arrests had been made. He asked if any of the teachers ever tried to touch me at any time. The answer was no, never. Part of me wanted to cheer about the arrests and the school's closing, but it saddened me to think how many young boys had been abused.

The night before Thanksgiving had a chill in the air, perfect for staying in. I was upstairs penning a letter to Berit when Sarah called me and asked me to come down. Frankie had arrived, and the two of them were hanging out on the patio. I knew why she wanted me, but shit, I didn't want the drama.

Sarah could be dramatic beyond the wildest measure, and the night before Thanksgiving must've seemed like a good time to upset the apple cart. "Frankie," she batted her eyes, oh for heaven's sake, "I wanted Bradley to be with me when I shared our good news. I *am* expecting. My doctor confirmed it; looks like we're gonna have a May baby." I glanced at Frankie and thought he might be sick.

"May, what a great time to have a baby," I said. What a stupid thing to say, but what do you say? "Congrats, y'all. I think maybe I should go inside now and give y'all some time alone to celebrate."

Frankie stood. "No, Bradley, maybe I better get going. I don't know what your sister is trying to pull, but I'm not having a kid at twenty-one. My parents will kill me."

Sarah started to cry, and I spoke quickly, "Sarah, shh, Frankie has every right to be upset, but it's not a time for anyone to be hasty. Frankie, sit. Are you upset because you don't think the baby is yours?" Her expression looked like she was gonna rip out my eyes, but that discussion had to come up eventually.

"No, no, I know Sarah hasn't fooled around with anyone else. That's not it at all. I don't think I'm ready for a baby. I'm too young. We're too young." He was extremely manic—running his hands through his hair, looking off to the side, changing positions at a remarkable rate, and almost wringing his hands. He was beside himself.

"How old was your mom when she had you?" I asked. "I know our mom was twenty when she had Sarah and twenty-two when she had me. People may be waiting a bit longer for kids, but y'all are both great, and I'm sure will be good parents. There's a learning curve, so I'm told." I chuckled to myself. "Come on. I know you love each other. You've been together for three years, and it's coming about before you expected it to, that's all."

Frankie started to relax, and I looked at Sarah. "Your body is already preparing you for this event, but you need to give Frankie time to catch up. The thing both of you also need to do is tell Mom and Dad. When you tell your parents, Frankie, do it together. With a unified front, they'll respect you more. They'll be upset at first, but after the baby comes, it'll all change. Who knows? Maybe they won't be upset at all." My time as their counselor was over, and I sure as hell didn't want to be around when she told Mom and Dad. Having Frankie with her was the right thing, not me. Boy, I couldn't wait to be back in New York. I went back upstairs to finish my letter.

Hoi my friend,

Miss you terribly. It's good to see the parents. Flew with Gran—she's funny. She reminds me of Sven in many ways. They have a lot in common, and I think they'd be fast friends. Maybe he could come with you for New Year's Eve. Just a thought.

My parents are different to me now that I'm older or something. Dad and I had a long and special talk, almost like two friends. We talked about being gay, and I acknowledged how they must be disappointed in some way and understandable. He said the f word, and I said the f word just like two guys, only he's my dad. It was cool. Mom and I had a heart-to-heart talk too, which was good, and I needed it. I love her hugs. I know what I sound like, but you know what I mean, you've had her hugs.

Hold on to your jockstrap, Sarah confided in me: She's pregnant. I know, I flipped, though not too much out loud. She wanted me to be with her when she told Mom and Dad, and Frankie. I helped with Frankie but told them they needed to talk to the parents as a unified couple. You would have been proud. I felt like you, wise and worldly. Strange. I hope I don't pressure you to be the sense of reason for my crazy ass. I know I did on your first visit here. I remember walking into some bar, ordering a drink, and having no money. Remember you canceled the order, got me soda or something, and had a-get-a-grip-Bradley conversation? I was such a pain in the ass and so freakin' insecure. Shit, I'm still insecure, just not as much. Stop laughing, swine (to coin you, my friend). Frankie didn't take it well at first and is probably still in shock. I know I would be, but if they have sex as much as we do, and they're bound to, most likely more since they see each other more, it was bound to happen. Berit, tell me you're using birth control, right? Okay, I'm a jackass.

Yes, I'm wound like a top, in case you're wondering. I could use some calming down right now. I wish you were here. As much as you like to eat, you would love Thanksgiving. Maybe next year. The more I've thought about the car dealership thing and us living here, the more I've come to terms with it. I never wanted to move back here, but we can have a life separate from my parents, Sarah, and their friends.

I'm beat and better call it a night. By the time you get this, I'll be back at school so you can answer me there, or we'll talk on Monday. Stay cool.
Friends always,
Me

Later that same evening, Sarah and Frankie made the big announcement to my parents in the kitchen. I could hear them talking downstairs, so I thought it better to stay in my room. I pulled *Huckleberry Finn* off the shelf, and a note fell out. I laughed—Huck, the perfect book for Berit the Cool. I unfolded the note.

You found it!
If you don't know me by now, then you'll never, ever know me, ba da ba da ba. Sappy, but it was on the radio and seemed to fit. Bradley, I love you more than I've ever loved anybody or anything in this entire world. All in the same thought, I'm happy I was the one to introduce you to the real you, but sadly I had to be the one. Perhaps you could've faked it in the straight world, but you wouldn't have been happy. You are who you are. Being gay can be filled with deception, betrayal, and hate. Straight men fear us and don't want to be close for fear that someone might think they're gay or that we might try to change them or try to touch them. Women love us for different reasons. Some believe they can change us with their bodies and feminine wiles, whereas others are fag hags because we're safe, and they view us as the perfect man. It can be convoluted at best.

I want to be your friend more than anything else. Friends are honest, open, caring, attentive, and interested only in their friends' wellbeing. A friend isn't self-centered, self-gratifying, or divisive. True friendship doesn't have any ulterior motives; it's pure. A friend doesn't lie to a friend, betray a trust, or purposely hurt. If I have ever hurt you, I'm sorry. If I have ever offended you, I have offended myself. I want to be there for you in every instance but know I can't.

I see a long life together—you and I—one filled with happy times, loving times, and sad times, but we'll be together to weather the storms. Love me for who I am, and I'll always love you for who you are.

Now I laugh at myself. When I first picked up the pen, I would write something provocative and sassy, but this came out. If you close your eyes and think of me, you can bring up all our wonderful memories together. You don't need graphic details; they exist in our memory. As long as you practice thinking of us together, we'll always be together though we're miles apart.

Repeat after me: Berit loves me, Berit loves me, Berit loves me.

Friends always

Berit

After I read it, I wished I had left some hidden love notes in his house, but maybe it's better I hadn't because he sold the house furnished to move in with Sven. Wouldn't that have been hilarious? Maybe not.

Dad called me downstairs to the living room. Mom, Sarah, Frankie, and Gran were sitting on the sofa. Had she told them I already knew, or should I act shocked? No one seemed perturbed or sad. The air wasn't heavy; it wasn't anything. No read whatsoever.

I sat down and looked around the room.

"We know you were the first informed of the coming addition to the family," Mom said. "We've called Frankie's parents and asked them to come over. We wanted you to know we fully support Sarah and Frankie. I hope his parents aren't too upset. Although it isn't ideal," she cleared her throat, "a baby is a blessing and never a mistake. We thought the whole family should be in on the conversation to show support, and what did you say? Yes, unity. Wise words, son."

Thoughts traveled through my mind, none of which I wanted to share. Did I have to be part of this ordeal? One good thing about having a gay son is that they didn't have to worry about me knocking someone up. Was I one day going to regret not having a child? As neurotic as I could be, I would've driven a child to lunacy, although Berit would've made a great dad. I wondered if he ever thought about it—conversation for another time.

The doorbell rang. Frankie's parents had arrived quickly. Did they suspect?

Dad answered the door. "Y'all, come on in." Dad showed Frankie's parents to the two fluffy chairs.

"Can I pour anyone a drink?" Dad asked.

"Should I want a drink?" Frank asked Dad.

"Maybe." Dad was calm.

"Bourbon and ginger, if you have it. If you don't have ginger, Coke will do. Wine, dear?"

The moms exchanged pleasantries, even though everyone in the room seemed to know. What else could it be with a young man and woman than a baby on the way?

Dad looked at Frankie with a stern nod. "Uh, Mom, Dad, uh, Sarah's, uh, pregnant," Frankie said.

His mom sighed, and his dad held his head in his hands.

"What were you two thinking?" his dad asked. "Wait, I know. You didn't think. Sarah, we feel close to you, and I have to say we're surprised. What's done is done." Frank looked at my dad and asked, "So, where do you want to go from here? Shotgun wedding or what?"

"I think it's up to Frankie and Sarah," Dad answered diplomatically.

"I feel Frankie needs to do the right thing. They want to act grown. Then they can accept the consequences. I know I had to, not that it's been a bad thing," he looked at his wife, "but life changes drastically, and they need to know it."

Time for a revelation. Frankie looked shocked. "Wait, what?"

"Oh, for heaven's sake, Frankie, do the math. I was three months on the way when Dad and I married," his mom said. Frankie's eyes jumped back and forth between his parents, trying to comprehend the news.

Gran got up and started for the kitchen. "Anyone interested in cheese and crackers?"

"I'll help," I said, making my exit. Gran was standing with the fridge door open, and I could see she had her hand over her mouth, and her shoulders were moving up and down a little. She seemed to be crying.

"Gran, it's gonna be okay," I said. But when she turned to me, she wasn't crying at all; she was trying to hold back laughing.

"I'd say little Frankie got knocked off his feet," she said. "He seems like a nice boy, but he has always had, in my opinion, a bit of a snobbish attitude like he thought his family was a little better than ours. Finding out that secret dropped him a peg or two. His dad is old school indeed. My thoughts, not that they matter, but we don't need to complicate this with a wedding. Babies are one thing, marriage another. Marriage is hard enough, but with a baby on the way, it's going to get rough. The kids need to hear it. Even though Sarah may be all dreamy-eyed about being a mommy, it's a hard road. None of my business, but I would've paid money to see Frankie's face with the 'do the math.' She's a funny lady." We managed to get the cheese and crackers served.

I fixed myself a bourbon and coke. The moms started talking about a December wedding. The dads were on another subject: Shit! Me. Good grief. The questions about life in New York and Columbia University popped up. I knew those answers and didn't have to lie or make excuses. After bullshitting with the men for a short while, I excused myself to my room and soon heard Gran come upstairs.

"Bradley," she whispered, "this is such a mess. You gave them good advice. Sometimes I'd swear you were the older between you and your sister. She's precious as she can be but too immature. The baby will be time to grow up. Going to be a rough ride." She winked at me, then kissed my cheek.

"Glad I'm in New York. Sorry for Mom and Dad and kinda for Sarah, but she was foolish." I wished her a good night and headed to bed.

Thanksgiving dinner the next day tasted as wonderful as ever, and the news from the night before didn't damper anything. No one talked about it, which was fine with me. They can wait until I leave town. I wondered if Gran would shorten her trip or balls it out.

She ended up staying, and I fled as fast as I could. Everyone knew I'd only be there a short while because I had to return to school.

Mom was tearful, driving me to the airport.

"Why the tears, Mom? You can visit me any time you want," I said. "You can stay with Gran, see your sisters, and spend time with me." I put my hand on hers.

"The wedding is the first thing on my dance card at present. You'll be home for a month at Christmas. By the way, are you planning on coming home for Mardi Gras?"

"No. I have to stay at school."

"What about spring break?" she asked.

"I'll see, but I know I'll be home for a couple of months during the summer."

"Okay. I just miss you, honey. It's hard having you away." She looked over at me with a sad smile.

We hugged before I walked to the gate. Mom needed to get back to her routine. Nothing was worse than sitting in an airport waiting for someone to depart. It had a morbid, sad feel like waiting for the inevitable.

I hadn't been back at school for twenty-four hours before there was a knock on my door.

It was Little Miss Washing Machine, who was pretty with long blonde hair and green eyes that had flecks of gold in them. She bordered on too thin but had a nice rack. Most guys would've gone for her in a New York second. "I brought a care package from home, and could you help me put the box on my top shelf?" she asked. I rolled my eyes and followed her.

The way she batted her eyes and swung her hips when she walked, I felt a set-up coming and was ready for whatever she threw out. In her room, there was, in fact, a box, and the shelf was out of her reach, but I felt something else was on the horizon. After I set the box, I realized my suspicions were correct.

"Thanks so much," she said. "Is there some way I can repay you? How about a blowjob, right here, right now?"

"It's only a one-time thing," I said. Wait, what was I saying?

"Okay, but more than likely, you'll be back for more."

"Probably not," I said. "However, you've caught me at a stressful time." I had two upcoming exams and a paper due that week, "You could give me some stress relief. No kissing or fucking, and I'm not doing anything to you." I was heartless and almost rude. I didn't want to be hounded or give the wrong impression.

She locked the door and told me to get on her bed. I unzipped my fly, and she went to town. Wow. She gave a blowjob like a guy; she was talented. Somebody had taught her how to give great head. Great, not like Berit, but better than Leonard, for sure. Maybe there'd be a next time, before an exam or something.

Not long after she started, I blew my load, and she swallowed.

"Can we still be friends?" she asked while wiping her mouth. "I just wanted to prove to you I wasn't a liar. Because I'm a girl, it's not cheating."

"Doesn't work that way; it's still cheating, but the difference being, I won't hide it, I'll tell him." I knew he'd be okay with it after the hospital nurse thing. He had not only fucked her once, but he kept doing it as long as Sven was in cardiac care—kissing her, taking her to dinner, everything from A to Z, or as he said Zed. One blowjob paled in comparison. I returned to my room feeling less stressed, but it made me miss Berit even more.

Back in my room, I re-read the note he had left in the book. Our phone call was less than twenty-four hours away, so I'd wait until we spoke to tell him. A blowjob didn't warrant a phone call. I reread the note and said aloud, "Berit loves me, Berit loves me, Berit loves me," I smiled. "And Bradley loves Berit." Something was bothering me; guilt rode me better than anyone else I knew. Hell, starving kids in Africa, guilty Bradley.

Monday didn't come fast enough. As soon as he answered the phone, I blurted out, "I let Miss Washing Machine blow me."

"Hi to you too," he laughed. "You've been obsessing over this, haven't you? What is wrong with you? Were you honest with her? How was it?"

"Exceptionally good; in fact, I told her she gave a blowjob like a guy, which she did." Berit didn't say anything.

"You good, Berit?" I figured he'd have some glib remark.

"Brad, make a point of talking to her. I'm willing to bet she's a victim of incest or sexual abuse. Girls don't give head like guys unless they're compensating for insecurity. I might be wrong, but make a point of checking her out. Let her know she doesn't have to do it to be your friend—unless she's a working girl, and then she would've charged you. Don't make it a big deal but talk to her." It was food for thought. I hoped I hadn't sent the same message. I had been such a dick with my no kissing, blah blah.

"She offered anal sex as well, but I said no thanks anyway. You know where my mind went? I thought for a split second that I could imagine you because all I'd be looking at was her back, but I didn't."

"Thank God you didn't; something is definitely amiss."

We talked for another fifteen minutes about the visit home, the pregnancy, and the idea of introducing Gran and Sven. On that one, he had to think it through. He didn't want to share my attention with anyone. How Bradley of him, I thought. We were merging our personalities. Scary. He mentioned at the end of the call to talk to the girl. I remembered I had one more question.

"Do you feel like you're missing out on having a child?" I had almost forgotten to mention it.

"What? I've never even thought about something like a child. Why, you?"

"I don't know," I told him, "I don't. I've never thought about it before, but with Sarah being pregnant—"

"Brad, neither of us is going to be pregnant. You realize that?" He laughed.

"No kidding. It was just a question but never mind, I'll talk to Miss Washing Machine. I miss you, and I love you. Friends always."

"You're always one for great questions. I love you too. Friends always."

Chapter 16

Miss Washing Machine turned out to be freaky fucking smart and on scholarship as well. I had spoken to her a few times and discovered she wanted to go to med school. We were in the same math class, so I stopped by her room after getting my exam grade. Our grades were close, but I figured she would be a point or two ahead of me, but close.

I knocked on her door.

"Coming. I'll be right there." I heard her say, followed by some shuffling. Maybe she wasn't dressed, but I didn't think that would have stopped her from answering the door. Perhaps I should say never mind and disappear.

She opened the door. Her face was downcast, almost forlorn. She appeared to have been crying—her eyes were red and watery. She wasn't her bold, confident self. She was timid and shut down. The door pulled open wider, and an old man was sitting on the bed. She looked to the ground like she was ashamed. "Hi, meet my grandfather, Harold."

The rotten smell of stale alcohol wafted my way, and I held back from covering my nose. "And who are you, may I ask? You one of Jackie's *boy*friends?"

I looked the bastard dead in the eyes and said, "We're classmates." I looked at her, "Just checking to see how you fared on the exam. Grades are posted."

She smiled and said, "Ninety-eight, you?"

I laughed, "How do you do it? I got a ninety-six. We can talk later. I think I know what two I missed, but later. Sorry to bother you."

"I was leaving," her grandfather said. "You two can talk your scores talk all night for all I care." He looked at her with a menacing expression. "You be home this weekend. No excuses this time."

"No excuses." He shuffled by me, smelling like a mixture of an ashtray and a bar floor.

"Are you okay?" I asked. "No disrespect, but that was weird." I was as diplomatic as I could be. I wanted to say what a horrible, miserable bastard, but I remained silent because he was her grandfather.

"Nothing I can't handle. It's a long story, Brad, and I'm exhausted."

"Can I come in for a minute?" I asked. She rolled her eyes and nodded, so I closed the door and held her. I stroked her hair softly. "You can tell me anything, ya hear?" She began to cry, and I held her tight. She was small, so small. I could feel the tears welling in my eyes. Then a lightbulb turned on in my head: The fucker was her abuser. Berit had been right. "You know it's not you, don't you?" She cried even more, so I scooped her up and put her on her bed. I sat at the end and held her feet on my lap. If we sat there all night, it was okay with me. She had to say something and let a piece of the bad go; it would be a beginning.

"I thought you were looking for—"

"A friend. I was."

She smiled weakly at me, "It doesn't work. I'm too fucked up."

"No such thing for a friend." I returned her smile and knew she saw my tears. "I can be a friend and a real good one, I promise. I'm not looking to be a knight in shining armor because I'm not. Just a friend. Can you come to my room? I have something I want you to see." She needed to see the Berit note. Maybe then she'd understand what I was saying.

She followed me to my room, and I pulled out the note and gave it to her to read. The most important part I told her was about being a friend. As she read it, she started crying.

"Your boyfriend is a good man, isn't he?" she asked through sobs.

"The best, most of all, he's my friend. My best friend, Jackie. Why don't we talk? You don't have to tell me anything you aren't comfortable with me knowing, but you can say anything to me without fear of judgment or pity. You may feel like a victim, but you have the strength of a victor."

She started from the beginning. She was eight years old when her grandfather had begun inappropriate touching. By the time she was twelve, he was raping her. She didn't need to go into the details. I could read between the lines.

Although she tried to look down as she explained the different ways he abused her, I raised her chin looked her in the eyes, and let her know she had the heart of a survivor. She put everything into schoolwork to escape.

"Have you ever told anyone?"

Jackie shook her head.

"What about your parents? Do they suspect?"

"Probably not."

"Yes or no, do you think or feel they know?"

Her chest heaved; she was having trouble catching her breath. I moved down to her and cradled her like a child. She cried in my arms, and I cried with her. I knew the answer; she didn't have to torture herself to say it.

"It's okay. I understand. Now just relax." I was going to make it my mission to keep her safe. She passed out from exhaustion in my bed. I also eventually drifted asleep.

I woke up a few hours later. I looked at the clock to find out what time it was in Amsterdam, and I quietly called Berit before he left for work. He was concerned when I called, and I reassured him and gave him a fast rundown with no specifics.

"You were right," I said. "How can I keep Jackie, that's her name, safe from her abuser? She doesn't want to report it to the police because she figures they'll turn it given her promiscuity."

"I understand how sensitive this can be," he said. "Is it a family member or friend? How long has it been going on? How severe?"

I used broad strokes to explain so he could understand without sharing details out of respect for her.

"Find out if she has any siblings, nieces, nephews, or cousins who she can confide in. If the predator was abusing her, I bet he's probably abusing others."

She started stirring, and I figured she had been listening to me for some time.

"Who's on the phone?" she asked.

"Berit, my friend, in Amsterdam. I wanted his advice. I haven't betrayed your trust in any way."

"Can I talk to him?" She asked.

I handed over the phone and told her it had to be quick.

"So, do you know about the blowjob?" she asked Berit. He and I had been through this before with Leonard, and he knew how to handle it. She was surprised to discover he knew and wasn't mad. He must've made mention of her boy-like talent.

"I am," I heard her say in a cocky tone.

I'm sure he was telling her that even though he didn't know her or her circumstance, if I had felt there was a problem, then there was a problem.

"You two have something different. Lovers and friends, hmm." She handed the phone back to me and sat on my bed.

"I know you gotta get to work. I love you and miss you, Berit."

"I love you, too. Man, your life is recently seeing plenty of drama."

I laughed. "No shit! Later, my friend."

What he said made sense.

I sat next to Jackie and grabbed her hand. "I wonder. Do you keep going back because you're concerned he's messing with other friends or family members? The only way you can stop the cycle is to report it."

"I don't know, but if I had to guess, I would say yes. Even though he's a drunk and nasty as all hell, he's connected," she said. "My family has influence."

"There will be someone in the police department not impressed by his pedigree or influence. The only way you can protect others is to tell the truth."

We sat in silence for a few minutes. I could see the gears grinding in her head.

She spoke first. "You told Berit about the blowjob?" She almost seemed amused.

"I told you I would. We're upfront. I brought you here to read our definition of friendship to give you an idea of what good looks like. If you think you're protecting others by being abused, you're not."

I hoped that our talk or Berit's note to me gave her courage. I copied it and gave it to her as a reminder.

The semester flew by, and I finished with a 4.0 GPA. I had four weeks between semesters for Christmas break, so I packed my room, not that I had much, and prepared to fly back home.

Sarah's wedding was the second Saturday in December, so Gran and I flew in the Thursday before. She would be heading back on Tuesday after the wedding. Berit made plans to attend the wedding and bring Sven.

I picked up Berit and Sven at the airport and took them to Frankie's dad's hotel, where they had reserved a room. (Berit and I would stay together on the sly, and Sven would have a room to himself.) Mom, Dad, and Gran had made their arrangements. Big Frank had comped them as well as given Dad a massive discount on the ballroom for the ceremony and reception. Due to the circumstances, they couldn't marry in church. I still thought marriage was unnecessary, but it wasn't my decision.

The families merged well, and my parents and Gran had accepted Sven into the fold. Gran and Sven were so similar. Sarah and Frankie were happy with the wedding and thrilled about their week's honeymoon. The world started to return to normal.

Back in the hotel room, Berit seemed utterly worn down, and he fell asleep fast. I wrote a love note and stashed it in his case to find when he unpacked. The next morning, he woke a bit better, but I had held him most of the night, "I don't want to leave you, Brad. Hold me tight and tell me you love me."

"Yes, I love you. You know I do." I couldn't keep it so serious. "Of course, it's only for your body and what you can do with it." I got a laugh out of him. I pinned him on the bed, "Let me see what I can do with that body." He seemed resistant, so I backed off.

"Sorry, it's me, not you."

"Eight hours from now, you're gonna say, 'Damn, what the hell was I thinking?' It'll be too late, my friend."

He smiled, and I could tell his mind was elsewhere, and he was just going through the motions.

I was sad the next day when we got to the airport, but I knew it would only be a couple of weeks until I would see him again. He was still quiet, and I wasn't sure what was bothering him before getting on the plane, so I pulled him to the side and asked. I didn't want it eating at me.

"I'm jealous, I think," he said. "I'm happy for Sarah and Frankie, but it doesn't seem fair that we'll never have a chance to get married. I know we've talked about it before and made our own vows, but sometimes I get sad, maybe even mad. I feel like the world ostracizes us, and it's not right. Not saying Frankie doesn't love Sarah, but I can tell you that I feel comfortable saying we love each other way more than they do. Like," he looked around pointing to a couple almost making out in the goodbye line, "can you imagine what would happen if we—"

"It's how the world is, and I don't like it, but we must play by the rules, Berit. Think, just because someone saw me coming out of a gay bar, an entire school screamed names at me and kicked my car. I can't imagine what would've happened if I had gotten out of the car or confronted the situation. I bet they would've beaten the shit out of me. We need to live in our love like you told me once."

He nodded but remained somewhat sullen. We rejoined Sven, who saw Berit's look and knew it well—he had been in one of those love-of-a-lifetime relationships, and it was even more challenging back then. I gave Sven an exaggerated hug and kiss on the cheek like a dad wishing his son goodbye and then turned to Berit and hugged him. I made it work for an extra-long hug, reminding him it would only be a couple of weeks. We'd stay on the same call schedule. I wished them both a happy Christmas.

Christmas flew by, and I realized how much I loved my parents.

The horrible things I had said to them or thought about them before haunted me. They were troopers—a gay son and a knocked-up daughter, hardly the ideal or a happily ever after—but they rolled with it.

Chapter 17

No city does New Year's Eve like New York. I was glad Sven had chosen not to come to New York for New Year's Eve. It gave Berit and me time alone together. We joined the throngs of people in Times Square for a celebration like none other. It was as crowded as Mardi Gras in New Orleans, minus the in-your-face-sex everywhere. We felt like kids; only we could drink. We both got pretty drunk, but not to the point of being disgusting, falling down, or throwing up, but our guards were down.

We felt jammed like sardines, I thought Berit grabbed my crotch, but it didn't feel like his touch. I touched the hand and realized it wasn't Berit's, and I crushed it. I bent it straight back at the wrist. Talk about me sobering up fast. Berit pulled him up by the scruff of his neck, flexing the hold I had on the jerk's wrist. The crack was audible, drawing the people's attention. The guy screamed out in pain. Some people in the crowd notified a nearby policeman who hauled the guy away while the crowd cheered. One less pickpocket off the streets, at least for the night.

"What happened?" Berit asked.

"I thought you were copping a feel," which made him laugh.

The atmosphere was electric, and we soon heard someone shouting at someone on the ground. It was the night for pickpockets, but the people of New York weren't having any of it. The bad guys were dropping like flies. I loved New York and the gutsy, no-nonsense attitude. They weren't rude; they were intolerant of stupid.

We stayed out until two or three and then made our way back to the hotel for some real celebration. Because we were tipsy, we were more playful. My boy was hands down the hottest thing in bed, drunk or sober. For the next two days, we stayed in bed, hungover and playing, making up for any lost time.

The last morning we discussed my schooling. Would it be better for me to complete my studies at Columbia and delay the move to New Orleans another year? We weighed the pros and cons of going to a local university like Tulane. By finishing my undergraduate degree and master's in architecture, the likelihood of having an alum hire me was good, especially given my grades. We mapped out the future between fondles. Nothing could compare to our first New Year's in New York City.

At the end of the spring semester, Jackie, also known as Miss Washing Machine, nailed her maternal grandfather. It was all over the news. Even though he had been a man of influence, rubbing elbows with celebs and politicians, she had made him a pariah. Not only was he arrested, but he also was found guilty and sentenced. He had abused her, her brother, her cousins, both male and female, and the worst thing of all, her mother when she was young. Her mother never came forward, even during the trial. We didn't speak much after the night of revelation, but she knew I was there whenever she needed me.

The following two years fell into place and were a carbon copy of year one. I ended my three years at Columbia with the highest grades possible, and Tulane accepted me for my master's program without hesitation. Things with the dealership were taking longer than expected.

Hell opened up when Sven suffered a fatal heart attack.

The phone call was one of the worst I've ever received. I, along with my parents, took the first flight to Amsterdam. Sven had left everything in his possession to Berit. A car met us at the airport, which was the first time he hadn't met me. Warning flags went up. I was more than concerned.

We arrived at Sven's house. I told Mom and Dad to stay downstairs. I went up to his room, but he wasn't in there. I found him in Sven's with the lights off in total darkness.

His voice was weak. "He fucking died on me, Brad, he died. How could he do that to me? He didn't even fight. He just gave in and almost looked happy to be dying. He wasn't old enough to die. He was only sixty-five."

I reached out to hold him, but he pulled away. He was unreasonable and wouldn't let me draw the curtains.

"He missed Luuk, Berit. Even though he had you, he missed his love. Look at this house; it's a shrine to him. He loved you like a son, you know that, and he didn't leave you. He went to be with Luuk. Acting like this is getting you nowhere, so get dressed and wash your face. Things need taken care of."

"Fuck you, Brad! I don't need you to tell me what to do. Fuck you. You have no idea what it's like to lose someone. You've had it made. Try walking in my shoes. And you call yourself my friend? Fuck you." I knew he didn't mean any of it, but he was hurting.

"I'll take whatever you want to throw at me, but you're getting your ass out of that bed. I dropped everything to be with you because I love you, and I loved Sven. I know you're angry and hurt. To love is to know hurt. Isn't that what Sven said to you once? To love is to know bliss, but it's also to know pain."

I went to touch his arm, and he swung at me. This *was* going to end okay, but getting there wasn't going to be easy. I swallowed hard and touched his arm. Again he swung. I caught his arm and held it; he sat up, swinging his other arm. I stopped it too. By this time, my eyes had adjusted to the darkness, and I looked into his eyes.

"Let me go, Brad."

"No. I don't want you to hit me or hurt me. I'd hate to have to kick your ass when you're downhearted like this."

"You kick my ass? Ha! Let go, Brad, now." He struggled to pull away. I wasn't letting go. A few years back, I could never have held his arms, but at Columbia, I was working out when I wasn't studying, and I now was strong, fiercely strong, and I knew it. He was far more of a fighter than I, but right then, his arms were immobile. We stayed in the same position at most for five minutes, although it felt like an hour. He yielded to me, and I went for it fast. I put my arms around him. At first, he was stiff as a board, but then he held on to me.

"I can't breathe, Brad. I got him to the hospital as fast as I could. Thank God we were but a few blocks away. I got him there, and they said faster than the emergency wagon could've gotten to him. He kept telling me that it was okay. He could barely speak. I shushed him and told him to save his energy. He smiled at me." Berit started crying. "He said, I love you, my son. Then he closed his eyes, and he was gone, just like that. He was holding my hand, and I felt it go limp. I felt the life leave his body. He left me, Brad." He sobbed on my shoulder, and I tried to hold the tears back, but it was to no avail.

"He knew you had me, Berit, and I love you. Let's get this thing done, okay? Can I open the curtains? Promise you won't hit me when I let you go." I was unsure and didn't want to deal with a crazy Berit.

"I promise. I'm sorry I said those horrible things to you. You know I didn't—"

"I know. I'm letting go now," I opened the curtains. Shit, Berit had wrecked the room—chairs overturned, pillows strewn everywhere, the mattress was barely on the bed, and the portrait above the bed was down and had what looked like a knee or foot through it. Wow. My beautiful friend was a wreck with swollen eyes from crying and a bruised wrist. I grabbed a hand towel and washed his face. I smoothed his hair and straightened his shirt. "There, you look like you. Mom and Dad are downstairs. Let's go down, okay?"

He straightened his shoulders, took my hand, and pulled me into him. "I love you. I'm sorry, truly." We walked out of the bedroom, and I grabbed one of Sven's hankies on the way out. Mom and Dad had heard some of the words but acted normal. I'm sure between themselves, they had commented about the house, especially the shrine.

When Mom saw Berit, she put her arms out. "Come here, my sweet boy," she said and hugged him. "I'm so sorry, love." He cried in her arms. Dad put his hand on his shoulder.

I put on the kettle and made some tea for Berit and my mom. Dad would never drink hot tea.

"Do you have ice?" Mom asked. I jumped up and grabbed the only tray in the freezer with a few cubes. "Put them in a washcloth and break them up with this knife handle." She put the washcloth filled with broken ice on his eyes. "Besides the swollen eyes, you look fine. The ice will help take the swelling away. Do you have anything like Preparation H? Apply a little under your eyes—works like a charm." I went upstairs to look, and while I was there, I straightened the mattress, chairs, and pillows. The painting was a whole different story and something he'd regret for a long time. I didn't hear my mom come up the stairs.

"Oh my!" she said when she saw the portrait. Was her reaction related to the big tear, the naked men, or Luuk's colossal penis? "Maybe you need to put the portrait in his closet." She mouthed, "Quite eclectic." I nodded. "Great portrait of you and Berit, by the way." She must have snooped around.

After settling the house, my parents went to the hotel. I had already told them to sleep or grab a bite and mentioned a few places right around their hotel. By this time, I may not have been a local, but I had spent some time there and knew my way around Sven's neighborhood.

We managed to plan Sven's service, and it went without a hitch. I know it made Berit feel good that so many were in attendance. The truth of it was Sven loved him like a son.

But Berit wasn't alone. He had me, and I loved him with every ounce of my being.

Epilogue

Before Berit made the final move to live with me in New Orleans, he decided to go it alone with the dealership. Heaven knows he had the means. I stayed with Berit long enough in Amsterdam to start the transition to America. Sven had left Berit quite well off, even though Berit was well to do independently. With Sven's inheritance, he was worth millions. When I left, Berit instructed me to find a house for sale in the French Quarter, and he would buy it with cash. He decided to keep Sven's place, which was officially now his but would be forever referred to as Sven's.

After finishing my master's in architecture, my income would be substantial and respectable, but nowhere near his. I found a place a few blocks from Leighton's. Berit said to buy it. He put the house in both of our names, which I told him he didn't have to do. I decided that once I was pulling in good money, I'd give him half the value—it was the right thing to do.

Soon construction for the Metairie dealership started. I kept a close eye on the progress, even though the car company built it to meet its specs. It was located on Veterans Boulevard, a plum spot for a car dealership because it was close to the biggest shopping center and a well-trafficked area.

Not long after, he made the final move to the bungalow I had purchased in the French Quarter on Chartres Street. Unlike many other areas of the Quarter, this area was residential and a tight-knit community.

Our life had its ups and downs like anyone else's life, but we were happy. Being gay was, in some ways, getting easier, but in other ways, it was getting harder. The Quarter was a fun place to live with a lot of festivities. The block we lived on was quiet and safe, but a change was in the air. Muggings a couple of blocks over were daily, and violence toward the gay community was on the rise. Scary things were happening in the world. Gay men started dying from the Gay Plague, later known as AIDS.

After a few years, we moved to the suburbs, but we kept our place in the Quarter. The big push to move came when I was walking home from the grocery store, and some ne'er-do-wells jumped me. I threw one to the ground, dug my thumb in the eye of another, and kicked the last one who grabbed my chain and ran away. I ended up with scrapes, a black eye, and a split lip. They picked on the wrong gay man. I went to the police station and made a report, but that's as far as it went. Berit started looking for a house the next day.

Violence toward gays escalated and worsened by the day. Some people were spewing hatred that AIDS was a judgment from God. "Adam and Eve, not Adam and Steve" was another slogan that brought out people's hateful parts. We watched as friends became sick and died. It took Stuart, Leonard, and many others we had met throughout the years. People were disappearing left and right.

Time went by; however, the memories failed to fade. I was still in love with the coolest person I'd ever met. Both of us sported graying temples and reading glasses, but we still laughed with each other and lived life to the fullest. For our thirtieth anniversary, I bought Berit a flashy red muscle car; it wasn't a Cutlass Supreme, but it had flavor. We'd ride with the windows down, the breeze blowing through our hair, just two regular guys having fun and living as friends always.

Acknowledgements

Many Thanks…

…to the love of my life, my husband, Doug. He's been my support through all my writing endeavors.

…to my children for their encouragement.

…to my brother, who I miss deeply.

…to Chad Sievers for his compassionate editing, eye for detail, and caring suggestions. Thanks for loving my friends so much. A big thanks to Paige Brannon Gunter, who has played the devil's advocate as well as cheering me on…thanks for the moral support.

…to Cyrus Wraith Walker for the cover and interior design. Once again, he had the patience of a saint!

…to the readers who follow my writing, thank you, thank you.

More Books by Corinne Arrowood

The Censored Time Trilogy
A Quarter Past Love (Book I)
Half Past Hate (Book II)
A Strike Past Time (Book III)

Be on the Lookout for:
A Seat At The Table
Price to Pay (2nd edition)
Untouchable Love

Please visit my website www.corinnearrowood.com
Reviews are always appreciated.

About the Author

Born and raised in the enchanting city of New Orleans, the author lends a flavor of authenticity to her story and the characters that come to life in the drama of love, lust, and murder. Her vivid style of storytelling transports the reader to the very streets of New Orleans with its unique sights, smells, and intoxicating culture. Once masterful event planner, now retired, she has unleashed her creative wiles in the heartwarming story…*Friends Always*.